DL GALLIE

To Vi,
Thank you for helping me nail down the plan for Doucheman's story ... option eleventy billion and one was the winner

To Bec and Margaret,
Thank you both for FINALLY getting back to this needy author and confirming that option eleventy billion and one was the winner

P.S. Doucheman, you really are a douche but I kinda love you and I'm glad you've been redeemed. Wren is a phenomenal woman to put up with your doucheyass ... good luck, Wren, he's all yours now.

WARNING

I Pucking Hate To Love You is a spicy contemporary hockey romance intended for adult readers.

Reader discretion is advised. I Pucking Hate To Love You contains content that may be triggering for some, including a loss. For a full list of warnings, please visit https://www.dlgallieauthor.com/content-warnings

Reading the list, may contain spoilers BUT your mental health matters. If you want to discuss any of the warning, my e-mail is always open, dana@dlgallieauthor.com

I vowed I'd never get involved with a client again. That was a lesson I thought I only had to learn once. When I'm assigned Stefan Däuchmen aka Doucheman, I realize I have a huge problem.

My number one rule is "never date someone from work" … or "a douche." One would think because he's an egotistical manwhore jerk, I would be safe from his charm. But my new, very attractive client has me questioning if rules were made to be broken.

I have to remind myself constantly it doesn't matter how good-looking he is. With his panty-melting smile, rich chocolate eyes, and washboard abs, or the heart of gold he hides under his douchey exterior. He's my client and I'm not going there—again. But the more time I spend with him, the harder I fall.

I pucking hate to love him, but I can't help it … I'm so pucking screwed.

1
STEFAN

"AND IN BREAKING NEWS, Stefan Däuchmen, the left defensemen for the New York Crushers has been caught with his pants down ... literally. The wild playboy was discovered in a compromising position with two young ladies earlier tonight in Hell's Kitchen. His antics since he and longtime girlfriend Chelsea Maxwell, daughter of head coach David Maxwell, parted ways last year have spiraled out of control. Sources say, he cheated on her and after what transpired last night and in recent weeks, my gut is saying it's true. Of course, this is pure speculation, but one has to wonder??? And going by his recent antics, you have to give some merit to those rumors. I bet right now, Stefan's agent, Jaxson Scott from Life's Too Sport, is in damage control. This leads us all to speculate if this latest scandal will have any repercussions on his trade to the LA Legends in the upcoming season."

Jaxson my agent shakes his head and flicks off the television, throwing the remote down onto his desk. "Are you trying to sabotage yourself and your career?" he asks me, shaking his head again and looking at me in that "what's wrong with you" kind of way.

"I'm living my life," I snap at him.

"Well, fucking live it behind closed doors. What possessed you to have a threesome in an alley?"

"They were hot and I was horny."

Jaxson sighs in that way he does when he's frustrated. "Stefan, you are the bane of my existence."

"You love me, Jax," I throw back at him. He might be the same age as me, but Jaxson Scott is a powerhouse agent, and I'm lucky to have him on my team.

"I really fuckin' hope this trade to LA is what you need to stay out of trouble."

"So it's still on?"

"Yes, it's still on. For some fucking reason, Leif Barber really wants you on his team but, Stefan, pull your head out of your ass. Another headline like that"—he points to the now switched off flatscreen—"and you just might lose what you've worked so hard for."

"As you said, LA will be the fresh start I need," I tell him. "Now, can I go? I have a hot date—"

"Are you fucking kidding me?" he snaps.

"You never said I couldn't date, you just said no threesomes in public."

"For fuck's sake," he growls. "Listen to me, Stefan, no fornication of any kind in public. That means no sex, no threesomes, no orgies, no blow jobs, no fingering, no anal ... fuck, I'm probably giving you ideas."

A chuckle slips out but I quickly school my expression when I see the seriousness on his face. "I promise not to partake in any of the aforementioned sexual acts in public."

"Thank you ... I'd like to go one week without seeing you appear on *What's the Buzz*."

"Challenge accepted," I singsong, but Jaxson and I both

know that's not going to happen. I'm Stefan Däuchmen. I can't help it if the ladies love me and men are jealous of what I have—on and off the ice. I'm at the top of my game. I'm being traded to my dream team, and I'm in one month, I'm moving from New York to LA.

Life is grand and nothing is going to squash that.

2
WREN

...six months later

I'M CHUCKLING as I pop my phone back onto my desk after hanging up from Marissa. Marissa is the receptionist in the LA office, and she's become a good friend of mine. Sometimes, I wished she lived closer so I could buy her all the drinks for going above and beyond her pay grade. She helped me relocate Stefan to LA earlier this year, and that was a feat in itself. While I'm here in New York, she does her best to try and corral Stefan into line but there's one problem with that, she's just too sweet and innocent for that man. He runs rings around the poor girl, and she doesn't even realize it's happening. Hell, he runs rings around me, and I'm no pushover. He really does live up to his "Douche-man" moniker, but I've never shied away from a problem client, and he will not be the first to beat me.

Speaking of the douche, he's once again in the headlines for being, well, a douche, and once again, we're in damage control. This time, he got into a fight with some guy at a bar for hitting on the guy's girlfriend. She stepped in to stop it, and in doing so, took an elbow to the face from her boyfriend. Thankfully, it wasn't Stefan who hit her, but as usual, the vultures—aka Margaret from *What's the Buzz* and other media outlets—are running with it and saying what they need for clicks. I'm working overtime trying to come up with something to turn the focus to the good, which is A. he didn't hit her, and B., ummm, yeah, this is why I'm working overtime to fix this before it blows into something bigger. When it comes to Stefan, there's very little good, which makes my job a billion times harder. If he wasn't such a stellar player, he'd be out on his ass by now.

"Knock-knock," Jaxson singsongs as he walks into my office without waiting for me to invite him. He drops into the chair across from me and lifts his feet onto the edge of my desk. Raising my eyebrows at him, he removes his feet with a smirk. He totally did that just to piss me off. Feet belong on the ground, not on my desk.

"What's up, bossman?" I say in greeting, and when I see the look on his face, I know something's up. I've only been with Life's Too Sport for a short time now, but I can read Jaxson like a book. For an agent, he has the worst poker face I have ever seen, but he somehow still manages to secure the best deals around.

Life's Too Sport, or LTS for short, hired me as their in-house image consultant. A lot of their clients only know how to play their chosen sport, they don't know how to handle themselves off the field or out of the pool, but that's where I come in. I help them with their image and teach them how to handle the press and potential sponsors. I coach them and mold them into superstars. I mostly work with those new to the fame game and, occasionally, I work with those who need an image overhaul and are wanting to reinvent themselves.

Well, I *try* to help them. Occasionally, you come across someone, cough**Stefan Däuchmen**cough, who always seems to do the opposite of what I suggest or they blatantly ignore my ideas. Cough**Stefan Däuchmen**cough. When it comes to Stefan, it's like speaking to a brick wall most of the time. Pretty sure a kindergartener listens better than he does. Mentally, I make a note for myself to arrange another face-to-face meeting with him. We were all hoping his move to LA was going to be good for him, but he's literally just swapped one playground for another.

"Is this about Stefan and his latest antics?" I ask Jaxson when he just sits in the tub chair and stares at me. "Because from what I'm hearing, witnesses back up that he didn't start the fight, but he was flirting with the girl so h—"

"It's not about that," he interrupts. "But it is Stefan related."

"You're dumping him as a client, and we no longer have to deal with the douche?" I excitedly ask, sitting upright in my chair. Excitement brewing at the prospect of no longer having to face the pretentious douche anymore.

"No, he's still ours but, umm," Jaxson hesitates and that's so unlike him. He's one of the best agents out there, and I was stoked when he employed me, but seeing him unsure right now has my spider senses tingling.

"Just spit it out, Jaxson."

"StefanNeedsAHandler" he says quickly, the four words tumbling out as one long word.

Once I decipher what he says, my head begins to nod. Leaning forward, I rest my elbows on my desk, take my chin between my thumb and forefinger, and ruminate his suggestion. "I like it," I tell him, as I rack my brain trying to think of someone who could handle this task, but I'm coming up blank. I feel sorry for whoever the sucker is. "Do you have anyone in mind?" I ask when I can't think of anyone up to the task.

"I do," he offers.

"Who?" I ask.

"You," he states.

Sitting here, I rapidly blink and process his words. "I'm sorry. I thought I heard you say me."

"I did," he confirms, his head now bobbling like mine just was.

"Me?" I screech like a banshee. "You want me to become Stefan's handler?"

"Yes, Wren. You."

"You want me to live with him? Babysit him? Keep him in line?" Jaxson nods emphatically. "But ... but I live in New York, he's based in LA." I pause. "I live in New York."

"It's only temporary, and LTS will cover all expenses."

"But why me? Do you hate me that much?"

"Wren, you're the only person who I would trust with this task. I know you won't fall for his charm and end up between the sheets with him. I think you hate him just as much as he hates the world and everyone in it."

"But why me?"

"Because you and I both know, Stefan Däuchmen will not change without constant supervision. Yes, you've done great with his image, but it's still not enough; he's still being Stefan, but he needs to rein it in, or he'll lose it all."

"LA won't re-sign him?"

"It's a possibility that at the end of his contract that they'll let him go."

Silence envelops us as I process all that Jaxson just dumped on me. The idea of being his handler plays over and over in my mind, and the more I think about it, the more I know it's the right move, but me? Why does it have to be me? It's because you are great at what you do. This will *not* be like the last time. You will move to LA, overhaul his image, and be back in New York in no time. Easy-peasy, right?

"Please, Wren," Jaxson begs, breaking the silence in the room and my internal thoughts/debate. "You and I both know that without twenty-four hour supervision, Stefan is going to continue to spiral. Leif Barber, Tania Clotsdale, and I all agree this is what's needed."

"You went above my head and spoke to them before me?" Tania Clotsdale is the owner of the LA Legends, and Leif Barber is their head coach.

"Actually, Tania called me and suggested it and, for what it's worth, Tania asked for you personally because she's seen how you handle Stefan firsthand. She has faith that you'll be the one the tame him ... and so do I"

"This is what I get for being the best," I mumble. Pausing for effect, I continue, "You know what, Jax?"

"What?"

"The only reason you're doing this is so you can retain your top agent status. Re-signing Doucheman to LA will be a massive feat, considering how much of a douche he is."

"That is a bonus, but I happen to agree with Leif and Tania. You're the best at what you do, Wren. It's why I hired you."

"But, umm, well, you know what happened the last time I was assigned something like this..." I drift off, not finishing that sentence because it's a time of my life I'm trying to forget. It's why I switched from dealing with movie stars and into working with sports stars.

"The past is the past," he emphatically states as memories of my last job and the shitshow at the end play on a loop in my mind. "Look, Wren, what happened previously won't happen again because I know you've learned your lesson. Imagine what you'll do for the agency, and your career, when you become the person to tame Stefan Däuchmen and his wild ways."

"This better come with a serious raise and a massive-ass bonus."

"Done," he agrees without blinking. *Dammit, I should have asked for more.* "Leif and Tania will be informing Stefan of this tomorrow morning. Your flight leaves for LAX at 6 a.m., and when you land in LA, there will be a car waiting to take you to meet with them. Then you and your new roomie will head to your new home by the beach and—"

"I'm leaving tomorrow?"

"Yep, we need to nip this in the bud, ASAP."

"I don't really have a choice, do I?"

He shakes his head. "No, you don't, and for what it's worth, I'm sorry you've been saddled with him."

"No, you're not," I hiss at him, but I know he is from the sheepish look on his face.

Jaxson gives me all the finer details and then wishes me the best of luck before leaving me to pack my things.

Looks like I'm moving to LA ... and in with Stefan Däuchmen, yay!

3
STEFAN

MOVING to LA was supposed to be a fresh start for me, but trouble likes to follow me around—well, that's not quite true. I like to test the limits; I mean, we only live once. Right? Besides, I can't help it if the bunnies want a piece of me. And what's not to love? I'm six foot two. I have muscles on muscles on muscles, all thanks to my vigorous schedule and routine. And not to toot my own horn, but I'm easy on the eyes, with shaggy dark locks and kissable lips. My eyes are the color of chocolate. I'm essentially the complete package. Oh, and I have a perfect dick and, like my hockey stick, I know how to wield it.

This is supposed to be the prime time of my life. Yes, professionally I'm at the top of my game, but personally, all I keep doing is fucking things up. No matter what I do, it's wrong. Yes, I know I control the decisions I make ... like having an orgy with three bunnies while my live-in girlfriend was away helping her friend, but they were hot ... and there were three of them. What sane male would turn down three hot bunnies with amazing tits? Exactly. No one.

The day God created tits: Best. Day. Ever. Well, it was, until my team won the Cup. THAT then became the best day ever.

Today, I've been summoned to meet with the team owner, Tania, and Coach Barber to discuss things. I'm not in the mood because I have a naked chick in my bed and a pack of condoms waiting for me to tear into. A meeting with the big bosses isn't what I want to be doing right now, but they sign my paycheck, so my dick will just have to wait. But as soon as this meeting is over, I'll be back at my beach-front condo, and before the front door clicks closed, I'll be balls deep inside the bunny I picked up two days ago.

Yep, whatever-her-name-is and I have been fucking for the last forty-eight hours.

I'm waiting in the conference room, and the assholes have the gall to be late. The chick waiting for me just sent a pic of her in my bed with her fingers in her cunt and a come-fuck-me look on her face. Readjusting my dick, I lean back in my seat and wait, but all I can think about is what's waiting for me in my bed—I can't wait to get back home.

Finally, the door opens and Tania walks in, followed by my coach, Leif. Tania is the team owner. She inherited the team when her father passed away, two years ago, but she has just as much passion for the sport as her late father did, making LA one of the top teams in the league.

"Stefan," Tania greets me. "Thanks for coming in on such short notice."

"Happy to be here, ma'am," I tell her. Even if it's far from the truth, but since she signs my paycheck and has final say in my contract renewal—fingers crossed—I'll play nice. "But I am a little confused as to why I'm here."

"Really, Stefan?" Tania growls. I don't think I've ever heard her take that tone. "You have no idea why you've been called in here today?"

There are so many potential reasons why, but I'm not about to list any, just in case they *aren't* the reason why I'm here today. Yes, a lot of my exploits end up in the tabloids, and that Margaret bitch from *WtB* always seems to be around, airing my dirty laundry for the world to see. This is the only downside of doing what I love. Hockey is in my blood. I was born to be a player, on *and* off the ice.

"Stefan, son." I hate it when people call me son. Hell, I even hate it when my dad does it. It's Stefan or Däuchmen, hell, I'll even take my nickname of Doucheman over son. "Are you listening?"

"Sorry, I was thinking about the next game."

"Bullshit, Stefan," Leif snaps. Coach is just as pissed as Tania today. "This is one of the many things we're referring to. You zone out. You do what you want, and you don't give a fuck about the consequences. All you care about is yourself and getting laid. You're a terrific player, Stefan, but your attitude is going to be your downfall. And *that* is why this meeting is happening."

"What *is* happening?" I ask them. And then I voice my inner fear, "Am I being fired? Traded?"

"If you were listening, Stefan," Tania interrupts because, right now, Coach is too pissed off to reply. "Your image consultant—"

"I already have one of those," I throw at her, but she glares at me, so I sit back, zip my lips, and listen.

"As I was saying, your image consultant from LTS is coming here. She will be moving in with you, and you will do what she says, when she says. Nothing more."

"Come again?" I hiss.

"Your image consultant is moving in to be your handler." She says this as if I'm going to be okay with some random chick living in my house. Pot. Kettle. I know since right now there's a random chick in my house, but that's beside the point.

"Like fuck she's moving in," I growl. "I don't need a babysitter. I'm out of here." Shoving my chair back, it topples over and I march toward the doors.

"If you want to keep playing for LA, you will sit down, shut up, and abide by the rules. You have until we start contract negotiations to turn your image around, Stefan." Tania's words stop me in my tracks. "You have eighteen months to show me that you are worthy of an LA jersey, otherwise, I will cut you loose. And losing you as a player would suck, but I have a brand image to uphold and, right now, you are tarnishing that image." Spinning back to face her and Coach, I stare at them, and from the serious look on each of their faces, they aren't messing around. "Stefan, this is your chance to show everyone who you really are. Take this opportunity and turn yourself back into something great. I know you can do it. As Leif said before, you're a great player, but your attitude and behavior stink. Wouldn't you rather your legacy be for your skill on the ice rather than for your antics off the ice?"

"Doesn't look like I have a choice in the matter." I huff like a petulant child. "But if my shit starts to go missing, this stupid deal is off."

Tania's phone pings, and when she looks to the screen she smiles. "Perfect timing. The consultant has just arrived. Let me bring her in."

"Awesome," I mumble, but we all know from my tone, it's less than awesome.

4
WREN

THE FLIGHT WAS UNEVENTFUL, thankfully, and like Jaxson promised, a driver was waiting for me when I exited the terminal to take me to my meeting. I'd pay to have been a fly on the wall when Stefan found out what's happening, I just hope his tantrum has subsided by the time I arrive.

LA traffic is shit at the best of times, and today it seems to be epically shit. What should have been a forty minute ride is nearing on two hours. I was hoping to have a moment to prepare myself before facing Stefan, but it looks like that won't be happening.

Since I have time, I shoot off a message to my brother.

WREN

How you doing?

Keeping it simple, I stare at my phone and await his reply, but I know it won't come immediately. His life is kinda hectic now. A few months back, he lost his wife, leaving him to be a single dad to my cute nephew, Fletcher. He's not coping very well, but Penn Brookes is a stubborn man; it runs in the Brookes genes. He won't ask for help or admit he's struggling. At least this move to LA will put me closer to him, what with LA being in the same state as Lockhart Falls ... even if it's still a seventeen hour drive.

Shocking me, my phone vibrates in my hand, and I see a reply from my brother.

PENN

I'm good ... how was the flight?

WREN

Uneventful

PENN

That's always a positive when flying. How's the new roomie?

WREN

On my way to meet him now. Traffic is a bitch

PENN

It's the universe preparing you for the wrath that is Doucheman

WREN

It might very well be but I can handle him, after all, YOU are my brother

PENN

I was an angelic brother

WREN

Yeah, so angelic you gave me a handful of ghost chilies and told me they were strawberries ... I can still feel the burn in my mouth

PENN

...and I can still feel the burn on my ass from the spanking I got

WREN

You totally deserved that

PENN

Yeah, I did, but if memory serves, you got your revenge when you put lightening cream in my shampoo and my hair went white blond

A snort slips out at that memory.

WREN

Yeah, that was awesome ... best yearbook photo of you ever

"We've arrived, Miss," the driver says. Nodding and smiling at him, I quickly shoot off a goodbye text to Penn, and he wishes me luck with an emoji thumbs-up ... which is eerily like him.

Climbing out of the car, the driver informs me he'll wait with my luggage, and after the meeting, he'll take me to Stefan's whenever I'm ready.

Staring at the arena before me, I take a deep breath and head inside. The first person I see is Marissa, and she envelops me in a hug. "Who did you piss off to get stuck with *him* as a roomie?"

"I must have done something seriously bad in a past life, but you know what?"

"What?" she asks, eager for my answer.

"I'm excited for this."

"Did the plane go too high in the atmosphere and cause you to go too long without oxygen to your brain? I swear I just heard you say that you're excited for this..."

"I am," I tell her honestly. "I'm excited to shape Stefan into the fine man we all know he can be."

"Girl, you're crazy, but if anyone can tame the beast

that is Stefan Däuchmen, it's you." She pauses. "Speaking of, he's in with Tania and Leif now. I've let them know you're here so you can head on in."

"Sounds like a plan. Mind if I use the ladies' first? I'd like to freshen up."

"Of course." Marissa links arms with me and leads me to the restroom.

After using the toilet, I change my clothes. Pulling out a royal blue wrap dress, I slip it on and thank the heavens for wrinkle-free material. Kicking off my ballet flats, I balance on one foot and slip on my good-luck heels—a pair of nude Karen Millen slingbacks. Shoving my dirty clothes back into my carry-on, I step out and wash my hands. Then I freshen up by applying some mascara and slapping on some lipstick. I'm a simple girl when it comes to makeup, hell, I don't even use foundation. Tinted moisturizer is as far as I go. Spritzing myself with my go-to fragrance, Versace Woman, I'm ready to go.

My phone pings with a text, and I smile when I see Evie's name on the screen.

EVIE

Good luck with the douche ... you've got this

WREN

Thank you ... I'm suddenly nervous

EVIE

Don't take his shit. Show him who's boss and then you can get back to New York and we can catch up properly.

WREN

Deal ... no shit will be taken

Evie Salvatore is a friend of mine from my college days.

We met in the library at USC late one evening, and we became study buddies: her in sports medicine and me in PR and image consultancy. She really is an amazing woman, considering the extraordinary life she's led. Her father is Roman Salvatore, head of the Irish mafia in Chicago. She left home when she was eighteen and has been on her own since then. We lost contact. Well, one day she was there and the next she was gone. I never saw her again. Not until we crossed paths again a few months ago. She started working for the Crushers after being head hunted by Doc for his sports rehabilitation program.

Looking at my reflection, I give myself a pep talk. "You can do this, Wren Brookes. He's just a client, a douche client, but you're going to turn him from douche to fantoosh. You got this." Blowing myself a kiss, I grab my bag and head out to meet my fate ... and my new roommate.

5
STEFAN

SITTING HERE, I shake my head. I cannot fucking believe they are sticking me with a babysitter. What am I, five? The door to the conference room opens again, and Tania returns with a chick who looks vaguely familiar. I watch her walk behind Tania, and my gaze roams over her. She's slim with a killer rack that's hidden underneath a wrap dress that hugs her curves and highlights her assets. She has brown, almost-black hair, doe eyes that are a vivid-blue, and ruby-red lips.

She shakes hands with Leif, and I sit here focusing on her tits. Tits I'd love to bury my face, or cock, in. Man, I would love to get more acquainted with her. Preferably naked ... and maybe with the chick waiting for me at home.

She turns her attention to me, and there's a scowl on her face. It looks like she wants to be here just as much as I do, and it makes me wonder why. Most people would kill to be in my orbit.

"Hi, Stefan," she greets me, taking the seat next to Leif.

"Why hello, gorgeous," I lay on the charm. "It's a plea-sure to meet you."

"We've met before, you asshole," she spits at me, venom lacing her words.

"We have?" Shit, have we already slept together? Surely I'd remember a bombshell like her ... unless she was a dud. You'd be surprised how many times the hot ones suck between the sheets. Luckily, I don't have that problem. I've been blessed with good looks, skill on the ice, and a stick I know how to wield.

"Several times and, for what it's worth, I wouldn't touch you if you were the last man alive."

"Stefan," Tania interrupts. "Wren is with LTS. She's your image consultant, and she's been trying to clean up your image, but her efforts from New York seem to have had little effect on you, hence this new arrangement."

"I don't need a babysitter," I hiss again. I cannot believe it's come to this. I'm a twenty-seven-year-old man for fuck's sake. I don't need a babysitter. Sure, I get into sticky situations at times, but what guy my age doesn't?

"The tabloids say otherwise," Tania states matter-of-factly. Then she follows up with a statement that stops me in my tracks. "Stefan, as part of your contract with LA, you're to maintain a positive public persona at all times. It should reflect highly on yourself, the team, and the sport. Right now, you're not reflecting highly on anyone." She pauses and gives me a look that means business. "You either take this or we terminate your contract. Right here. Right now. And then I'll sue your pretty ass for breach of contract, and let me tell you, my lawyers will eat your lawyers for breakfast. I suggest you listen to Wren and take this chance because I will only be offering it once."

"How long?"

"Until your image is overhauled and not a minute sooner."

"But that could take years."

"Then she will be your roomie for years."

Wren makes a sound that has my head snapping toward her. From the look on her face, it seems she's as impressed with this arrangement as I am, because the scoff that just passed through her lips was felt on the other side of the world.

"Look, Stefan," Wren says. "You can do this. There was once a time when you were a pleasant person to be around, and like many young guys, sometimes the fame becomes too much and they act out—"

"I'm not acting out," I snap. "I'm living my fucking life."

"But you're in the public eye. You cannot live your life like a regular Joe, but I can help you—"

"Yeah, to become boring."

"It will only be boring if you make it boring. I've worked with many clients who I guarantee do not live boring lives. You just need to find a balance, and with my help, I can do that for you."

"You're pretty sure of yourself," I throw at her.

"And you're an egotistical asshat douchehole who is about to lose everything if you don't pull your head out of your ass. From where I'm sitting, everything you've worked so hard for is going to be taken away from you. Wouldn't you rather be remembered as LA's amazing left defenseman than the douche from LA who threw it all away?"

When she puts it like that, it causes me to stop and listen. I've worked too fucking hard to get where I am, and from the looks on both Tania's and Coach's faces, they mean business, but can I do it? Can I tame my wild ways?

"Stefan," Coach states. "You can do this. I believe in you. If you take your talent and willingness to learn and utilize those skills in your personal life, you'll become the person we all know you can be. Listen to me on the ice, and listen to Wren off the ice."

"Fine," I relent. "It's not like I have a choice in the matter."

Letting out a sigh, I realize I have no choice. Looking to Wren, I see that she wants the best for me, and since I have no choice here, I offer a suggestion. "Look, my house isn't roommate worthy right now. Can you give me a few hours to clean up"—and get one last fuck in—"and then we can start our new arrangement?"

"That's fine," Tania answers for her. "We have some paperwork to fill out, and I'd like to discuss a few things with her."

"Perfect," I state.

Throwing my keys at Wren, I smile at my new roomie and before anyone can say anything further, I hightail it out of there ... and home to my bunny.

"Fuck me harder," the bunny purrs. She's bent over the back of the sofa, and I'm fucking her from behind. I never fuck them face on, eye contact means feelings, and feelings are the last thing I need or want from a bunny. She was on her way out, and when she bent over to pick up her purse and I saw her naked ass and the salacious look on her face when she stood back up, I had to have her again.

She's moaning like a porn star, and from the corner of my eye, I see Wren standing in the doorway to my home. Shock etched on her face. Turning my head to face her, I smile at my new roomie and continue fucking the bunny. The bunny reaches her peak, well, I think she does, and gives an Academy Award winning scream as she tumbles over the edge.

After a few more pumps, I empty my load into the condom. Pulling out, I remove the condom and pull my pants back up as the bunny rights herself and pulls her dress back into place. She turns around and that's when she sees Wren. "You could have joined us," she purrs to a scowling Wren.

"Pass," Wren replies.

"Your loss," she throws back at Wren. Then she looks my way. "Call me."

Nodding, I stand here and watch her walk toward Wren. She turns before exiting, "You don't have—" But before she can finish her sentence, Wren slams the door in her face.

"You had to clean the place, huh?" She sneers at me.

Nonchalantly shrugging, I smile. "Welcome home, roomie."

6
WREN

CLENCHING MY TEETH, I have to remind myself I don't look good in orange but most of all, I refuse to heed to Stefan's doucheness. Standing here, I watch as his muscular ass clenches with each thrust into the bimbo he has bent over the back of the sofa.

The pig that he is catches me watching, and with his eyes locked on mine, he brings his whore to climax, then he empties himself inside her. *I hope he's wearing a condom*, I think to myself, and no sooner do I finish that thought and he pulls off a condom and pockets it. *EEEEW!*

His bimbo spins around and notices me as she pulls her dress back into place, and she makes an offer that has me quickly passing and holding back vomit. *EEEEW!*

"Your loss," she singsongs. Then she looks to Stefan with stars in her eyes. "Call me," she purrs before she marches across the room like she's on a catwalk in Paris, but Stefan is paying no attention to her. His stormy gaze is locked on me. His bimbo is out the door and turns around, but I don't want to deal with her anymore. With a fake smile, I kick the door shut, slamming it in her face. When I spin back around, I come face-to-face with a smirking Stefan.

"You had to clean the place, huh?"

He shrugs and smiles. The urge to slap him in the face is strong, and it rises when he says, "Welcome home, roomie."

You don't look good in orange. You don't look good in orange, I chant to myself as I walk farther into Stefan's home. Making my way toward the floor-to-ceiling windows, I stare out at Venice Beach. I've always loved the beach, and as much as it pains me to say this, this view is stunning and the view alone is the reason I know I'll survive this.

A knock on the door startles me, and I jump in fright. Stefan walks over, opens the door, and steps outside. I can hear muffled voices, and then Stefan returns with my two suitcases.

"So, which room is mine?" I ask. He goes to open his mouth, and I just know he's about to say something douchey, so I raise my hand to stop him. "If you say your room, I will knee you in the balls."

He raises his hands in surrender but from the smirk on his face, I know I was right. "For your information, I was going to say, up the stairs and to the right."

"Thank you," I tell him as I grab one of my cases and head to the stairs.

"Let me," he offers, and before I can protest, he grabs both cases and starts up the stairs. Standing here, with my purse in hand, I watch him ascend the stairs. Seeing him being helpful gives me hope that I can get him back on track ... that is, until he says, "What you got in here? Glass dildos and anal beads? These things are heavy as fuck."

Shaking my head, I don't answer. I stomp up the stairs and follow him. "Where's that go?" I ask, pointing at the door just past the entrance of the master suite. Yep, Stefan's room has a grand fucking entrance.

"To the rooftop deck."

"Nice," I voice. A silence envelops us, and we stare at one another. "Guess I better get unpacked then."

"I'll leave you to it." Without another word, he leaves me in my new room to unpack.

A few hours later, I'm all unpacked. I haven't seen or heard from Stefan, and it's been peaceful, maybe this arrangement won't be so bad after all. Making my way back downstairs, I find Stefan in the kitchen. He has an apron with the cartoon image of a woman with huge boobs on it tied around his waist, and he's cooking. My stomach rumbles and the amazing smell permeates the air. The rumble is so loud Stefan hears.

"Hungry?" he asks.

"Famished," I tell him. I haven't eaten since the plane, and it's nearly dark now. I'm surprised I'm not hangry and biting Stefan's head off.

"Dinner's nearly done. I hope you like buffalo chicken mac and cheese."

"I've never had it before, but I'm sure it'll be delicious considering the smells coming from the kitchen right now. Can I help with anything?"

"You can set the table if you like ... or we can eat here." He points to the barstools.

"Here is good."

"There's white wine in the fridge or red wine on the rack over there."

"What are you having?"

"Water, but I'll have a glass of what you're having while we eat."

Nodding, I open the refrigerator and grab the white. "Moscato," I say. "I would have pegged you as a dry wine drinker, like maybe a chardonnay."

"Ugh, that's like drinking wood."

"That's from the oak it's soaked in."

"Are you a wine connoisseur?"

"Ha," I laugh. "Not me. If it tastes good, I don't care what variety it is or how much it costs."

"Same," he agrees with a nod. "I think the best wine I ever had was when I was in Australia; it was like six bucks a bottle."

"Gotta love a bargain."

Pouring two glasses, I place them in front of two stools, and with a lucky guess, I open the cutlery drawer and grab two forks.

Stefan plates the food, brings it over, and takes a seat next to me.

We dig in and quietly eat. When we've finished eating, he insists on cleaning up but I help. After we top off our wines, we head up to the deck I was admiring when I arrived.

"Sorry for being a dick earlier," Stefan says, breaking the silence.

"I get it. It was a shock to be stuck with this, but you do know, they and I, only have your best interest at heart?"

"I'm not a child," he huffs.

"Says the man currently huffing like a child." He eyes me. "Look, this can go one of two ways. You follow the rules, things pan out, and then I can leave. Or, you can fight this and prolong my stay, but in fighting this, you also risk losing your job and facing a massive lawsuit from Tania and, between you and me, that woman scares me."

"Between you and me, that woman scares me too."

"Then looks like it's option one," I reiterate.

"Looks like it."

"How about tomorrow after your morning practice, we sit down and work out some ground rules. I don't want this to be awkward—"

"What's not awkward about a twenty-seven-year-old needing a babysitter?"

"What's not awkward about *being* a twenty-seven-year-old babysitter overseeing a twenty-seven-year-old hockey player."

"Touché." He raises his glass in my direction.

I tap my glass against his and watch Stefan as he takes a sip. Maybe this won't be so bad after all.

7

WREN

"YOU'RE A FUCKING ASSHOLE, STEFAN!" I shout at the man standing before me. I have never met a more arrogant, egotistical, self-righteous douchehole in my life.

The peace of our first night together was a fluke. A one-off. A blip in the time-space continuum because ever since, Stefan has had me angrier than I've ever been before.

This morning after my run along the beach, I came home to find some bimbo blowing him goodbye by the front door. What ever happened to a nice wave and a peck on the cheek?

For three weeks now, it's been a revolving door of women and bar fights. I swear he's been with a different girl every night, and I'm learning so many new sexual positions.

"And you're a fucking bitch," he snaps. His breathing is hurried, and if this were a cartoon, flames and steam would be coming from him by the bucketload.

"Did you just call me a bitch?" I know I should let it slide since I called him an asshole first, but it's the truth ... he's an infuriating asshole.

"If the bitch shoe fits," he throws back, and then he shocks the ever-loving shit out of me when he slams me into the wall beside the stairs. My mouth opens in shock, and he takes the opportunity to push his tongue into my mouth. I know I should push him away or knee him in the balls, but I find myself kissing him back because the man can kiss. Holy shit can he kiss.

Draping my arms over his shoulders, I pull him into me and kiss him with everything I have but as quickly as the kiss started, it stops. He steps back from me, breathing deeply. Silently we stare at one another, and then without a word, he turns away from me and heads upstairs, taking them two at a time. He marches across the landing and into his room, slamming the door behind him.

The click of the lock echoes around the house, and I slide down the wall, my legs giving way after the best kiss of my life. How do I keep finding myself in situations like this? I never should have agreed to this move. Stefan is ruining my life ... and my stress levels.

My phone rings, and in a stupor, I stand up and grab it off the counter where I threw it earlier. "Hello," I say without looking to see who's calling.

"Wren, you okay?"

The sound of Jaxson's voice snaps me out of the daze I was in. "Umm, yeah, I just got back from a run."

"Ohhh, lady of leisure, are we?"

"No," I snap into the phone. "I needed to go for a run and clear my head before I murder our client."

"Things are going well then?"

"You and I both know they are *not* going well."

"Yeah, I just saw the latest from the lovely Margaret."

"Fucking Margaret." I sneer. "That woman is vile. If anyone deserves to get bitten by fire ants, it's her."

"That's harsh," he declares.

"It's deserved. I would like to state that after getting Stefan's side of the story, this one has been blown way out of proportion."

"You defending him now? Has hell frozen over?"

"Hardy har har, Jaxson. You know I wouldn't unless there was proof."

"And what proof do you have?"

"Stefan was *not* in that bar because he was here, fucking three chicks on the living room sofa. I walked in mid-gang bang."

"Photos or it didn't happen," Jaxson teases.

"No one needs photographic evidence of that ... I'm still trying to bleach my eyes."

He laughs. "I bet that was a sight to see."

"Please," I scoff, rolling my eyes, thankful this isn't a FaceTime call. "You're such a man."

"Yes, yes, I am." We both chuckle at that. Jaxson is definitely all man, and if he weren't my boss, I could definitely see myself with someone like him, but in saying that, he's too metrosexual for me. I prefer them rugged and manly ... *like Stefan.* I quickly shake off that thought and focus back on the call with Jaxson. "But it's good to know that Margaret is off her rocker this time around." He pauses. "Should we issue a statement of refusal? Demand a retraction?"

"Ummm... in this instance, I think silence is the best course of action. If we defend it, he will look guilty, and demanding a retraction doesn't feel right in this instance."

"I trust your judgment, Wren, and can I say, you're doing an amazing job. This is the first time Doucheman has been in the news since you moved out there."

"What can I say? I'm amazing at my job." There's a McMassive smile on my face right now because Jaxson is right, I *am* good at my job and there's proof to back it up. My minor blip in my last role hasn't affected me one bit.

"Modest would be a word that comes to mind," Jaxson teases.

"It's only modest when it isn't true, and in this case, it's true."

He chuckles. "Alrighty then. I'll leave you to it, and keep me posted on any new developments or issues that come about. Seriously, Wren, thank you for doing this. It was a lot to ask, but you really are a lifesaver and this is off to a great start."

Hearing this praise from Jaxson is a massive kick in the guts. Yes, I'm doing a great job, but I just made out with my client when I vowed never to do it again, but it's a kiss I cannot stop replaying.

Holy kiss, Batman.

My lips are still tingling from it, and it pisses me off because why does a douche like him have to kiss like that? It will never happen again, and if it does, I will kick him in the nuts so hard, they'll come out his nose.

Jaxson and I say our goodbyes, and I head upstairs to shower. Once I've washed off my run, I head into my makeshift office in the corner of my room and go over the details for the meet-and-greet Tania has set up with a local peewee hockey team, but I can't focus on the task at hand. All I can focus on is that kiss. It can never happen again, but at the same time, a part of me wants more. There was a softness to it that is so not Stefan, but I can't get involved with a client again. I just can't.

8
STEFAN

WELL, I didn't see that kiss coming, but seeing her so angry just now did something to me. I needed to shut her up, and kissing her was the only thing I could think to do. I'm lucky she didn't knee me in the balls. Wren seems like the ball-smashing kind of girl. With her doe eyes and blunt razor cut, she's sexy as fuck, and her mouth ... totally kissable ... and I was right. That angry kiss was off the charts hot, but I cannot shit where I sleep. I need to keep her and everyone onside. I need to focus on the end goal: playing hockey. To keep playing hockey, I need to behave and overhaul my image. Once that's done, I can get rid of my new roomie and get back to living life ... but why do I keep thinking about her?

She's always on my mind, and when she goes running in those tight little outfits, I have to think of fat naked grannies, otherwise, the woodie of all woodies pops up to say hello.

It's time to leave for practice, and if I don't want to be late, I need to haul ass. I quickly grab my gear and make my way to the garage, thankful, I don't pass Wren along the way.

As I slide into my G-Wagon, Big Bertha, "Poker Face" by Gaga comes on, and it reminds me of the times the JJ would sing in the showers when I was with the Crushers. Can't believe I'm saying this, but I miss the camaraderie I had with them, even if they pissed me off most of the time. The guys here in LA aren't as friendly, but they train hard and push themselves, and that's something I admire.

Big Bertha is a matte black, top-of-the-line G 63, and I love her to pieces. Along with my beachfront condo, she's my most prized possession—oh, aside from my hockey card collection that includes an ultra-rare Wayne Gretzky rookie card.

When I arrive at the stadium, I turn off the car, grab my things, and as I'm walking in, I bump into Rick. Maverick "Rick" McQueen is the owner and assistant coach of my old team. A year or so ago, he lost his wife suddenly, leaving him a single dad with four kids. "Coach, what are you doing here?"

"Catching up with Leif while, ummm, K—" He stops himself and furrows his brow and a silence engulfs us. "You played well against Vancouver over the weekend."

"Thanks, everything fell into place in that game. The team and I were seamless ... better watch out come the finals."

"Bring it," he states. "But you and I both know, that Cup is ours again."

"Bring it," I repeat.

Coach and I say our goodbyes, and I head toward the locker room to change and get out onto the ice.

Coach Barber didn't appear today, and today's session was left to the assistant coach but, between you and me, he's a complete loser. He doesn't know shit when it comes to hockey, how he got this job is beyond me.

After a less than productive session, the guys and I decide to meet at my place for an impromptu team barbecue and game of beach volleyball. On my way out to my car, I run into Coach Barber and Rick. I extend an invite them too, but they both decline.

Like earlier, I notice Rick isn't his usual self, and when he and Coach say goodbye, Coach brings Rick in for a hug. It isn't your usual "catch you later" hug, this is something more. When they pull apart, Rick sees me and immediately schools his expression as he makes his way over to me. "How was practice?"

"Shit," I honestly tell him. "You're a far better assistant coach."

"Thanks," he replies. "Well, I better get a cab and head off..."

"I can drop you back at your hotel, if you like?"

"I, umm—"

"It's no trouble, Coach, and I'd really like to catch up. I ... I miss New York."

He stares at me, and just when I think he's going to turn me down, he nods. "That would be great, thank you."

We silently we fall into step and head toward my G-Wagon. Climbing in, I start the engine and quickly turn down the volume. "Sorry, I like my music loud. Gives me time to think."

"Yeah, I do that too," Coach agrees. His tone morose.

"So, where too?"

"City of Hope Comprehensive Cancer Center—"

"You have cancer?"

He shakes his head. "A, umm, friend's mom does."

"I'm so sorry, Coach."

"Thanks, it's not looking good ..."

Not knowing what else to say, I focus on the road and getting Coach back to his friend. After dropping Coach off, I swing by the liquor store to stock up on beer and White Claws. Then I head back to my place. When I arrive, some of the guys are already here and setting up on the beach. Like moths to a flame, the ladies gravitate toward us.

The guys ask Wren to join us, but she declines. Instead sitting on the lower deck with a glass of wine and a book. She doesn't seem to be getting too much reading done, though because each time I look over, her eyes are on us. Me, specifically. And each time I flirt with someone, I swear Wren's jaw clenches.

Ever since our kiss the other day, she's been avoiding me. Which is fine by me, less time in her presence means I can continue to have fun, but I must admit, taunting her is a new hobby of mine. And from the look on her face right now, this afternoon is going to be fun with a capital F-U-N.

9

WREN

"HEY, HEY, BABY SISTER," my brother says when he finally answers his phone.

"Hey, hey, big brother. How's that cute as fuck nephew of mine?"

"Cute as ever," he replies, and I can hear in his voice how happy he is. It's been a while since I heard him like this. It's been a rough time since we lost Maddie, but my brother has managed to pull himself out of the ashes and is living again.

"What's up?" he asks, snapping me from thoughts of my late sister-in-law.

"Nothing, just calling for a chat," I tell him.

"Why do you sound like your dog just died?"

"Because Stefan is going to die ... by my hands. I swear, Jaxson hates me and that's why he stuck me with this douche." I've been here for a few months already and just when I think I have Stefan on track, he goes and does something stupid and newsworthy. Then within the same breath, he's down at the Children's Center being human and nice. I always knew this assignment would be hard, but he might be the first client I cannot overhaul. This man gives Jekyll and Hyde a run for their money, but it's the good side of him that keeps be persevering with my assigned task.

"Or he stuck him with you because you're the best at what you do. Oh, and FYI, Mom has a feeling about you two."

"Mom and her feelings, but I swear, this time she couldn't be more wrong."

"Mmmhmpf," he tells me, and if I know my brother, he'll be rolling his eyes. "You and I both know Mom is never wrong."

"This time she is wrong with a capital W-R-O-N-G, wrong ... and with twenty gazillion exclamation marks at the end. I would rather glue my vagina closed with Gorilla Glue than ever, E V E R, let Doucheman and his dick or lips near me." Near silently, I add, "Again." I'm glad I can hear *Bluey* in the background, and I send a silent thank you to my nephew for the distraction because he hopefully didn't hear my slip of the tongue. My brother yells at my nephew to turn it down, and I imagine the glare he'll be throwing his dad right now. Apple doesn't fall too far from the tree there. My brother and his son are two peas in a pod, and it seems *Bluey* wasn't loud enough because my brother asks, "Did you quietly say again?"

"No," I hiss. "Why would you even put that thought into the atmosphere? My vagina and his cock will never meet."

"Again," he can't help but add.

"Ugh, you're just as annoying as him."

"Yet you still love me, Wren."

"Not right now I don't, but forget about me, how you doing?"

"I'm actually doing okay," he replies, and I can tell from the tone of his voice, he means it.

"That's so great to hear. I was worried about you for a while there."

"To be honest, I was too, but Fletch and I are finding a new norm, and we're slowly getting there. Don't get me wrong, there are some days when it hits me like a linebacker, but those days are few and far between now. I don't think I'll ever get over her loss, but each day is getting easier."

"Good, 'cause I'd hate to have to come there and kick your ass."

"I'd like to see you try."

"Daaaaaaaaaaaaaaaad," Fletcher shouts. "We can go. *Bluey* is done."

"Where you guys off to?"

"You'll be so jealous, Sis. Fletch and I are off to the store to get stuff for dinner."

"Totes NOT jealous," I say with a laugh. I despise grocery shopping with a fiery passion, and I guarantee you if home delivery groceries weren't already invented, I would have invented it. "Why don't you just online shop? No pants or bra are needed, and you can do it drinking a beer."

"I don't want to think about you pantless or braless."

"I'm both of those right now," I tease, and if I weren't still working, I totally would be.

"I'm hanging up now, love your face."

"Me and my pantless and bralessness love you too."

Tossing my phone down onto the coffee table in the living room, I fall back into the sofa and sigh. This thing is like a hug so I take a moment to appreciate it. With a smile, I think of my brother and how far he's come of late. Losing

Mads was hard for him, and we nearly lost him too, but thankfully, we were able to stage an intervention just after I moved here and get him the help he needed to get back on track.

...My MacBook starts to ring, and I race up to my room to answer. Today is the day we confront Penn. It's time he pulls his head out of his ass and starts living again. He has a little boy to think about. He lost his mother, he doesn't need to lose his father too.

The front door opens and Penn steps inside. I'm stuck here in LA so I'm attending this intervention via FaceTime. Without him uttering a word, I can feel the sass from him through the screen. This isn't going to be easy, my brother is stubborn at times.

"What's going on?" We're all silent as we watch Penn walk farther into the room, "Someone wanna start talking?"

"Hello, Penn. I'm Dr. Nina. Your family is concerned—"

"I'm fine," he interrupts, sneering at the doctor that Mom and Dad reached out to. He looks around at each of us, his eyes land on mine through the screen and he gives me a look that says, I hate you right now. *His gaze flicks around the room again before he repeats, "I'm fine. Really."*

"Penn, you're kidding yourself if you think you're fine. You are anything but, and we're worried about you," I say.

"I'm fine," he hisses again, throwing his hands up in exasperation. Then proving just how not fine he is, he marches into the kitchen, grabs a beer from the refrigerator, pop the top off, and takes a sip.

A scoff slips out and it echoes through the speakers. "You're so fucking fine that you're drinking a beer at nine fifteen in the morning. You look like a fucking hobo. When was the last time you shaved? Showered? Huh?"

"What do you know? You're however many fucking miles away in Los Angeles."

"I have eyes, moron, I can see you're falling apart. You need help."

"I'm fucking fine," he growls again. I feel like throwing that line from The Italian Job about what fine stands for, but Dad beats me to speaking.

"Penn!" Dad shouts. "Enough is enough. You need help."

We go round and round, and it feels like I'm dealing with Stefan and not my brother. But when Dr. Nina asks him a question, you can see the light bulb go off in his mind and then he utters the words we all wanted to hear, "I ... I need help. I'm so sorry for acting like—"

"A stubborn jackass douchehole," I interrupt, causing him to laugh. A real Penn laugh.

"Yeah, that."

"Penn, there's only enough room for one stubborn jackass doucheman in my life, and that position is already filled. I, we, we all want happy-go-lucky Penn back. I know it's probably been said, but Maddie wouldn't want you wallowing like this. She'd want you to be the best dad/mom you can be for your son, and she'd want you to be happy."

He drops his head and focuses on his feet, well, I thought it was his feet. "Mads loved this rug. As soon as she saw it, she fell in love but it was a thousand bucks. She refused to pay that much for 'something people are going to walk over' but I saw that sparkle in her eyes so I went back the next day and bought it. She was so mad at me for spending that much money on a rug. I suggested we put it down, see it in place and then we could return it. I didn't want her to be upset over an area rug but as soon as it was down, that glint from the store was back. She was glowing and I knew we were keeping it. We made love right there and then on this thou-sand-dollar rug, and it just so happened to be when we *conceived Fletch. Funny story, he got his name from this rug 'cause it's called The Fletcher."*

"Eeeeew," I screech and gag. "I walk on that thing ... with bare feet."

"Then I probably shouldn't tell you Mads and I have also done it on the couch, the bed in the spare room, the kitchen island."

Conversation turns to the specifics so I log off. I can't do much from LA, and as I said earlier, I already have one douche to look after.

Shaking off the memory of that day, I head into the kitchen to grab a drink of water and start on dinner. Glancing down, I catch sight of the rug beneath my feet and my eyes widen. "It's a Fletcher," I mumble. It's the same one as Penn's, and seeing it hits me in the chest like a freight train. Why did my sister-in-law have to die? Why is my nephew without a mom when there's child molesters and rapists roaming free and breathing? Why is Doucheman able to be a douche and Mads is six feet under?

Dropping to my knees, I cry at the cruelness of the world.

Arms wrap around me and a deep voice murmurs "Shhhh" over and over. The sound of their voice calms me, and when I look up, I'm shocked at who I see.

10
STEFAN

COACH BARBER WAS in fine form today, and my body aches all over. He really put us through our paces in practice today. What I wouldn't give for a rubdown from Lexi. That girl has magical hands. Man, I miss teasing JJ about her and her hands. Last I heard, the two of them were ridiculously in love again. But if you ask me, love is for suckers. I was in love once, it didn't end well—totally my fault—but being in love made me realize you're vulnerable. That your heart is fragile, especially when it breaks. Looking back, not only did I break her heart but I broke her soul. At the time, I was spiraling and I didn't want to drag her down with me so I acted out. Could I have ended things in a better way? Probably, but in the end, it worked out for the best for her. Even if her new partner is a complete jackass.

Kallen-fucking-Jones is the star goalie on my old team. Everyone loves him, including my ex.

Waving bye to the team, I grab my gear and head home. I'm going to head up to the rooftop deck and climb into the hot tub and soak my sore muscles.

It's funny, when I'm up there, even though I live right on the beach and there's heaps of people wandering around three levels below, when I'm in that tub, it's like I'm in my own oasis.

Traffic was light and I make it home in record time. Walking inside, I come to a stop when I see Wren on her knees in the middle of the room crying.

Dropping my bag, I walk over to her, and without uttering a word, I pull her into my arms and comfort her as she falls apart. Holding her tight to my chest, Wren sobs her heart out. Running my hand up and down her back, I'm at a loss of what to say but I know that chicks dig hugs, so I quietly sit here holding her as she lets it all out.

Eventually her sobs stop and we silently sit here in the middle of my living room. Wren is snuggled into my chest, and it hits me that this isn't awkward. She fits against me as if we were created within the same mold. She lifts her head and looks up at me. Her cheeks are tear-stained, and without thinking, I lift my hand and wipe her wet cheeks. "Are you okay?"

She nods and smiles at me, but it's forced. "It's just hard."

"What's hard?" I ask ... holding back the urge to make a joke about *being* hard.

"She's gone—"

"Who's gone?"

"Mads," she replies as if I know who Mads is. Then she adds, "And Penn's all alone and Fletch doesn't have a mom."

"Who are Penn and Fletch?"

"Penn's my brother and Fletch is my nephew."

Nodding, I process what she's saying. "When did you all lose Mads?"

"It was before I moved here, she was killed in a car accident. One day she was here and the next she wasn't. Fletch's mom is gone, and now Penn is a widower."

A chuckle escapes me, and Wren looks at me with daggers. "Sorry, I know this isn't a laughing matter but you're Wren, you're brother's Penn. Clearly your parents liked rhyming names."

"It's been a running joke all our lives."

"I can see why, but what happened today to cause you to fall apart in the middle of my living room?"

"A few months back, we staged an intervention for my brother. He wasn't coping. He's fine now but during the intervention, we talked about his rug, the same rug you have. It's called The Fletcher. It's how my nephew got his name 'cause they conceived him on that rug, and with that memory in my mind, it hit me that she's gone and well—"

"You broke down."

"Yep." She nods, letting the 'p' pop.

"Tell me about her?"

"You wanna know about Mads?"

"Mmmhmpf."

Wren smiles and begins. She sits in my embrace and I hold her tight as she tells me all about Mads, her brother, and her nephew.

"You can let me go now."

"I know I can, but I'm oddly comfy."

"Me too," she agrees. "I really need to pee, though."

"Why don't you go pee and then join me in the hot tub? You can tell me more about you and your family."

She nods and mumbles, "I'd like that."

Shocking me, I miss her being in my arms when she stands up. She offers me her hand, and I take it, but when she tries to pull me up, it ends with her falling on top of me. Her hands land on my shoulders and our gazes catch. Our breaths mingle together and before I do something stupid, like kiss her again, she pulls away and races up to her bedroom. Leaving me sitting here confused about what just happened.

A soft voice from the second floor garners my attention. When I look up, I see Wren standing before me in a sexy as fuck, black halter one-piece swimsuit with cutouts on the side and a towel draped over her shoulder. "You coming?"

"Yeah, just getting drinks. You want one of your girly cans?"

"Please ... and we both know that you love the girly cans," she air quotes girly cans, "more than I do. What with your sweet tooth and all that."

"Photos or it didn't happen." But she's right, my sweet tooth does like the girly drinks. When she first moved in, I played off the White Claws in my refrigerator as leftovers from a party when in they are, in fact, mine.

Grabbing a watermelon White Claw—my favorite—for Wren, a beer for me—because I *do not* drink that girly sweet shit—and a bag of chips, I make my way up and meet her on the second floor. She takes her drink from me, and together we head up to the rooftop deck.

The sun is shining brightly today, there's not a cloud in the sky. This is one of the things I love about living in LA. Days like this happen more often than rain, and it never snows here. I don't miss that, not one bit.

Wren climbs into the tub and she sits in *my* spot and I frown. She notices the expression on my face.

"Is this your spot?"

"No," I quickly refute, but she knows I'm full of shit. Her raised eyebrows give it away. "Fine, yes, it is my spot but it's okay, you can sit there." With a chuckle, she stands up and wades over to the opposite side and sits back down. "You didn't have to move."

"Yes, I did. You'd pout about not sitting in *your* spot, and we can't have you pouting."

Flipping her the bird, I climb in and sit down, in *my* spot. Leaning back, I rest my head against the edge and I stare up at the sky. "This is my happy place," I state, breaking the silence.

"I can see why," she agrees, and when I lift my head, I see her doing the same. She looks much more relaxed now, and as I sit here and watch her, I find myself enthralled by her. Wren comes across as this hard as nails chick, and she is, but underneath her tough exterior, she's a softie.

"Stop staring," she utters.

"I'm not," I defend. "I'm admiring the view."

"Of me," she snaps.

"Well, you are in my line of sight, and I can't help but look." I point to the sky behind her. "There's not a cloud out there, and that blue is so, well, blue."

"Funny that the sky would be blue," she teases, but she sits up and spins around. Resting her arms on the edge of the tub, she lowers herself down and stares out at the sky. "It really is a stunning shade of blue," she murmurs. Wren starts mumbling about light refracting and purple and shit, but I'm not really listening. I'm just staring at her.

She looks so carefree and relaxed right now, the opposite of how I found her earlier.

When I walked in and saw her like that, I thought someone had died. It reminded me of that day when I was fifteen and I came home and found my nanna in a similar state, but unlike today, someone did die. Well two someones died, my mom and my younger brother.

...Waving bye to my coach, I trudge up the front stairs. My body aches, I stink and I'm starving. Mom said she was going to cook my favorite for dinner, buffalo chicken mac and cheese. Opening the front door, I step inside and stop mid step when I see my nanna in the middle of the foyer on her knees. She's crying, full-on sobbing crying. She senses my presence and lifts her head. Tears are cascading down her cheeks. "Stefan," she blubbers my name and breaks into another round of sobs.

Dropping to my knees, I pull my nanna into my arms and hold on to her as she breaks down. She wraps her arms around my waist and continues to cry into my chest, but when she breaks the news about my mom and brother, the roles reverse. It's her turn to hold on to me tightly while I break down over the loss of my mom and brother.

"Hey," a soft voice pulls me back from the memory. "You okay? You have tears in your eyes."

"I'm fine," I snap at her.

"You know, what fine stands for?" I stare blankly at her. "Freaked out. Insecure. Neurotic and emotional."

"I am *none* of those things," I refute, but she gives me that *Wren look* that lets me know she knows I'm full of shit. "Okay, fine. I was thinking about my family."

"Tell me about them," she says.

"You want to know about my family?"

"Yep," she replies before taking a sip. "The more I know about you, the easier it will be to work with you." She waits for me to continue, but before I can tell her, she adds, "And the sooner we get your image overhauled, the sooner I'm out of here."

Her "out of here" comment pisses me off and makes me want to clam up tighter than a nun's cunt. Then, Wren being Wren imparts more of her wisdom. "Studies show that sometimes talking about things is good for the soul."

"So you want to hear me talk about statistics and plays?"

"I'll listen to anything you have to say to me. I'm not a monster, Stefan, I only want the best for you."

"Why?"

"Why what?" she asks, confusion marring her face.

"Why do you care?"

"Well, it's my job to listen—"

"So it's just about the money then?" My hackles are raised, of course she only cares because she's getting paid.

"Not everything is about money, Stefan. I care because everyone deserves to be happy, but we're all built differently and that's what makes each of us unique. Some people are academics. Some are book smart. Some can cook, some can burn water." We both laugh at that. "Some people are a natural at what they do, like you on the ice. Even though they excel in areas, they lack in others and that's where I come in. I mold people to be the full package."

"So you manipulate situations—"

"No." She shakes her head and chuckles at my remark. "It's not manipulating, it's making people see things differently and giving them the tools to thrive. A garden can't grow without water and fertilizer. Think of me as fertilizer, helping you to sprout and grow."

"You want me to think of you as shit?"

"Metaphorically, yes."

"You are quite phenomenal, Wren Brookes."

"And you, Stefan Däuchmen, aren't as tough and mean as you portray."

"Let's keep that between us. I have a reputation to uphold."

"Considering my job is to overhaul said reputation, I don't think that'll be possible."

"Maybe we can meet in the middle?"

"Maybe," she agrees. "Now, go get another round of drinks and then let's play twenty questions."

11

WREN

"HE DID NOT!" He laughs, slapping the water.

"Oh, he did. I can still feel the burn in my mouth from his chili strawberries all these years later whenever I think about it."

"So do you like real chilies and strawberries?"

"Strawberries, yes. Especially a strawberry margarita. But you can stick chilies up your ass."

"That might burn," he throws back at me with a chuckle.

"Not my ass, therefore, not my burning problem."

"Harsh."

"It's not harsh, it's the truth," I tell him matter-of-factly.

"Touché. I do believe we have one more question each."

"We do, so, hit me with your final question."

"Hmmmm, let me see ... favorite sexual position?"

"Of course you'd ask that," I reply with an eye roll.

"You stated at the beginning that nothing was off-limits."

"Well, that just bit me in the ass."

He laughs and takes a sip of his water. He switched from beer to water about five questions ago. Me? I'm still on the White Claws but I think I should switch to water because I'm feeling lightheaded and a little tipsy.

"Position?"

"Cowgirl," slips out before I have a chance to hold it back.

"So you can take the girl out of the country but you can't take country out of the girl?"

"I'm not country," I reply, splashing him.

"Lockhart Falls by all definitions *is* a country town."

"Touché," I throw back at him. "Now, it's my turn."

"Hit me." He leans back in his seat, lifting his arms out and resting them along the edge.

My other questions were all safe ones. Like favorite color—black. Summer or winter—both. Sweet or savory—sweet, no surprises there. So, for the last one, I'm gonna go deep. "Why did you sabotage your relationship with Chelsea? You two were the sweetest couple and then—"

Before I can finish my sentence, he's standing up and glaring at me. "None of your fucking business," he hisses and without another word, he's out of the tub and storming away from me. The door inside slams shut, and I can hear him stomping down the stairs, and then another door slams.

Dropping my head back, I stare up at the dark sky. "Fuck," I mumble. That one question ruined what was turning out to be a great afternoon.

Climbing out of the hot tub, I grab my towel and wrap it around my body. Picking up the empties, I drop them in the trash and then I head inside.

The door to Stefan's room opens, and he's dressed in jeans and a button-down. His hair is styled in that messy on purpose way. "You're going out?" I ask.

"Yep," he says, letting the 'p' pop. "Don't wait up."

Before I have a chance to reply, he's off. "Fuck," I hiss.

Racing down the stairs, I head into the garage just as his G-Wagon screeches out of the driveway, narrowly missing a car already on the street. Running out to the road, I stand there in my towel and watch him fly down the pavement until he turns onto a side street.

Heading back inside, I grab my phone and dial Tania to give her a heads-up that I fucked up and Stefan is probably gonna do something stupid. She tells me it's not my fault but no matter what she says, it *is* my fault. I pushed him too far with that question and really, it's none of my business. What happened between him and Chelsea is exactly that, between him and Chelsea. If Joe from down the road did that to Mary-Beth no one would give a shit, but because Stefan is an athlete and in the public eye, everyone feels like they're entitled to know everything about his life.

And we aren't.

Heading up to my room, I take a shower and slip into a pair of yoga pants, a white tank, and my fluffy slippers. I hate walking around barefooted, and these slippers are like a second skin. If I could wear them out of the house I would, but slippers are for inside use only.

The doorbell rings and I jump ten feet in the air before I call out, "Coming." Not that they'll hear me, this place is soundproofed like a recording studio.

Heading downstairs, I smile when through the glass entrance windows I see Tania standing there. When she sees me, she gives me her megawatt smile and holds up her hands. She has a bottle of wine in one hand and a bag of takeout in the other.

"What are you doing here?" I ask her as I open the door.

"Stopping you from blaming yourself."

"I'm—"

"Don't even try to deny it; it's written all over your face."

A laugh escapes me and I shake my head. Stepping aside, I usher her inside and she whistles as she takes in Stefan's place. "Fancy," she singsongs. "Clearly I'm paying my players well."

"I'm not complaining. The view certainly makes up for my roommate."

She laughs and goes about opening cupboards till she finds the wine glasses. Opening the bottle, she hands me a glass and pours another for herself. Raising her glass up, she makes a toast. "To kick-ass woman and the men who need said kick-ass women to keep them in line."

Tapping my glass against hers, I nod, mumble "Cheers," and take a sip. Closing my eyes, I savor the flavor and let out a moan.

"Shall I leave you and your wine alone?" Tania teases.

"If you leave the bottle on your way out, sure, but I would much rather hang with you."

"Good answer."

Tania and I have an amazing night. Stefan never returns, and for the next week, I don't see him at home ... but I do see him in the tabloids.

12
STEFAN

THE LAST SEVEN days have been a blur.

It's been a week of booze, bunnies, practice, and playing that one question over and over in my head—*Why did you sabotage your relationship with Chelsea?*

That's the million-fucking-dollar question, and even to this day, I still don't know why I did what I did that weekend. I'd like to blame it on the booze, and yeah, it played a part in it but when I look back, I was at the height of my career but something was missing. Yes, Chelsea Maxwell is the sweetest person ever and I fucked her over in the worst possible way, but she and I were never going to make it. We were never couple goals. We were cliché, the coach's daughter and his player. I'm just glad Nanna isn't alive to see what I did to her, but I will never find myself in that situation again. If I bunny hop, feelings won't get hurt, and I get to enjoy life, one bunny at a time.

Dropping my head back, water hits my face and cascades down my body. I ache all over. I was on fire tonight and together as a team we were seamless, and we deserved the win.

With my towel around my waist, I walk back into the locker room and when I look up I see the Three Stooges—Tania, Leif, and Wren—waiting for me. "Oh, look. It's Larry, Moe and Curly," I state as I come to stop in front of my locker and the trio.

"I call dibs on Curly," Tania shouts, tousling her long curly hair. Then she looks to me with her I-mean-business look. "Get dressed and then we need to talk."

"Ohhh, goody," I singsong, earning myself a glare from all three of them.

"Stefan," Wren says my name with a disappointed tone to it. It's the first time I've seen her in person since the hot tub incident seven days ago. She looks tired and worn out, and for a microsecond, I feel bad, but then I remember her question—*Why did you sabotage your relationship with Chelsea?*—and any remorse I feel for her dissipates. She should have kept her nose out of my business. Therefore making my antics this week her fault.

"Cut the shit," Coach Barber hisses when I make no move to heed their request. "Get dressed so we can chat."

"Fine," I nonchalantly reply.

Dropping my towel, I stand buck naked before them. Wren's eyes widen, and her cheeks turn pink. Tania's mouth drops open while Coach just rolls his eyes and shakes his head. Seeing dicks and balls is par for the course in the locker room.

"Put your junk away," Coach says. "It's nothing to be impressed by."

"That's not what the ladies have been saying this week," I taunt as I pull on my sweats and make an exaggerated move to tuck my dick in.

"It is impressive," Tania mumbles, and when she realizes she said that out loud, she spins on her heel and marches into Leif's office. Wren follows while Coach waits for me to finish getting dressed. No doubt to make sure I head to his office and not sneak out.

"You really like toeing the line, don't you, son?" he asks me as I slip my feet into my slides.

"What did I do now?"

He looks at me with a deadpan look on his face. "Really? You have no idea what you might have done?"

"Nope. We won tonight and I was on fire."

"Yes, you were, and yes we did, but maybe this has something to do with your actions over the last week off the ice."

"I haven't missed a practice."

"No, you haven't, but you have arrived reeking of booze and sex." I smile at that because he's right. This week has been one long extended party.

"I don't see a problem then."

"Stefan, the fact you don't see the problem *is* the problem. You were doing so well but this past week, you've gone off the rails."

"I'm fine," I snap at him.

"Fine is a relative term, Stefan."

"What more do you want from me?"

"I want you to uphold your end of the bargain and stay out of trouble. Yes, you're coming to practice and, I agree, you played phenomenally tonight but off the ice, you're a hot mess. Tania has given you this opportunity to turn yourself around and you're pissing it away. Things need to change or she will terminate your contract early, if she so desires. Th—"

"You coming?" Tania shouts, interrupting Coach.

"Coming," he replies.

Not having a choice in the matter, I slam my locker closed and follow Coach into his office where the three of them lay down the law.

"No booze. No bunnies. No sex. You will not eat, sleep, or move without Wren's say-so." Tania is looming above me as she lays out the new rules. This feels like déjà vu. Why are people in my life always telling me what I can and cannot do? I'm not doing anything illegal. Well, what I did with that chick last weekend is probably illegal in five countries but at the end of the day no one got hurt, no one died, and no one got arrested.

"Can I shit without checking in?"

"Your bathroom habits are your own, I don't need an update on that," Wren unhelpfully adds.

"How nice that you don't want to follow my bowel movements. Just every other fucking aspect of my life."

"That's what they're paying me to do."

A silence falls over Coach's office, and all eyes are on me. Normally I love the spotlight, but not this time. I can see why I need to rein things in, but this is over-the-top. I was hoping Wren would be gone by now, but I guess they mean business. I mean, she's still here, and now there are more rules in place to keep me in check.

"Look, Stefan," Tania interrupts my inner thinking. "We've said it countless times. You're a great player, and no one is questioning that. We only want the best for you, and while you're an employee of the Legends, you will do as I say. The season is nearly over and with the way things are going, we won't be making the playoffs this year."

"You keep reminding me," Coach cries.

"And I will keep reminding you until we bring the Cup home."

"Next season," he nonchalantly states and a look passes between the two of them, making me think something is going on between them.

"Hello, I thought this was about me and not the Cup?" I interrupt their eye-fucking.

Tania turns her attention to me, and the look she gives me has me quaking in my boots. "Just think, if you put just as much effort into playing as you do getting laid, we'd have that Cup in our sights."

Without another word, Tania exits Leif's office.

"She means business, Stefan."

"I know that," I snap, then I lower my tone. "I know that."

"Show us you know that and we won't be in this predicament again. See you tomorrow for practice before we head down to San Fran."

Coach walks out and now it's just Wren and me left.

"I'm sorry," she utters, breaking the silence. Turning toward her, I furrow my brows.

"Why are you sorry?" I hiss at her. "You get paid regardless of what happens to me."

"I don't give a fuck about the money, Stefan. Yes, I get paid to do this but at the end of the day, I want to see you succeed and Tania is right. You're a God on the ice but off of it, you're a..."

"Hot mess," I finish for her.

She chuckles. "Something like that, but I was apologizing for asking that question. It's none of my, or anyone's, business, so I propose we leave the past in the past and focus on the future."

"It's not like I have a choice." The look on her face is defeat, so I quickly add, "But I know I need to buck up. I promise to do better."

She nods and smiles at me, but I can tell she doesn't believe me. To be honest, I don't believe me, but I want to go out on a high so I'm going to try.

...a few months later

"GREAT WORK, STEFAN," I tell him as we leave the stadium to head home.

Even after all this time, it's weird to call his beach house home but it has become somewhat of a home for me. I've even made friends with a girl a few doors down. Fern and her fiancé, Bradford, are so loved up it's sickening at times. He may be twenty-years her senior but he adores her. He's book fiancé material ... and mighty fine on the eyes for a silver fox.

"It was horseshit," he hisses at me.

Stefan just did a podcast for a couple of kids who are diehard LA Legends fans. They were so starstruck to be on air with Stefan that it was a train wreck from the start. I will give it to him, he was an absolute legend—pun intended— and I have no doubt, those kids will remember today for the rest of their lives.

"Give em a break, they're twelve."

"When I was twelve, I was a gun on the ice."

"Brag much?" I throw at him as he opens the door to his G-Wagon for me. "Thank you," I say as he waits for me to climb in.

"And it's not bragging if it's the truth," he replies before closing the door.

Currently, we're in one of Stefan's good phases, but I'm waiting on the bench for the horny shoe to drop. Going on previous history, he does so well and then boom, Doucheman Stefan is back and we're at square one with his image again. In the last few months, he's really turned his image around. He's attended many charity events, without whining, and he's spent countless hours down at the group home. He's great with the kids, and I think he actually enjoys himself.

After Stefan was caught having a threesome in an alley behind a club, Tania and I felt that in order to keep this polite version of Stefan around during the offseason, he and I would hide away in Bumfuck, Colorado at Emerald Creek, the ranch Tania owns ... because, of course, she owns a hockey team AND a ranch. FYI, she also owns her own private jet, an island in Fiji, and a chateau on the French Riviera—Tania Clotsdale is one rich lady. Her wealth aside, we all thought it was a good idea for Stefan to hide away so we relocated from the beach to her ranch.

Stefan and I were getting along great and he was actually being nice ... and a normal human being. Then the ranch hands arrived for the summer season and it all fell apart.

Stefan had gone weeks without hooking up and drinking excessively and in less than twenty-four hours, he worked his way through a bunch of ranch hands and caused three of them to quit. Well, they were fired for fighting ... over Stefan ... and who blew his mind the best.

After that, as "punishment," and I use the term loosely, Tania sent us to her island in the Pacific. Waking up to crystal-clear water being just a hop, skip, and a jump from my front stairs was ah-may-zing in every way, and I forgave Stefan for his fuckups and luring us into this "punishment" in paradise.

With the new season just around the corner, we're back in LA and diving headfirst into things. Currently, we're heading into the LTS office in downtown LA to meet with Jaxson and run through a few things. He and I have been collaborating on new ways to overhaul Stefan's image and keep him in-line without losing who Stefan is as a person, and we think we've found the perfect solution.

"This is fucking brilliant," Stefan shouts, slapping the conference room table. He's smiling a genuine smile, and I think we finally found the "thing" that will make Stefan happy and keep him on track. "When do we start?"

Stefan, in conjunction with Hockey Inc., is releasing a sportswear line. He's always complaining about something not fitting right or this being too long/loose/tight. I happened to mention it in passing to Jaxson a few months ago. Well, Jaxson being Jaxson knew someone and then BOOM, discussions were had. And now Hockey Inc. is meeting with Stefan to finalize the details, but there is one part I'm not sure Stefan will go for.

"Stefan," I broach, finally putting my big girl panties on. "As part of this arrangement, ummm ..."

"Just spit it out, Wren."

"They want you to donate a portion of the proceeds to underprivileged kids."

"Too easy," he says without missing a beat.

"You will also have to help raise extra funds, atten—"

"Attend their galas and spend time with the kids down at the group home, which, by-the-way, I've already been doing. I can do all that," he states matter-of-factly. He hasn't argued any of the finer details regarding this deal and he actually looks excited for this.

"And you're okay with that?"

"Mmmhmpf." He nods.

"Really?" I ask, shock laces my tone as I stare across the table at Stefan. Going by the look of glee on his face, he means it. He *really* is excited for all of this.

"Really-really," he replies. "It may come as a shock to you, but I wasn't raised with a silver spoon in my mouth. I had to work hard for everything I have. Sure, when Mom passed there was an inheritance but there were kids on my team and around me who didn't have what I had. Now I'm in a position to help them achieve their dreams too."

Stefan goes on about ideas of what he can do but before he gets carried away, we need to actually get this off the ground.

"I will arrange a face-to-face with Steph at Hockey Inc., and then we can go from there," Jaxson interrupts Stefan, who is listing all the things he wants to do in the future regarding this venture.

"Awesome," Stefan agrees. "Let me know when and where and I'll be there. So, what else you got for me?" Stefan asks, shocking the two of us.

"Just that for now," I tell him, while Jaxson adds, "Let's see how much time this takes and then we can go from there."

"Cool." He looks to me. "Ready to head home?"

"I'll drop her home later," Jaxson answers for me. "We have LTS stuff to discuss."

"Cool, cool." Standing up, he shakes Jaxson's hand, smiles at me, then spins around and exits the conference room. The door clicks closed, and Jaxson and I sit here silently. Each of us has a quizzical look on our face.

"Did that just happen?" I ask, breaking the silence surrounding us.

He nods. "Yep, Doucheman wasn't a douche, and he jumped at this opportunity."

"Can you pinch me?" I ask, holding out my arm. He reaches over and pinches me. "Ouch, why did you do that?"

"You asked me to," he says with a shrug.

"It's rhetorical, you dick, but seriously, I must be dreaming cause ... wow."

"Maybe you're rubbing off on him after all."

"Let's not count our chickens yet. Do you really think he can be the face of this and not fuck it up?"

"With you monitoring him, I think he can do anything. You may not think you're getting to him but, Wren, that's a different guy than the one who left New York."

14
STEFAN

"OH MY GOD," I complain. "This is fu—" Wren slams her hand over my mouth before the naughty word can pass through my lips.

"There are children around," she rasps between clenched teeth, and then quickly pulls her hand away. "Eeeew, did you just lick me?"

Nodding, I chuckle as she wipes her licked palm down my face. "Ohhh no, not my slobber."

"Shut up," she hisses, slapping me in the arm. "You're doing great, Stefan. Just mind the language."

"Yes, boss," I reply with a salute. "Shall we get a drink?"

"Sure," she replies and we make our way over to the drink table. I rest my hand on her lower back as we walk, and I feel a heat radiate from her to me. She lifts her gaze to mine when we reach the drink table and she smiles. Wren really is beautiful, but before I can tell her, a little hand grabs mine and tugs.

Looking down, I see a little girl with pigtails and a plastic princess crown staring up at me. Dropping down to her height, I smile at her. "What can I do for you, princess?"

"That lady wants to speak to you." Looking over to where she's pointing, I see a woman. She has her back to us, and I take a moment to appreciate her sexy as hell ass in her figure-hugging, bright orange dress. Long bleached-blonde hair skims her shoulders, which are muscular and sexy. And her legs, they go on and on and on. How I missed her before is beyond me.

"Thanks, sweetie," I tell the little girl, and before I can say anything else she skips away.

Standing back up, I keep my eyes on the blond hottie who wants a word with me.

"Stefan, you cannot screw that woman here," Wren warns from beside me.

"I wasn't even thinking about that." *Kinda. Sorta. Maybe.* She turns her gaze to me, and from the look on her face, she knows I'm full of shit. "Come on, Wren, it's been weeks since I got laid."

She looks at me. "Fine, just not here ... or at home, I don't need to hear that."

"You jealous that you can't have a piece of me?"

Her gaze roams over me, her cheeks darken, and I'm about to say something inappropriate when Wren's eyes widen to the size of saucers and she whispers, "Fuck me."

"Now who needs to mind their language?"

"Not the time, Stefan," she snaps. I don't know how we went from *having fun* Wren to *snippy* Wren in the span of three point five seconds. I haven't done anything but then she lifts her hand, grips my chin, and turns my attention to the woman now facing us. My gaze roams over her and she looks somewhat familiar, then my eyes land on her belly.

Her pregnant belly.

My eyes widen like Wren's, and then I flick them back

up to the woman's face. Her gaze locks with mine and she smiles. Memories of her on her knees smiling up at me flash before my eyes, as she starts to make her way over to Wren and me.

My eyes drop back to her belly and are locked on her bump when she reaches us.

"Stefan," she purrs when she reaches Wren and me. She rests her hand on her bump and murmurs, "Surprise."

SURPRISE IS FUCKING RIGHT, I think, but somehow my brain to mouth filter kicks in and I don't voice it. Wren would be so proud, but I think the pregnant woman before us will trump my little vocab win just now.

"How? What? Is it mine?" I stammer, my eyes flicking between the woman and her belly and Wren.

"We had sex. It's a boy. And yes, he's yours."

Nodding, I take in what she just said.

From beside me, Wren says, "I'll, umm, leave you two to chat."

"Your girlfriend can stay," the chick says.

"I'm not his girlfriend," Wren informs. Shit, I don't even remember her name but I do vaguely remember her lips around my cock. She sucked dick like a Hoover, if memory serves correctly. There's something else in my mind regarding my night with her too, but I can't put my finger on it right now. All I can think about is her lips on my dick. "I'm Wren. I work with Stefan."

"I'm Alicia."

"I'll, ummm, ahhh," Wren stammers. "I'll be over there."

"It's fine, you can stay," Alicia nonchalantly says. "I just wanted to let Stefan know he's going to be a daddy." Her hands once again rubbing her bump.

"How did you find me?" Not really the question to ask but my mind has been blown, and not in the fun sexy way.

"I saw it in the local paper," she tells me.

A silence overtakes us because right now I can't form words. I don't know what to say or do, I haven't ever been in this situation before.

"How far along are you?" Wren asks, breaking the silence.

"Six months."

"Six months," I repeat, my head moving up and down as I try and think back six months ago. That was just before Wren and I were shipped off to Emerald Creek and paradise.

"Anyway, I'm off." She turns to leave and I reach for her wrist.

"Wait," I call out. "We, ummm, we need to discuss this."

"I don't want anything from you, Stefan."

"Then why tell me?"

"Because it was the right thing to do."

"And the right thing to do is for me to be there for my son."

"That's if he is your son," Wren mumbles under her breath.

Alicia's gaze snaps to Wren's, a murderous look crosses her face. "Excuse me," she hisses. "Are you calling me a liar?"

"I'm not calling you a liar," Wren defends, "but what sane man would just take the word of anyone when it comes to this?"

"Stefan and I had sex and I got pregnant. End of story."

"Stefan's had a lot of sex," Wren throws back at her. "You're not the first to tell him this—"

"I'm not a liar," Alicia says with a snarl. She snaps her gaze to mine. "Are you going to let her talk to me like this?"

"Well, she has a point." Alicia goes to interrupt me but I raise my hand. "But until we can get a paternity test, I will do what any father would do, and I'll be there for you and our baby."

"Really?" Her eyes widen in shock at my words and, to be honest, I'm kinda shocked too. Contrary to what Wren just said, I have never been in this situation before. I've always wrapped it. During health at school someone said, "If it's not on, it's not on" and that statement resonated with me. Ever since I lost my virginity to Velma Jones during senior year, I have never gone bareback—not even with Chels and we were a couple for years. I've also never had an STI or a pregnancy scare. Which is kinda amazing when you think about things.

"Really," I confirm. "Give me your number and we can meet up tomorrow. I'll get my lawyer to draft an agreement—"

"And you'll need to sign an NDA," Wren interrupts.

"Why do I need to do that?" Alicia voices.

"Because Stefan doesn't want his business spread about. This is a private matter, and the world does not need to know. If and when Stefan wants to make his impending fatherhood public knowledge, the two of you can come to a new agreement. Until that point in time, you can't talk to anyone about it."

"And if I don't sign?" Alicia asks.

"Then you'll get nothing from Stefan."

Her face blanches at that. "I need to discuss this with Tyrone."

"Who's Tyrone?" I snap, suddenly pissed that there's another guy in this scenario.

"My boyfriend."

"Couldn't he be the father?"

"No ... he and I were, umm, ahhh, on a break then."

My head starts to move up and down as I process her words, and doubt begins to creep in, and as if she can read my mind, Alicia steps closer to me. She takes my hand and presses it to her swollen belly. Her hand rests on mine, and I can feel movement. My eyes drop to our joined hands, and I quickly pull mine back. "He's yours, Stefan."

"I believe you," I mumble. From beside me Wren scoffs but tries to cover it with a cough. Alicia glares at Wren but when she looks back at me, her features soften. "Give me your number and I'll text you when we can get in to see my lawyer."

"Do you have a pen?" she asks.

"I do," Wren replies. She pulls one out from her pocket. Her always having a pen is something I've noticed she's started to do so if a fan comes up to me, I can sign things for them. *She really is great at her job,* I think to myself as Alicia writes her number on a piece of paper. Handing it back to me, she smiles. "I'll wait to hear from you."

Nodding, I stand here and watch her walk away. Before she exits the room, she looks over her shoulder and she smiles. The door closes and I turn to Wren. She has a look of shock on her face, and when she notices me staring, she turns her head toward me and says seven words that shock me, "Stefan, I don't think you're the father."

16
WREN

"DO you really think you're the dad?" I ask Stefan in the car on the way home. Traffic is a bitch this afternoon due to an accident on the freeway, and the silence in the car became deafening. Ever since Alicia dropped the baby bombshell, Stefan has been quiet. I've never seen him like this before, so I'm expecting shit to hit the fan in the next few days … or tonight.

"Why wouldn't I be the dad?" he replies, his voice full of shock.

"Come on, Stefan, think about it," I deadpan as traffic begins to flow again. "Out of nowhere a chick appears and claims you're the dad."

"Why would she lie?" Stefan growls again, "What does she have to gain?"

"Really?" I scoff, he takes his eyes from the road for a moment and looks incredulously at me and then focuses back on the road. "She has a shit ton to gain, Stefan."

He flicks his gaze to me briefly again. "But what if I *am*

the dad? I won't be one of those deadbeats who turns their back on their kid just because I'm not with Alicia."

"Really?" I'm shocked at his words.

"Family is everything to me," he tells me. "When I lost my mom and brother, my nanna stepped up and raised me when my dad shut down. She showed me love and affection, and I will do the same for my kid too. My dad shutting me out hurt, and I always said that when I become a dad, I will be present. Sure, becoming a dad is not happening how I envisioned, but I will be there for my son."

"That's very admirable of you, Stefan."

"I may be a douche, but I'm not a complete douche."

Debatable, I think to myself but I don't voice it because right now, I'm seeing Stefan in a completely different light.

Finally, we pull into the driveway and before we climb out, I reach over and put my hand on his arm. "Just, please be careful. Something is off with all of this."

"Why can't you trust me?" he growls. My words have pissed him off, and without another word, he climbs out of the car and heads straight to the kitchen and grabs a beer. He chugs it back and before he's finished the first one, he's grabbing for another just as there's a knock at the door. Looking up, I see Fern standing there with a bottle of wine and an infectious smile.

Once a month Fern and I get together for wine, cheese, and a chat. This month it's at my, well, Stefan's place.

"Hi, Fern. We only just got home, I'll be ready in a sec."

"Traffic a bitch?" she asks, stepping inside and heading straight for the wine glasses.

"Hey, Fern," Stefan says, saluting her with his beer. "I'll leave you two to it." And without another word, he heads upstairs to the rooftop deck. He seems to retreat up there when he needs to think.

"He okay?" Fern asks as she opens the drawer to grab the wine opener.

"Long day," I offer and I start to work on the choo-choo platter. I know that's not the right term but charcuterie is hard to pronounce, plus choo-choo is way more fun to say.

Fern pours the wine and slides one of the wine glasses over to me before she pulls out a stool and sits down. Lifting her glass, she tilts it to me in a salute and I do the same before I take a sip. The crisp flavors dance on my tongue and I smile.

"So, what's on this week's choo-choo?" she asks before taking another sip.

"This week we have salami, spicy chorizo, feta stuffed olives, a Dutch smoked cheddar, and I made a cheeseball—"

"Please tell me it's your mom's recipe? That was the best thing I've ever tasted."

The other week Mom and Dad visited for the weekend and it happened to be the weekend Fern and I get together. Mom joined us and she made her famous cheeseball, I'm pretty sure she discovered the recipe back in the Stone Age but whenever she found it, I'm glad she did. It's become a staple in the Brookes household, and now in the Halstead, soon-to-be, Manning household too.

"It's not as good as Mom's 'cause no one makes them as good as my mom does, but it's a close second."

"I'll be the judge of that."

She grabs a cracker and cuts into the ball. Popping the tasty morsel into her mouth, she moans and groans and I grin. *I did good.* "Shall I leave you and the cheeseball alone?"

"Yes," she replies before laughing. "Do you think Bradford and I can serve this at the wedding?"

"It's your wedding, you can serve whatever the hell you want."

"I knew I liked you for a reason."

"I thought you only liked me for my cheeseball?" I tease.

"That's just an added bonus."

Sticking my tongue out at her, I grab the choo-choo board and we head out to the lower patio. From here, we can see out onto the beach and it just so happens the college boys are playing beach volleyball this afternoon—total coincidence. **WINK WINK**

Fern and I finish the platter and wine and are on to a second bottle when Stefan comes back downstairs. From my spot on the lower patio, I watch him for a moment. He seems to be lost and in his own head. This baby thing is affecting him more than he's letting on. I know he's saying he's okay with it all, but this is Stefan Däuchmen we're talking about. He never takes bad news lightly, and while this isn't bad news, per se, it's news that'll change his life forever.

"What's going on between you two?" Fern asks out of nowhere.

"Come again?"

"You and him." She nods inside to where I was staring. "The relationship between you two has changed. Dare I say it, you even like him."

"I do like him," I confess.

"Like like? or just like?" Her questions stump me.

Previously it was just like, more like barely tolerate, but the more time I spend with him, the more I like him, but I cannot go there again. He's my client and most of the time he's a douche, but then there are times when he's sweeter than pie. "He's—" Before I can answer, Stefan shouts and throws his phone against the wall.

"Excuse me," I offer and head inside. "You good?"

"Do I fucking look good?"

"Well, no, you don't, but there's no need to be a jackass."

"Fuck off, Wren." Before I can prod him for more details, he stomps upstairs, leaving me standing here confused as to what just happened. A few moments later, the door to his room slams shut. The force rattles the painting on the wall underneath his room.

"I'm gonna get out of your hair," Fern says, joining me inside.

"You don't have to go," I tell her, but we both know that it'll be for the best if she does.

"Call me if you need anything." With that, she kisses me on the cheek and heads out, leaving me to deal with Stefan.

Returning to the patio, I bring in the empty platter and our glasses. I've just popped the bottle of wine back into the fridge when Stefan enters the kitchen. He's shirtless and water cascades down his bare torso. My eyes watch as a droplet races down his skin into the towel wrapped around his hips. I bite my lip to swallow down the groan that wants to slip out.

Thankfully, he didn't notice me checking him out.

He opens the fridge and grabs himself a beer and, being a gentleman, he grabs my bottle of wine and refills my glass.

Nodding my thanks, I take a sip. "You good?" I ask him.

"Yes. No, I don't know," he answers.

"Wanna talk about it?"

"Yes. No, I don't know," he repeats, and I can't help but laugh at his reply. My laugh causes his lip to lift slightly. "I saw that," I tease.

"You saw nothing."

"Mmmhmpf," I reply with a nod.

"Wanna watch a movie, eat popcorn, and forget about the world for a few hours?"

"Depends on what movie?"

"You're choice."

"My choice?" he repeats and I nod. "I can pick anything I want?"

"Yep."

"Okay, *IT*."

"Nope, no fucking clowns." He knows how I feel about clowns. He discovered my fear when we went to the local fair when we were at Tania's ranch. A clown came up to us, and I screamed like I was being murdered. Now that he knows of my aversion to them, he likes to taunt me. One day I will find what he's afraid of and it will be game on.

"You said anything," he retorts.

"No. Fucking. Clowns," I hiss between clenched teeth.

"I'm just messing with you. You know I hate scary movies too, but I couldn't help messing with you again."

"You're a jackass." I throw the tea towel in my hand at him.

"Ohhh no, not a tea towel." Flipping him the bird, I emphasize it with a poke of my tongue too. "Ohhh no—"

"Shut it or I'll make you watch *Inside/Out* again."

Stefan and I had a cartoonfest when we were in Colorado, both of us teared up in that movie when Bing Bong sacrificed himself. We both agreed it's one of the saddest movie deaths, up there with Thomas J in *My Girl* and John Coffey in *The Green Mile*.

"That's just mean. How about you get the popcorn started and I'll go change. Then we can scroll until we find something to watch?" he suggests.

"Deal," I agree.

Stefan turns and heads upstairs to get changed, and I get to making the popcorn. Before Stefan returns, I head upstairs and change into yoga pants and a Lockhart Falls

Fire Department sweatshirt. I bump into him on my way out and together we head down to the living room.

The two of us get comfy on the sofa and we binge watch *Grown Ups* and *Grown Ups 2*. We've just started *Tag* and my eyes become heavy. The next thing I know, it's morning. My head is in Stefan's lap, his hand is resting on my ass, and his morning wood is poking me in the cheek. Carefully I sit up, avoiding his dick, and I smile when I realize he pulled the blanket on the back of the sofa over me.

Sitting here, I watch him sleep and then I furrow my brow when I start to wonder what this pregnancy is going to do to him. He's either going to embrace fatherhood or it's going to implode like Hiroshima and there will be no saving him or his image.

17
STEFAN

"ONCE AGAIN, Stefan has shown us that he's still the party boy player we all know and love. Last night he was seen in a bar downing shots and having a good time with the locals," Margaret from *WtB* says to her viewers. "Later that night, he was found passed out on the beach in Venice in only his boxer briefs. Bystanders tell us he went for a midnight swim before promptly passing out. Word on the street is Stefan's contract with LA is on the line and his handler, Wren Brookes, is close to losing her career and reputation after not being able to tame her wild client."

"Fucking bitch," Wren hisses from beside me.

Flicking off the television, she throws the remote onto the coffee table and it flies across the wood, landing on the rug below. "I'm not losing my job but I might end up in jail." Wren turns her murderous gaze to me as I bend down and pick up the remote. "What the fuck were you thinking, Stefan?" Opening my mouth to defend myself, I pause because I really don't have a defense. I got news that rocked me to my soul and when Alicia and Tyrone—who by the way, is more of a douche than me—met up the following day, it didn't end well. He pissed me off with the way he was treating Alicia. He was being a massive dick to me and giving me attitude, it took everything I had not to punch the fucker in the face. After that I went out for a drink and before I knew it, I was drunk. Leglessly drunk. I ended up going for a night swim, and then I passed out on the beach.

End.Of.Story.

If it was any other person, no one would give a shit, but because I'm a God on the ice, what I do off the ice is everybody's business. When this baby news breaks, it's going to be everywhere. Margaret will have a fucking field day with this. "Please tell me, Stefan, how we went from an amazing afternoon of you hanging with the kids followed by a movie night. You then went to training them and BOOM, you acted like a frat dick from rush week combined with spring break. What gives?"

"I'm going to be a dad," I snap at her.

"And is that how a father behaves?"

"Well, no but—"

"No, no buts, Stefan. You need to man up and be the dad I know you can be. Now more than ever you need to change your ways. You're going to be a dad, Stefan." Her words "you're going to be a dad" slam into me like a freight train. "Ohhh," she adds, breaking the silence that fell between us. "Speaking of becoming a dad, I've already spoken with Sebastian."

Sebastian is my lawyer from Nobel and Hayes. He's the son of the owner and knows his shit. He's a little quirky and not my kind of guy, but he's a cutthroat lawyer and I'm glad to have him on my team. He has my back and my best interests at heart. He doesn't care that I'm a millionaire hockey player. He only cares about me and my estate. I've managed my money well since I started playing professionally and aside from my Venice Beach pad, I have my car, a bike, and a sizable stock portfolio. It's funny, I tried to hit on his sister, Soraya, once but she's a ballbuster and put me in my place. *The chick is hot, can you blame me?*

"Why did you speak with him?" I ask her, confused.

She raises her eyebrows in a *really* kind of way. "You have an appointment with him Tuesday morning after practice for Alicia to sign the NDA. He's also going to draft an agreement regarding the paternity and your rights and what you're willing to cover an—"

"Everything," I snap at her. "I will cover all expenses."

"Stefan—"

"Everything," I repeat. "I will not be one of those dads who isn't involved."

"I wouldn't expect anything less from you but, Stefan, just think about adding a clause that if you're not the father then all expenses must be returned."

"I'll chat with Sebastian and go with what he says. He's always had my back and this time will be no different."

"Good."

"Good," I reply. "Now, I'm going to head upstairs and soak off this hangover."

"You do that," she tells me. "I need to fix this shit you've found yourself in once again." Just as she says that, her phone rings and she curses before answering. "Jaxson, what can I do for you?"

From where I'm standing I can hear him yelling and I take that as my cue to leave.

Heading up to my room, I change into my board shorts and then climb the last flight of stairs up to the rooftop and slide into the hot tub.

Sitting in my spot, I stare out at the ocean as the water bubbles away around me. It eases the ache in my muscles from sleeping in an odd position on the beach last night.

Considering how much I drank over the evening, I feel pretty good.

It still blows my mind that I'm going to be a dad, guess my wild ways have finally caught up with me. I would have thought I'd be shitting my pants over the prospect of becoming a dad but, if I'm being honest, I'm kinda excited. I'm going to have a son. I'm going to be a dad to a little boy. I can picture he and I skating around the rink together. Hanging on the beach together in the offseason. This could be fun. Do I wish it was with someone I was in a committed relationship with? Well yeah, I do, but I have to accept the cards I'm dealt and that means I'm having a baby with Alicia.

I'm trying to remember our night together. She mentioned a club opening, and if my memory is correct, it was the night I was caught having a threesome in the alley, which resulted in Wren and I being shipped off to the mountains together. It was me, her, and another chick. I was fucking Alicia from behind and fingering her friend, we were about to swap positions when we were interrupted and that was when all hell broke loose.

A noise snaps me back to the present, and when I open my eyes, I see Wren standing there. She's wearing a red swimsuit that should be illegal, with a glass of wine in one hand and a beer in the other. She looks like a goddess in the afternoon sun and she's fucking hot.

We stare at one another for a few beats and then she asks, "Mind if I join you?

18
WREN

"FUCK MY LIFE," I grumble after hanging up with Jaxson. He was pissed over Stefan's antics from last night, but I've managed to get him back on team Stefan without telling him about the baby. I did so by mentioning an ex-bunny resurfacing and Stefan and, well, then he handled it how Stefan does, by self-imploding.

Stefan and I agreed it's best to keep the baby news and details of Alicia quiet until he meets with his lawyer. He has an appointment to meet with him on Tuesday, and Jaxson and I are scheduled to chat again after the lawyer visit. Depending on how that goes, we may or may not tell Jaxson, it's up to Stefan to make that decision.

Before we hung up, Jaxson asked me what I think of this woman who's popped back into Stefan's life. I told him exactly what I think, "Jaxson, that woman is a scheming conniving bitch. I don't trust her as far as I can throw her. I'd bet everything I have this is a ploy for fame and money."

He agrees and then asked me to pay attention to Alicia,

but I'd already decided to do that. My spidey senses are on high alert when it comes to this woman. Now I need to find a way to broach the topic with Stefan that will not cause him to go off the rails, again.

Needing a drink, I walk into the kitchen and grab a bottle of water from the fridge, but then I see the wine in the door and decide wine is what I need. I pop the water back onto the shelf, grab the wine, and pour myself a glass. Taking a sip, I instantly relax. Leaning against the counter, I sip on my wine and think over the day. I did *not* have this on my Stefan bingo card.

Finishing my wine, I think about what I want to do for the rest of the afternoon. My book and another wine up on the rooftop sounds like a fabulous idea, but then I remember Stefan's up there. Like Stefan, the rooftop has become my spot to get away and forget the world. I hem and haw as to whether I can interrupt him and decide that I deserve a break too.

Racing up to my room, I change into a bright red, halter one-piece. I'm about to head up to the deck when I realize I left my drink downstairs, so I head back down to the kitchen and grab it. I decide to grab a few beers for Stefan too, a peace offering of sorts.

With drinks in hand, I head back up. I'm huffing near the top and decide Stefan needs to put an elevator in. I'm pooped by the time I make it back up the two flights of stairs, and when I step outside, I see he's in his spot with his head back and eyes closed.

Standing here with our drinks in hand, I watch him for a few beats. His face is tense, and I guess that's due to the baby bomb. He must sense my presence because he lifts his head and stares at me.

"Mind if I join you?" I ask, but he doesn't answer. "I

brought drinks." I lift the drinks in my hand up. He still doesn't say anything, he just watches me but finally he nods and speaks.

"Well, you brought drinks, I can't turn you away now."

Smirking at him, I shake my head and place the wine and his beers into the mini fridge up here. Refilling my glass, I grab one of the beers for him and hand him one before I place my glass on the edge. Lifting my leg up, I climb in but my foot slips and I lose my balance. My arms flail about and I begin to fall and then I'm not. I'm held suspended in the air by a pair of muscular arms. Stefan leaped up and saved me from falling out of the hot tub and cracking my head open.

He holds me in his arms and I gaze up into his brown eyes. "You have gold flecks around your pupils," I mumble.

"And yours are an electric blue in this light."

We continue to stare into each other's eyes. The moment is almost romantic but as quickly as that thought appears, I'm back on my feet and Stefan is shuffling back to his side of the hot tub.

"Thanks for saving me," I tell him as I take my seat. Lying back, my body relaxes and I sigh in contentment.

"You'd do the same," he replies, taking a sip from his beer.

Looking to the side, I frown because during my recent trip, I knocked my wine over and now I have no drink.

"Why do you look like your dog just died?"

"Because I knocked my wine over and now I have to get out and get another one." But before I can blink, Stefan jumps up and climbs out. Water sluices down his body, and I watch with rapt attention as the water droplets cascade over each ripple of his abs.

Shaking off the last of the water, he walks over to the fridge and grabs my wine bottle. Then he opens the freezer compartment and pulls out a bucket and adds some ice from the ice maker because, yes, he has a built-in ice maker on his rooftop deck. Placing my bottle of wine and a couple of beers into the bucket, he walks back over to the tub.

Reaching out, he picks up my glass and refills it. He hands me my glass and when our fingers brush, a spark jolts between us, but as quickly as it was there it's gone again. Placing my wine back into the bucket, he grabs himself another beer.

Climbing back in, he returns to his spot and leans back. Sipping on his beer he stares off into the distance, returning to his thoughts from before I disturbed his peace.

"You okay?" I finally ask, the silence becoming too much.

"Mmmhmpf," he replies.

"So that's a no then?" He opens his eyes and stares over at me and shrugs. "Wanna talk about it?"

"What would I even say?"

"Whatever you're feeling," I honestly tell him.

"You want honesty?" Nodding, I wait. "Okay then, I'm feeling every emotion possible at the moment. I'm pissed at her for not telling me when she first found out. I'm excited at the prospect of having a son but at the same time, I'm scared fucking shitless at having a son. Then there's the worry about how the world is going to react. Everyone is going to say 'ha, the puckhead finally came unstuck' and they're going to want to know everything about my lil' man and there's nothing I can do to protect him from vultures like Margaret. That enough for you?"

"Do you feel better after getting all of that off your chest?"

He stares at me and thinks over my question. "Actually, I do."

"Then my job here is done."

"So you're moving out?"

"Well, that portion of my job is not done and with this new development, I think you need me more than ever. You feel like you're spiraling, you come to me. You don't do what you did last night. Is that how you want your son to see you?"

"God, no," he refutes. "I want him to look up at me with awe."

"Then listen to me and we can make that happen."

He nods and takes another sip of his beer. "Thank you," he murmurs.

"For what?" I'm kinda confused now as to why he's thanking me.

"For always having my back. I know I'm not the easiest person to be around and I sometimes do stupid things—"

"Only sometimes?" I cheekily interrupt.

"Hardy har har, Wren. But seriously, the old me would still be out on my bender but when I was lying on the beach, I started thinking about SJ."

"SJ?"

"Stefan Junior," he says with a smile.

"That's corny, even for you."

"Well, I need to think of a name for him and that's all I've got for now."

"It's a great name, Stefan," I deadpan, we both chuckle. "But I think you better discuss names with his mother." At the mention of her, I decide to just rip the Band-Aid off. "Speaking of her, what are you going to do about her and her partner? And are you..." But I stop myself before I blurt out what I really think because I don't want to upset him again but, at the same time, I need him to think clearly.

"Are you what?"

"Are you sure he's yours?" He mutely stares at me, processing my question. "You said it yourself, Stefan, you vaguely remember your night with her and you've always stated that you wrap it every time."

"Why would she lie?"

"Are you really asking that?"

"Yeah, I am."

"Stefan, you're a big-time hockey player. You earn in one game more than she's likely to earn in her entire life. This could be an easy cash grab for them."

"Or she really could be pregnant with *my* son, and if I come across as a cunt I will miss out on seeing my son grow up."

"Don't use the 'c' word, it's vulgar."

"What should I use then?"

"In this instance, there are many options. Asshole. Douche. Fuckface. Fucktard. Douchehole. Twat. Take your pick but whatever word you choose, get a paternity test before you fall in love with him ... or even her."

"Are you jealous?" he snaps at me.

"Why would I be jealous?"

"I see the way you look at me."

"And how's that?"

"Like you want to fuck me and live happily ever after with me."

"You really think that highly of yourself, don't you?" He shrugs and that shoulder movement pisses me off more than his words. "Fuck you, Stefan," I hiss.

Standing up, I climb out of the tub and grab my towel. Wrapping it around my body, I storm toward the stairs but before I head back inside, I turn back to him. "For what it's worth, I really hope you are the dad because when you talk about the baby, you get a glow in your eyes that I have only ever seen when you're on the ice. This could be good for you but at the same time, I worry you're being taken for a ride and as your friend, I want you to be careful."

With my piece said, I head inside and go to my bedroom. Closing the door behind me, I lean back against the wood and shake my head. He really is an egotistical douche but at the same time, he's really sweet. No wonder bunnies fall for his charm—not that *I'm* falling for him.

19

STEFAN

"ALL DONE," my lawyer states after Alicia finally signs the NDA. He's pushing for a DNA test but I want to speak with the doctor to make sure it won't harm the baby. I've googled it and it's pretty invasive and can be harmful to the baby, and that's the last thing I want to do to a child, mine or not.

Alicia was hesitant to sign at first but after my lawyer laid down the law—go Sebastian—realized she had no choice. Hell, even I signed quickly when he passed me the document. Sebastian is good at what he does and he can get anyone to sign anything. Hell, I'm pretty sure he could convince the sluttiest of sluts to join a convent.

Sebastian goes through all the paperwork and now that the I's are dotted and the T's are crossed, it's all done.

Tyrone didn't come with her and Sebastian has asked, well demanded, that he come in and sign one too. Alicia tried to argue he doesn't need to as is this between her and me, but Sebastian reminded her that if she wants anything from me, he will sign the NDA. His isn't as stringent as hers but it's still watertight.

With the paperwork and agreement finalized, Alicia and I exit the Nobel and Hayes offices. While we're waiting for the elevator to arrive, an uncomfortable silence envelops us. The only sound is the snapping of her gum as she chews loudly like a cow.

"You wanna grab lunch?" I ask her out of nowhere.

"Ohh, I'm, I can't. I have a scan to get to."

"Can I come?" The words pass through my lips before I have a chance to even think about it.

"You wanna come?"

"Yes, I do. I meant it when I said I want to be a part of my son's life. I'm not a total asshole."

She looks at me and just as the elevator arrives, she nods and mumbles, "Okay."

Nodding, we step in and I press the button for the garage and the car whisks us down to the underground lot. Escorting Alicia over to my car, I rest my hand on her lower back and I think of when I did this with Wren the other day. The heat and connection I felt with Wren, but now with Alicia, the mother of my unborn child, there's nothing.

We climb into my car and I reverse out of my spot. Round and round we drive till we appear on the street again. "Where to?" I ask.

She rattles off the address and I enter it into the navigation system. We leave downtown and head into Hollywood. With each mile that passes, the buildings become more and more derelict and the number of homeless people increases. An audible gasp leaves my lips when we pull into the parking lot of the doctor's office. The building before me looks like it's about to fall down. The once white exterior is covered in graffiti. The windows have bars on them and the path leading to the entrance is cracked with weeds growing between them.

"We aren't all millionaire hockey players," Alicia hisses when she sees the expression on my face.

"I ... I'm sorry," I stammer. Looking over at her, I take her in and she really is an attractive woman, not Wren attractive, but still attractive nonetheless. I can see why I hooked up with her. "I mean no offense, it's just, is this a safe area?"

She laughs. "Stefan, it's Hollywood not Skid Row. I've grown up here, this is home and it's where I'm going to raise my baby. If you don't like it, leave, I don't need you."

"I'm not turning my back on my child," I snap at her. "But seriously, does this doctor actually know what he's doing? This isn't some back alley thing, is it?"

"Oh My God, your privilege is showing, Stefan. And, yes, Dr. Sanchez knows what he's doing. His mom delivered me and he learned all he knows from her."

"So why isn't she looking after you?"

"Dr. S. was killed during a break-in. Some junkies looking for drugs attacked her when she was leaving one night. She put up a fight but one of the little punks stabbed her and she bled out."

"So safe," I deadpan, earning myself an eye roll from her.

A silence fills my car but it's broken when Alicia says, "Shall we?"

"Mmmhmpf," I reply, but I'm still not one-hundred-percent sure about any of this. Alicia climbs out and I follow suit. Meeting her by the hood, I pull on my cap and I tag along behind her into the building before us.

Thankfully, the inside is much nicer than the outside.

It's your typical sterile waiting room and I see two other pregnant women in various stages of pregnancy. They both eye me with suspicion and considering I'm the only male here, I don't take offense.

Alicia checks in with the nurse and then we take a seat. No sooner does she sit down and her name is called. Not wanting to overstep, I don't move. I just sit here and watch her walk toward the nurse. "You coming?" she asks over her shoulder.

The sound of her voice snaps me to attention. I jump up and follow her down the corridor and into the doctor's office. She walks over to a table and hops up. Resting her hands on the edge of the examination table, she swings her legs back and forth while I lean against the wall and we wait.

A few moments later, a young guy walks in. Is he even old enough to be a doctor?

"Alicia, good to see you again," he greets her. A huge smile is on his face and he gives me creepy vibes. "How ya doin', Alicia?"

"I'm good, Dr. Sanchez."

"How's the sickness?"

"Sickness?" I ask. "You didn't tell me you were sick."

"Morning sickness," she snaps and then looks back to the doctor and sweetly answers. "It's starting to settle down now, that medication is helping."

"Good, good. Well, let's have a look at your baby." He hands her a gown and pulls the curtain around the table she's sitting on and while she changes, he turns his attention to me.

"Good game on the weekend," he says while Alicia is changing.

"Thank you," I reply with a smile. After all these years, it's still so surreal to have strangers say things like that to me.

"And you are?"

"The dad," I outstretch my hand. He takes it and shakes.

"Nice to meet you."

"I'm ready," Alicia calls out.

Dr. Sanchez pulls back the curtain and I see Alicia on the table. She's got the gown on backward, I go to tell her, but then the doctor pulls the gown open and starts pushing around on her belly.

"Won't that hurt the baby?" I ask, fear lacing my voice.

"Not at all," he replies. "I'm just checking to make sure everything is where it's supposed to be, and it all feels good." He smiles and I nod. He presses a few buttons on the machine beside him and then he looks back at me. "You ready to see your son?"

Nodding my head, I stand here and watch as he squeezes gel onto Alicia's bump and then presses the wand thing to her stomach. The screen across from us flickers to life and before me I see a baby.

My baby, well, our baby.

I've seen this in movies and TV shows before but seeing it in real life is completely different. My eyes well with tears as I see the lil' dude kicking about. Without thinking, I reach out and grab Alicia's hand and squeeze.

"It's amazing, isn't it?" she murmurs, her eyes glued to the screen.

"It sure fucking is," I reply. "Shit, I shouldn't swear anymore, should I?"

"I think you'll be fine now but after he's born, yeah, might wanna curb the swears."

I chuckle at her words.

My eyes return to the screen and they are glued to the image of my lil' man, when it goes blank, I let out an audible, "Wow."

Dr. Sanchez laughs and then he hands me a strip of images. "Your lil' man," he says.

He and Alicia chat but I don't pay them any attention. I'm focused on the images Dr. Sanchez handed me. I already feel a connection with him. I don't need a test, he's mine. I feel it. I see movement out of the corner of my eye and when I look up, Alicia is sitting on the edge of the bed topless, the gown screwed up in her hand, and Dr. Sanchez is nowhere to be seen.

Quickly I avert my gaze and she laughs at me. "What are you being so bashful about, Stefan? You had your mouth on my nipples and your dick between my tits when we hooked up. Looking at them shouldn't be a problem."

"This is going to sound bad but, I kinda don't remember that night."

"Maybe we can recreate it one time?" she offers.

My mouth opens and closes, I'm at a loss over what to say but when she laughs, a deep belly laugh, I furrow my brows in confusion.

"I'm messing with you, Stefan."

Nodding my head, she pulls her shirt back on and hops off the examination table and heads to the door. Before she exits, she looks over her shoulder and seductively adds, "But anytime you want to suck or fuck them, I'm just a phone call away."

She exits the examination room, leaving me standing here stunned ... and a little aroused.

...a few weeks later

IT'S NEAR ON SUNSET, and Fern and I may have had a cocktail too many this afternoon. We are up on her and Bradford's deck, which is just as awesome as Stefan's but instead of the hot tub, theirs has a fireplace. Not that you need a fireplace in LA but the ambiance of drinking by a fire is great.

Arm in arm, she walks me out and the two of us are giggling like schoolgirls. "Thank you for this afternoon. I needed it."

"Youd may not says that tomorrow when you wake with the hangover from hell but we can blame José for tasting so good," she slurs.

"Yesd, tis José's faults," I hiccup and then giggle when I realize, I too am slurring.

Pulling her in for a hug, I lean back and stare at my gorgeous friend. "Dis was the bestest afternoon but next timed, don't drops de cheesedball."

"Hey, snot mys fault Mr. Woolley gots dit before meds."

"Goods shluck wis that. I've hearded dogds shits are, well, shitty to cleand up."

"Pissed off homes, you wench."

"Loves youd tood, wench," I singsong as I open the side door and make my way down to the boardwalk.

She sings out, "Tood-a-loo musderfucker" and I chuckle. Waving over my shoulder, I step onto the board-walk and head home. Fern begins to cackle like a hyena when I stumble over my feet. I just shake my head and flip her the bird. She's a crazy gal but she's a crazy gal I've come to love, and when her bestie, Calliope, or Cali as everyone calls her, comes for a visit, she's even crazier.

The fresh sea air slams into me, and my drunkenness amps up. I'm a little more drunk than I thought I was but, thankfully, Stefan's place is only a few houses down so it doesn't take me too long to walk—stagger—home.

When I reach the house, I hear muffled voices from down the side alley. Peeking around, I see Alicia and her boyfriend, Tyrone. They look to be having a hush-hush but heated argument. Not wanting to intrude, I walk backward away from them but in my drunken state, I trip over my feet. Ending up on my ass, I stare up at the sky and in the process, I garner the attention of the arguing couple. Tyrone marches over to me, his large frame looms above and he stares menacingly down at me. "What did you hear?" he hisses, spittle flying out of his mouth.

"Huh?" I ask.

"What. Did. You. Hear?" he growls again.

"Nnnnothings," I stammer. "Iiis justs gots here'd," I tell him but before I can say anything else Stefan arrives.

"What's going on?" he shouts and when he comes over and sees me on the ground, a murderous look appears on his face. "Wren, what happened? Why are you on the ground?"

Before I can answer, Tyrone answers for me. "She's drunk and fell over. I was just about to help her up when you arrived." And playing the "helpful hero" role, he reaches out and grabs my upper arm. Squeezing tightly, he wrenches me up to my feet, causing me to once again stumble.

Pulling my arm free, I lose my balance and fall into Stefan. He wraps his arms around me. "I got you," he murmurs and when I lift my gaze, I see concern etched on his face.

"You's shaveds," I drunkenly stammer and I run my fingers over his smooth scruff-free jaw.

"And you're drunk," he replies.

"I'ms fines," I tell him and no sooner do I say that, everything turns black.

"Ugh," I groan as I roll onto my side and into something hard. My eyes snap open, and I see a muscular back before me. "Shit. Shit. Shit," I hiss. Who the fuck is in the bed next to me? I don't remember much after leaving Fern's last night but surely I came straight home. I wouldn't have stopped off at a bar, would I????

"You're awake," a deep voice growls. They roll over to face me and my eyes widen in shock when I see it's Stefan. Relief at knowing the person filters through me and I relax a little. Then my eyes widen once again when I realize Stefan is in my bed and, I'm lifting the covers quickly, I see I'm in a Legends shirt that is not mine. My gaze snaps back to his and the asshole has a smirk on his face.

"Did we..." I quickly ask. My heart races as I await his answer.

"Have sex?" he asks, there's glee in his tone and I hate it. Nodding, I anxiously wait for him to answer me. "No, we did not. I prefer my partners to be awake when I fuck them. Somnophelia is not really my jam."

An unladylike snort slips out. "So there *is* something that Stefan Däuchmen won't fuck."

"Excuse me, I may be kind of a manwhore but even I have standards."

"Kind of? I'd say you're the president of the manwhore association."

"I like to think of myself as king of the manwhores."

"Shall I get you a crown?"

"I won't say no to a crown."

"Conceited much?"

Nonchalantly he shrugs before he climbs out of bed. He's only in a pair of black boxer briefs. The material hugs his ass perfectly and when he turns around, my mouth drops open. His morning wood is proudly standing to attention and it's poking out the top of his briefs. The mushroom head of his thick dick glistens in the morning light.

"Put some clothes on," I snap and cover my eyes, but I peek at him through the slits between my fingers because, hello, half-naked hockey player. He really is a fine specimen ... even if he is a douche. The day he was created, the angels were have a fan-fucking-tabolous day.

"I can see you peeking," he teases as he pulls his pants on.

"Was not," I quickly refute. I run my fingers through my hair but I don't get far due to the knots that are no doubt forming a bird's nest right now. How's that for fate, a half-naked hockey player and I look like a homeless bum.

"Let's agree to disagree." He chortles and then points to my bedside table. "There's water and headache tablets there for you."

"Thanks," I tell him. That's a really sweet gesture and it's confusing me. Like I know he can be sweet, I've seen it, but this is like super sweet. "Stefan," I ask. "Why are you here?"

"You were drunk, Wren. I wasn't going to leave you alone. What if you vomited in your sleep and you choked on it and died? Who would ride my ass when I do stupid shit if you were gone?"

"Stefan," I deadpan. "There's a long line of people who would like to ride your ass and I—"

"That's stating the obvious," he cheekily informs me with a waggle of his eyebrows ... and a smirk that has the potential to melt panties.

"Oh My God, you're so vain."

"No, that's a song by Carly Simon. I'm confident in my body ... and I know how to use my dick."

"Definition of vain," I inform him, but my eyes drop to his crotch. The cocky douche smirks at me before pulling his shirt over his head, making an effort to showcase his abs and dick.

Turning my back to him, I can't help the grin on my face. He *does* have a spectacular physique, but I'm not going to stroke his ego by admitting that out loud. Reaching over, I pick up the pills he left and uncap the bottle of water. Popping them into my mouth, I take a sip and swallow. My mouth feels less ashtrayish now, but my head is throbbing as if I'm at a rave.

"You feel like eggs?" he asks.

Nodding, I sit here and watch as he walks out of my room, closing the door behind him. Stefan constantly surprises me, and when douche Stefan is not around, I can actually stand the guy. He's really not half bad ... I must still be drunk to be thinking that but deep down, I know I'm not. Stefan *is* a nice guy, and I'm starting to become confused about my feelings when it comes to him.

I'M COOKING breakfast for Wren and me when there's a knock at the door. Looking up, I smile when I see Jaxson standing there. Sometimes I appreciate the clear entrance but other times, I wish it was frosted so I could hide away and not answer it.

Walking over, I let him in. "Jaxson, what are you doing here?"

"I think you know," he states and pushes his way past me. "I'll take a coffee, black. No sugar."

"Please, come in," I snarkily retort. "Can I get you a coffee?"

Jaxson just laughs and makes himself at home on one of the stools at the breakfast bar, while I turn on the coffee machine and make him his coffee.

"Thanks," he says, taking the mug from me. I turn back to the stove and add the eggs to the pan.

"That smells good, what you whipping up for me?"

"I'm making eggs for Wren," I reiterate her name.

"She not well?" he asks, taking a sip of his coffee.

"Hungover," I tell him.

"I'm not hungover," a soft voice says from the stairs.

We both turn toward the sound of her voice, and my eyes widen when I take Wren in. No longer is her hair a bird's nest, and there's no trace of the panda eyes from when she first woke up. She's in those jeans of hers that mold to her body and highlight her ass. She's wearing a Legends tee and blue Converse that match the team colors.

"Jaxson," she says his name by way of greeting and walks over to the coffee machine. She makes herself a cup. "So, what are you doing here? You hate the beach."

"I was in town for a friend's wedding yesterday."

"You have friends?" I cheekily tease just as Wren sits next to Jaxson with her coffee in hand.

"Yes, I have friends ... even if he is a client of mine."

"Anyone I might know?" I ask him.

"Marshall Kerr."

"I heard he was getting married. The playboy of racing has finally settled down. You want some?" I lift the pan of eggs up and he nods. Getting out another plate, I dish three plates up and slide two over to Wren and Jaxson.

Before I eat mine, I hand Wren her bitch juice, aka her morning OJ, and make her another coffee—black, no milk or sugar. I made that mistake once and my balls are still frightened each time I make her one. Fearful that a speck of sugar or a splash of milk will have made its way into her cup of black tar. Don't get me wrong, I like coffee but it needs to have Italian sweet crème added. Yes, I know, it's not what you'd expect someone like me to drink but it's mother's milk. Chefs kiss if you will, but then again, it's no secret that I like White Claws.

Leaning on the counter, we all dig in. Silence surrounds us as we eat but as soon as Jaxson is finished, he places his cutlery down and turns to Wren. He has a look on his face I cannot read. "Something you want to tell me?"

She furrows her brows and looks at Jaxson. "Ummm, no?" It comes out like a question.

"So Stefan isn't about to become a dad?"

"Ohh that," she replies.

"You didn't think as his agent I should know something as important as that?"

"We're dealing with it," she matter-of-factly tells him.

"And how are you dealing with it?" He air quotes the last three words.

"Stefan and Alicia are still hammering things out but it's been amicable so far, and Stefan will be there every step of the way."

After we've explained things, he's changed his tune. Jaxson's dad is a deadbeat dad and this is hitting close to home for him, so once he has the complete story and realizes that I'm going to step up, his demeanor changes.

"Are you sure it's yours and this is not a play for fame and money? Have you considered a paternity test?"

"He's mine," I growl between clenched teeth.

"How can you be sure?"

"The doctor we went to all but confirmed the conception date is when she and I hooked up and because I trust her. I get you and Wren have my best interests at heart but I also have a brain, and I know he's mine."

"Like you can remember every hookup you've had," Jaxson throws back at me.

"I. Trust. Her." Emphasis is placed on each word. My fists clench and unclench at my sides, and I tell myself that I cannot hit my agent. No matter how much of a douche he's being right now. Why does no one trust me about this? Sure, I've made shitty decisions in the past but when I step up and be a man about the situation I find myself in, everyone doubts me. I cannot win, no matter what I do, the people around me don't trust me.

Jaxson nods and turns and focuses on Wren. "Wren?"

"It's Stefan's decision. He knows how I feel."

"And how is that?" Jaxson questions her. Wren doesn't answer him and she avoids my gaze. "Wren," he warns. "What are your thoughts?"

She lifts her gaze to mine but quickly averts it and focuses on Jaxson. "Stefan trusts her, therefore, I trust him trusting her."

"I call bullshit," he snaps at her. "No one trusts him, and the fact you're saying you trust him tells me that you don't trust him."

"You asked for my opinion on the matter and I told you. I trust him trusting her. And for what it's worth, since he found out, have you seen him in the headlines?" *Well apart from the first night but Jaxson doesn't know that was the cause of that bender.* "No, you have not. As much as I'd like to take credit for that, it's the baby bombshell that did that." She takes a deep breath. "I really think this baby is a good thing." Her mouth opens and closes like she has more to say, but in an unlike Wren fashion, she stays quiet.

"Very well then," Jaxson voices. "Seems like you have it all under control."

"That we do."

Silence falls over us but it's broken when Jaxson's phone rings. He looks at the screen. "I have to take this, excuse me." He stands up and walks through the living room and out onto the lower terrace.

The two of us sit here, still not saying anything.

"Thanks for having my back with Jaxson just now," I tell Wren as we both begin to clean up the kitchen.

"Mmmhmpf," she nonchalantly replies. I get the feeling she's not telling me the truth when it comes to Alicia. Come to think about it, Wren and I haven't really spoken about it in detail. Every time it's come up, something has interrupted us.

"You do mean what you said, right? You trust me?"

She pauses wiping down the countertop and when she looks to me, I know I'm not going to like what she has to say. "I do trust you, Stefan. You've really changed these last few weeks but when it comes to Alicia, just be careful."

"Why does no one trust me regarding her?"

"I trust *you*. It's *her* I don't trust."

"Well I do, Wren," I snap, pissed off because I thought she had my back.

"That's all well and good, Stefan, but you are blindly believing what she's telling you. You're a mega-rich athlete, and she's well, not a mega-rich person. I still agree with your lawyer; you really need to consider a paternity test. Yes, the doctor confirmed the dates match up, but I can't believe you think her word is concrete and she wasn't screwing anybody else."

"I was there for the sonogram, Wren. That baby is mine. When I saw the grainy image on the screen, I felt a connection. Why can't you believe it?"

"I want to believe it, but there's just something I don't trust about her and Tyrone. I really think you need to be careful when it comes to Alicia."

"That's your opinion but Alicia is a part of my life, and we're having a child together. You need to accept that or you and I are going to have a problem."

Throwing the tea towel down on the counter, I storm out of the kitchen. Little did I know, it would be *me* with the problem.

22
WREN

I'M ready for today to be over.

Actually, I'm ready for this year to be over and this just now, is the icing on the shitcake that is my life right now.

Not only do I have to deal with *him* but now I have to deal with *her* as well. There is something about Alicia that has my spidey senses tingling, but she seems to have Stefan wrapped around her pinky finger. I will give her credit in that he's been less of a douche recently, but we lost douchey Stefan and have gained bitchy Alicia ... not sure which is worse.

But right now, those two are the least of my concerns, some jackass hacked my credit card so I've spent the last million hours down at the bank getting that sorted. Thankfully, Stefan lent me his car so I didn't have to rely on public transportation but it left me to the traffic that is LA, and it's almost as sucky as my life right now.

To top my day off, on the way home after stopping for groceries, some moron sideswiped the bus in front of me, causing me to nearly run into the ass of said bus because I wasn't completely paying attention. I was listening to Margaret rattle on about the recent nuptials of Kallen and Chelsea, and that they are all on bump watch since she looked "chubby" the other day when they left the stadium. Who does this woman think she is? I'd love for someone to report on each and everything she does and eats. See how she likes it.

After finishing with the police since I was an eyewitness, I'm allowed to leave but due to the time of day now, I'm stuck in peak rush-hour traffic and it takes me almost an hour to travel three miles. At least I had my Spotify playlist to keep me company, and I had my very own rock concert. The stereo in the G-Wagon is amazing.

Finally I pull onto our street and I cannot wait to relax. I'm going to grab a bottle of wine, my Kindle, and head up to the hot tub to unwind. However, that feeling of relief at being home dissipates when I pull into the driveway and see Alicia's car.

Letting out a frustrated sigh, I mumble, "Great." Before I climb out, I flick the stereo's volume to the upper limit so when Stefan gets in tomorrow morning for early practice, it will blast TayTay at him.

Leaving his car in the driveway because I hate parking the monstrosity in the garage, I head inside. When I walk in, the two of them jump apart and from the look on each of their faces, I walked in on something. It's like I caught two teenagers doing things they shouldn't have been doing.

"Hey, guys," I greet them and walk into the kitchen to dump my bag and unpack the groceries I picked up.

"Get it all sorted?" Stefan asks me, walking over to where I'm standing at the kitchen island, leaving Alicia in the living room by herself.

"Yeah, but I have to wait for them to investigate, and it'll be a week or so till I get new cards and whatnot."

"Let me know if you need anything."

"Thanks," I tell him with a smile. Alicia clears her throat and both Stefan and I turn to face her. She has a scowl on her face and looks pissed off. "Sorry, did I interrupt something?"

At the same time they both answer with different responses. She replies with a snarky "Yesss," hissing the S, while Stefan matter-of-factly states, "No." Sensing it's about to get heated in here, I walk over to the wine cabinet and grab a bottle of merlot. "I'm just gonna head up to the hot tub, I'll leave you both to it."

With my bottle of wine in hand, I walk up the stairs and leave the two of them to get back to whatever they were doing when I walked in.

Walking into my room, I change into a teal one-piece with side cutouts. Slipping a cover-up over me, I grab my Kindle and when I exit my room, from below I hear heated and hushed voices. Quickly, I head to the rooftop and leave the two of them to it.

I'm on my second glass of wine when Stefan appears. Holding my breath, I wait for Alicia to appear behind him, but he's alone. Relief floods me at it being just him but the relief disappears when Stefan growls, "I don't know why you're so rude to her."

"Excuse me?" I snap in defense, he did not just accuse *me* of being rude.

"Just now. You were rude to Alicia."

"I never said a word to her."

"Exactly," he huffs.

Removing his shirt, he tosses it on the table and climbs into the tub with me. Each of us sitting in our unofficial proclaimed spots, reminding me of Sheldon and *his* spot in *the Big Bang Theory*.

"So your pissed because I didn't say anything past hello?"

"I'm not, but Alicia is," he tells me.

"Well, have her say something to me."

"I would but she, umm, doesn't really like you."

"Why? I hardly know her."

"That's what I said and then she got all pissy, threw a fit, and left."

Nodding, I sip on my wine and process his words. "You don't find it odd that she hates me for no apparent reason?"

He shakes his head. "Nah, I just presumed it's a chick thing."

"Stefan—"

"Don't go there, Wren. I know you don't trust her but whether you like it or not, she's a part of my life. She's the mother of my child, and I will be there for my child. I may be an asshole, but I'm not going to let an innocent child be caught in the crosshairs of my life."

"You sure it's your child?" I mumble under my breath, but going by the murderous look on Stefan's face, he heard me.

"Why are you so quick to judge?"

"Why are you so quick to believe her?" I throw back at him. "Stefan, use your brain, and not the one between your legs. Her word isn't proof that you're the baby daddy. I hope I'm wrong but something with her and Tyrone rubs me the wrong way."

"What will it take for you to trust me?"

"A paternity test. Find out once and for all if you are the father. Once there is irrefutable proof you are the father, then I will support you, but until that happens, I cannot support something I don't believe. Now, if you'll excuse me, I need to go before I say something else to piss you off."

"I'm not pissed, I just wish people would trust me."

"Then do stuff to earn that trust. Stefan, look at your past, you have not done one thing for anyone to trust you."

"I'm trustworthy," he hisses.

"Saying it and proving it are two different things, Stefan."

With that, I climb out of the hot tub, grab my towel, and head back inside. Before I close the door behind me, I look over at Stefan and I find myself smiling. He really is trying to be a better person. I just wish it wasn't because of a lie. And I know it's a lie. I will catch Alicia, and when I do, all hell is going to break loose.

23
STEFAN

IT'S the second intermission and we're leading Vegas, three to one. I've scored two of our three goals. I'm on fire tonight, and the crowd is going wild. The bar after the game is going to be cray-zy. Normally when I'm in Vegas, I skip the bar and hook up with this chick named Raquel. She's one of the bunnies I was with when Chelsea came home. Raquel fucks like a rabbit and sucks dick like a Hoover. I've been avoiding her calls and texts all day but just before the game, she sent a photo of her and a friend naked together. I'm sorely tempted to head over to her place after the game, but I've promised Alicia I'll behave while I'm away. I'm not sure what's happening between the two of us, but I kind of want to see where this will go. I mean, we share a child. I know she's with Tyrone, but surely baby daddy trumps boyfriend, right?

"Stefan," Wren shouts, running into the locker room. She *never* comes into the locker room during a game or after practice, not since she walked in to see Brayden Sharpe doing the helicopter with his dick. That guy is hung like a fucking donkey and after hearing him and his wife going at it in an alley while out one night, he knows how to used said monster cock.

When I look up, she's got an expression on her face that I don't recognize. "What's up?" I ask when she reaches me.

"It's Alicia," she pants, "she went into labor."

"But the baby isn't due for another five weeks."

"Babies come when babies come," my teammate, Johannes Innes, and dad of three states.

"But there's still a period to go," I state like a fool.

My heart is racing and not from exertion from the game. It's thumping away at the prospect of meeting my little man. I'm about to become a dad. Ever since Alicia dropped the baby bombshell, I've been excited and now it's here. There's going to be a mini me out in the world.

"Family always comes first, Stefan," Coach Barber says. "Go meet your baby. We've got this."

Nodding, I stare at my coach and process his words. Then I smile brightly because I'm about to meet my baby. I know I sound like a sap, and the old me would totally be teasing me for being such a pussy.

Then it hits me, I'm about to be a dad. I'm excited and scared. So fucking scared. What if I fuck this up? I'm not the most responsible of people, but I have made strides since finding out I'm going to be a dad. Even Wren said so, and she doesn't offer me any kind of praise whatsoever. Okay, well, that's not entirely true.

"Okay," I mumble.

"I'll meet you outside," Wren says and then she's walking away from me.

While I strip out of my gear and change into my street clothes, the team passes on their congrats. While the guys retake the ice, I race out of the locker room to meet up with Wren. With my bag over my shoulder, I step out of the locker room and find Wren in the hallway with her phone to her ear. She's glued to that thing but where I play stupid games, she's working. Non-fucking-stop.

When she sees me, she smiles and wraps up her call just as I join her. "I've arranged a car for us to get back to LA, since we travelled here on the team bus. It should be dropped off here in the next fifteen minutes."

I'm glad Wren is here with me because I didn't even think about transport back to LA. "Thank fuck you're here, Wren, I'd be stuck if it wasn't for you."

"Just doing my job," she says.

"No, Wren. This is over and above. Your job is to keep my ass in line, not get me back to LA so I can meet my baby."

She looks at me pensively, something passes between us but as soon as it arrives, it's gone again and the sound of her phone receiving a text pulls her gaze from mine. "Car's here," she informs me, and then she turns on her heel and walks toward the player entrance.

Five hours later and we're back in LA. An hour after hitting the city limits, we reach the hospital. LA traffic sucks at the best of times but when you really want to be somewhere, it's even shittier.

"You should be a race car driver," I tell her as she pulls up in front of the hospital. "Maybe you need to get Jaxson to sign you with Marshall's team."

Putting the car into park, she lets out a breath and unclenches her fists from the steering wheel. "Pffft, I don't think so, besides, all I did was drive ... maybe a few miles over the speed limit."

"And what about the weaving between cars once we hit the city limits?"

"It was just driving," she says. "But I got you here. That's the main thing." Her voice is timid but I guess she's tired after the long drive.

Sitting here, I don't make a move to get out. Suddenly I'm anxious and not sure if I'm ready to do this.

"In you go," she says, breaking the silence.

"You're not coming in?" I ask but she shakes her head.

"Apart from Alicia not wanting me there, this should be a moment between mom, dad, and the baby."

"You sure?"

"Positive, but call me when you want me to come get you."

"Thanks, Wren." I reach out and cover her hand sitting on the gearshift. She drops her gaze to our joined hands and lifts it back to mine. She smiles but it doesn't reach her eyes. I climb out before the moment becomes awkward.

Gazing at the building, I just stand here and stare at nothing in particular. The sound of the car pulling away garners my attention. Turning around, I watch it drive away. A part of me wishes I was still in the car with Wren. When it's just the two of us, it's peaceful and I feel contentment, but out here it's a wild world. Generally due to my actions and right now, the biggest consequence of my life is about to become a reality.

I'm about to become a dad, and as much as I'm excited for it, I'm also shit fucking scared. My life is chaotic at the best of times. Add a baby into the mix and it's going to be volatile. Alicia and I have spoken about what's going to happen, but what if it all turns to shit? What if this is the catalyst for the end of my career and life?

24
WREN

PULLING AWAY FROM THE CURB, I head out of the hospital parking lot and I stare at Stefan in the rearview mirror. He stands there, watching me drive away, and just before I pull out onto the street, he turns and heads into the building to meet up with Alicia and his child.

On autopilot, I drive home. Parking the rental in the driveway, I grab my handbag and walk down the boardwalk to Fern's place. I don't want to be alone right now. I don't know why.

"Wren, what are you doing here?" Bradford asks when he answers the door.

"Hi, umm, is Fern here?"

"Yeah, come on in." He closes the door and calls out, "Fern, Wren's here ... I think you need wine ... or tequila."

Normally I'd laugh at that, but not tonight, Fern steps into view and as soon as I see my friend, I burst into tears. She walks over to me and wraps her arms tightly around me as I fall apart.

"Wren, babe, what's going on?" she asks when I finally stop crying.

"Alicia went into labor," I tell her.

"Is everything okay with the baby?"

"I don't know. I dropped Stefan off and I left. I ... I just couldn't be there."

"Because you like him more than you want to admit?"

"Yes. No. Maybe." She looks at me. "Okay, fine, yes I like the douche more than I should but..."

"But what?"

"He's my client."

"Don't give me that shit." Fern scoffs. "Bradford was my boss when we first got together."

"That's different," I throw back at her just as Bradford arrives with two glasses of wine.

"I'm going to head over to Carlton's. I'll, ummm, leave you two girls alone to, ummm, chat." He looks to me. "For what it's worth, Wren, I say fuck the rules. Rules are meant to be broken and, sometimes, breaking the rules leads you to the best thing to ever happen to you." With those words of wisdom imparted, he kisses Fern and leaves. Leaving me to process his words.

"He's right you know," Fern agrees.

"I know he is but—"

"Do not finish that sentence unless you're going to tell me that you're going to give it a go."

"I was going to say it's not that simple when my livelihood is on the line."

"Hello, I fucked my boss. The man who signed my paycheck. The man who held the power to fire me."

"But you two are different. You two are meant to be. Stefan and I ... we'd be a mess."

"A pucking hot mess," she unhelpfully adds. "That man

is H O double T hot, and with the number of bunnies he's had, he clearly knows how to use what God gifted him."

"Oh. My. God. Fern, don't let Bradford hear you say that."

"He's happy for me to window-shop but, umm, have you seen my man? I know where I'm supposed to be ... just like you do, too."

Shaking my head, I take a sip of my wine and sigh, what the puck am I going to do?

25
STEFAN

AFTER ASKING FOR ASSISTANCE, I follow the directions given and I make my way up to the maternity ward. The elevator is taking forever so I enter the stairwell and walk up the four flights of stairs. Pushing the door open, I'm met with the sound of crying babies. "Guess I better get used to that," I mumble as I walk over to the nurses' desk.

My looming presence garners the nurse's attention, and she lifts her head. Then she does a double take when she realizes it's me. "You're ... you're S-s-s-stefan D-d-d-d-däuchmen," she stammers.

"In the flesh," I reply, offering her a smile. Her cheeks darken, and I know I've found a fan, possibly even a bunny. If I wasn't here to meet my baby, I'd take her in the closest room and give her a moment to remember forever, but that's the old me. The new me is a responsible dad. "I'm here to see Alicia Rockwell."

"Ohhh." Her face drops when I mention Alicia and then something passes over her expression. "Are you..."

"The dad," I answer with a smile when she doesn't finish the sentence.

"Ohhh, umm, shit." *Okay, this just got weird*, I think to myself. "Room seven," she says and points down the hall.

Nodding, I turn and head to room seven to meet my son.

Reaching number seven, the door is closed. Pausing, I wonder if I should knock but I decide not to in case the baby is sleeping. Lifting my hand, I press down on the handle and when I step into the room it's quiet. Alicia is lying in the bed with her back to me. My gaze darts around, looking for my lil' man, but I can't see a bassinet anywhere.

Walking farther in the room, Alicia stirs and when she rolls toward me, it stops me in my tracks. Her eyes are red, swollen, and bloodshot from crying.

"Alicia, what's wrong? Where's the baby?"

My question causes her to burst into tears again. She's sobbing uncontrollably as I climb onto the bed and pull her into my arms. She presses her face into my chest, her tears soak my shirt but I don't care. I just want to know what's going on. Finally she calms down. "Alicia, talk to me, sweetheart. What's with the tears?"

"He ... he died," she murmurs.

"What?" I hiss, it's louder and harsher than I intended and Alicia flinches in my arms.

"He didn't make it. The birth was so quick, and I did that final push and then there was nothing. He ... he didn't cry and when I looked at the doctors and nurses, I knew something was wrong."

"He ... he died?" I repeat and she nods. Tears stream down her cheeks again. Reaching out, I wipe under her eyes but it's fruitless. "How?"

"Something called birth asphyxia."

She doesn't elaborate and, right now, I'm okay with that. All that matters is that we lost our little boy.

Alicia and I lie here, wrapped in each other's embrace. She's drifted off to sleep and I focus on the steady inhales and exhales of her breathing.

Slipping my phone out of my pocket, I google birth asphyxia. I'm shocked to find that this affects around nine-hundred-thousand babies each year. There's no rhyme or reason as to why it happens, it just does. There is literally nothing Alicia could have done. I'm guessing that must be killing her right now because I know I feel helpless. I can't make the pain go away for either of us, I can't wave my bank account at the doctors and say fix him. All I can do is hug her and be here for her.

Placing my phone back in my pocket, I stare up at the ceiling. My eyes are starting to droop when there's a knock on the door. Lifting my head, I wait for them to enter but instead of the door opening, they knock again.

"Come in," I whisper-shout but it must have been enough because in walks Tyrone. When he sees Alicia in my arms he growls and glares at me. Carefully, I shuffle out of the bed. Alicia stirs but curls into a ball and falls back to sleep. She's exhausted, physically and mentally. I cannot imagine how she's feeling right now. She went through the pains of labor, only to have our little man taken away from her.

"What are you doing here?" Tyrone snaps at me when we step into the hallway.

"I was here to meet my son, but that didn't quite pan out." He stares back at me and is about to say something when a guttural scream comes from the room behind me.

Spinning around, Tyrone and I both bust into the room. Alicia is sitting upright in bed, one hand covers her mouth and the other her stomach. Tears are once again pouring down her cheeks. Taking a step forward, I'm shoved to the side when Tyrone races over to her. Enveloping her in his arms, she cries into his shoulder, just like she did for me earlier. "Ohhh, baby," Tyrone coos and he holds on to her. "It's okay, it's all going to be okay."

Awkwardly I stand here and watch her break down ... in the arms of her boyfriend.

"It's my fault," she blubbers. "It's my fault he's gone."

"Alicia," I voice, causing both of them to look at me. "There is nothing you could have done. I googled it. This is just one of those things that happen. It's not your fault."

"He's right," Tyrone agrees with me. He gives me a look of thanks, and he stands up, letting me get closer to Alicia.

Walking over to them, I take her hand and squeeze it. Reassuring her that I'm here.

"This is my fault. It's all my fault," Alicia cries as she pulls her hand away. She turns her back to Tyrone and me and curls herself into a ball. "This is my penance."

"Penance? For what?" I ask, confused. Sitting on the edge of her bed, I rub my hand up and down her arm and she continues to cry into the pillow.

Taking a deep breath, she looks over her shoulder at me. "He wasn't yours, Stefan. I lied."

"What?" I ask, pulling my hand back from her arm. Standing up, I run my hands through my hair as I process her words. "He wasn't mine?" I voice the question, not expecting an answer but when she does, my world once again falls apart.

"Tyrone is the father. He and I saw a way to make a few bucks."

"What? How? The doctor confirmed everything was going well. Yes, he was on the larger side but we put it down to him taking after me."

"I lied about the conception date. I lied about everything, and now, I lost my baby for being deceitful."

Standing here, I stare at the woman before me. At the woman who lied to me.

"You lied to me," I whisper. "You fucking lied," I hiss louder. "You made me fall in love with a baby that wasn't even mine." My voice is like thunder. "I grieved over losing my son when he wasn't even my son." My hands are clenched into fists at my sides. The longer I stare at her and Tyrone, the more my anger builds. "You're a fucking bitch," I sneer at her.

"Watch your mouth," Tyrone snaps at me.

"Fuck off, cunt. That bitch here has just ruined my life. She—"

"Sir," a voice from behind me commands. "I'm going to have to ask you to refrain from language like that or I'll have security escort you out. This woman has been through enough—"

"This woman here," I interrupt the nurse, "this woman here lied. She fucking deserves everything she's going through and then some." Turning back to Alicia, I shake my head. "That kid deserved better than to have you two as its parents. I never want to see either of you ever fucking again."

Before I say anything else, I storm out of the room, kicking a chair in the hallway on my way past in frustration. The plastic item sails through the air and crashes to the floor with a loud bang. Seconds later, babies cry from within the rooms around me and before security is called, I exit the maternity ward and hospital. I head to the closest bar to drown my sorrows ... and my pain.

26
WREN

"WHERE THE FUCK HAVE YOU BEEN?" I growl at Stefan when he finally surfaces ...three days later. The last I saw of him, he was standing outside the hospital about to go inside to meet his son.

Then nothing.

No one could find him, but of course, Margaret from *WtB* did. Since he went missing, she's plastered numerous images of a drunk and passed out Stefan all over the socials. She's speculating as to what's caused his recent spiral but as of yet, she hasn't discovered the why ... and neither have I.

"Fuck off, Wren, I don't need this right now."

"The fuck I will," I shout at him. "Stefan, you've been gone for three days. Three fucking days of radio silence. If it wasn't for Margaret, we'd have no clue what's been going on. I know you celebrate after a baby is born but this, this is wild, even for you."

"Don't, Wren," he warns. "I've had a rough few days. I don't need you riding my ass too."

"Newsflash, Douche, it's my job to ride your ass. Now, explain."

He stares at me and just when I think he's going to ignore my question, he lets it all out. "The baby died and I'm not the dad."

"What?" I exclaim, totally confused right now.

He walks over to the wet bar and grabs a bottle of bourbon. Taking a swig, he turns to face me and then he explains what happened. When he's finished, I kind of feel like a bitch for going off on him like I did just now but before I can say anything else, he takes another swig. Turning his glassy drunken gaze to me, he adds. "Now, if you'll excuse me, I need to shower and then I'm heading to Club Mudd to drown my sorrows."

"What about hockey? You missed the game, and Leif is pissed."

"My son died," he growls. "I'm allowed to grieve."

"I'm not saying you can't but you have responsibilities. You need to let people know what's happening." I pause. "Let us help you, Stefan." As much as this guy grates on my nerves, my heart is breaking for him right now. I knew this woman would fuck him over, and she's done a spectacular job of doing it. Now it's to me to save him before he does something *really* stupid.

"Fuck the responsibilities. Fuck people. Fuck life and fuck you. My son died and his bitch of a mother lied to me. I think I'm entitled to take a few fucking days."

Without uttering another word, he storms up the stairs and slams the door to his room behind him.

"Fuck my life," I mumble.

Jumping up onto the kitchen counter, I try and come up with a game plan but this is new territory for me. My phone rings and it's Leif.

"He's here," I say in greeting.

"Well, that's good. What did he say?"

I fill Leif in on what Stefan just told me.

"Fuck me," is his response. "But why is he melting down?"

"Because he's gutted, Leif. He was so excited to be a dad and, right now, her betrayal hurts just as much as the baby dying."

"That's fair, but does he need to act like a toddler about it?"

"He is Stefan DOUCHEman," I tell him, earning myself a chuckle but, unfortunately for me, that also happens to be when Stefan comes back downstairs.

"Tell me how you really feel," Stefan snaps as he stands on the last step and stares at me. Hurt is all over his face, and I think it's more from my words than from what's happened with Alicia and the baby.

"Stefan," I say his name but from the look he's giving me, it confirms it's my words that hurt him. "Don't let me stop you from the gossip session," he says with a snarl and before I can say anything, he turns on his heel and stomps back up the stairs to his room, once again slamming the door.

"I'll call you back," I tell Leif.

"Good luck," he states before we disconnect.

Standing here, I stare up at his room, wondering how I can fix this. He's right to be hurt and angry but there's a correct way to do it. I just wish I knew how to get through to him. Letting out a sigh, I head up to my room to take a shower.

Great ideas often come to me in the shower, but today, nothing comes to me. All I can think about is the hurt radiating from Stefan. I cannot believe Alicia did that, well, I can. A small part of me feels sorry for her; she lost her baby and Stefan. Then again, she was only using Stefan, so she's probably not upset over that loss.

Climbing out of the shower, I dry off and pull on my comfy yoga pants and a racer-back tank. My stomach growls so I head down to the kitchen to get a snack but when I enter, I find Stefan sitting on the floor. He's holding the ultrasound photo from the fridge in one hand and a half empty bottle of bourbon in the other.

"Ohhh, Stefan," I voice as I squat down in front of him. Taking the bottle from his grasp, I place it on the counter and grab a bottle of water from the fridge. Uncapping it, I hand it to him and, shocking me, he drinks it.

"You're so good to me," he drunkenly slurs.

"And you're an asshole to me," I throw back at him.

"Yep, but as they say, boys who tease girls like them."

"Mmmhmpf." I nod. "Let's see how you feel in the morning."

"I'll still be me."

"One can hope you will change overnight but, luckily, dreams are free."

"Why do I need to change? Why can't everyone else?"

"Because you're the one with a chip on your shoulder. Stefan, you have the world at your feet but when shit happens, you implode."

"She lied," he growls at me.

"I told you she was lying."

"I don't need an 'I told you so' right now, I just need—"

"To put on your big boy panties and get back to your life."

"I think I'm entitled to a few days grace."

"There's grace and then there's being a doucheface asshat, guess which category you fall into?"

He chuckles and shrugs at me. "And just so you know, Leif wants to cut you from the team. He doesn't feel your skill is worth the hassle, but luckily for you, Tania has a soft spot for you. She's rooting for you to pull your head out of your ass."

Somehow I manage to wrangle a drunk Stefan upstairs and into the shower. Leaving him to wash himself, I change his sheets because who knows what's in them or who he's had between them recently. I've just spread out his duvet when he appears. "Feel better?"

He nonchalantly shrugs and I pull back the covers and he climbs in. Smiling at him, I turn to exit but he reaches out and grabs my wrist. "Don't leave me, please," he begs.

My heart breaks for him, even if he is making my life a living hell right now.

The fallout from the baby bombshell is crazier than I ever imagined. I didn't realize how much Stefan was invested in this baby. In the baby I knew wasn't his. I hate that I was right because dad-to-be Stefan is—was—the kind of guy I envision myself with one day. He was doting. Caring. Loving. Three adjectives I don't think have ever been used to describe Stefan Däuchmen before. Conceited. Egotistical. Douche. Those are the three that immediately come to mind.

He tosses the duvet aside and taps the mattress beside him. Against my better judgment, I climb in next to him. He shuffles us around so his head is resting on my chest, his arm is over my waist, and his leg is thrown over mine. He's effectively pinning me to the mattress next to him.

He snuggles into me and when I feel his body start to shake, I run my hand soothingly up and down his back. "He died, Wren," he blubbers. "But what hurts the most is he wasn't mine. I was in love with another man's baby because she lied. She should have died, not him."

"You don't mean that."

"I do. I hate her, Wren. She's ruined my life."

"No, Stefan, you're doing that all on your own. Yes, what's happened sucks, but you're an adult and right now, you're acting like a child."

"But—"

"Nope, no buts, Stefan."

"I'll get your butt one day."

"Hell will freeze over before anyone gets near my ass, let alone you. Now, close your eyes and go to sleep. Tomorrow we will work on getting your life back on track."

"You're the best, Wren. I love you."

"I'll remind sober Stefan of this tomorrow."

"Mmmhmpf," he mumbles, and in the next breath, he's fast asleep cradled in my arms.

Lying here with him, I run my hand up and down his back. He sighs in his sleep, and when I look down at his sleeping form, my heart hurts for him. The next few days and weeks are going to be tough, but I made a vow to stick by him. Together, we'll get him through this ... right?

27
WREN

AFTER CONSOLING STEFAN LAST NIGHT, it seems I too fell asleep and I spent the night in his bed. "Shit! Shit! Shit!" I mumble in shock when I find us spooning. Him being the big spoon and me the little spoon. His morning wood is digging into my ass, well, I presume it's morning wood but since he's still asleep, I'm not sure. What the hell do I know about dicks and morning wood?

Climbing out of bed, I leave a sleeping Stefan and I head over to my room to shower for the day.

Stepping under the warm water, I shake my head at the fact that spooning and sleeping with Stefan wasn't as unpleasant as I envisioned ... Then I shake my head and mentally slap myself upside of the head for thinking that.

I cannot fall for him.

I will not fall for him.

Letting out a frustrated sigh, I finish up my shower and once dressed, I head down to the kitchen and make myself a coffee. While I'm waiting for my drink, my phone pings with a message; it's Evie.

EVIE

Just checking in to see how you are doing?

WREN

I'm not rocking an orange jumpsuit so I'll call it a win

EVIE

That bad, huh?

WREN

He's the douchest douche there is, but then he's also nice … it's all confusing. I just wish he'd pick a persona and stick with it. Would make my life that much easier.

EVIE

Well, he is a man

A fine specimen of man, I subconsciously think to myself.

EVIE

Just keep doing what you are doing and soon you will be free.

WREN

I feel like I'm going to be stuck here forever but there are worse places to be stuck.

EVIE

That's the spirit … chat soon … and remember, there's no wine in prison.

A snort slips out at her message, and I shake my head. Turning my attention to the coffee machine, I finish making my drink. With my mug in hand, I decide to head up to the rooftop to enjoy my morning coffee in peace.

His bedroom door is still closed as I pass by, and I wonder if I should check on him, but last night was pretty emotional for him and he needs the rest. So I shuffle past and head up the stairs. But when I step outside into the morning sun, I stop mid step when I see Stefan on the lounger ... and a bottle of champagne sitting on the table before him.

From the look on his face he's passed out, but then my eyes widen in shock when I round the lounger. There's a half-naked woman between his legs. She's trying to get his pants down and his dick out. Her top is missing and she's wearing a really short skirt that shows everything, and I mean everything, because I can clearly see her vagina, as she's not wearing any panties.

Where the fuck did she come from? I was only away from him and in the shower for thirty minutes, if that.

She finally manages to get his fly open and dips her hands inside his pants. He doesn't even flinch when she rubs his dick. She pulls his briefs down farther and his cock springs free but it's softer than butter. She pumps her fist but he's not getting hard. It's moments like this that piss me off. He's clearly drunk and if it was a man doing this to a woman, all hell would break loose. She leans down to suck his dick into her mouth, and that's when I lose it.

"What the fuck do you think you're doing?" I growl at the chick.

She squeaks and spins around. "Who are you?" she breathlessly asks.

"Who I am doesn't matter, but I think you should leave."

"You can't tell me what to do, besides, Stefan wants me here."

"Really?" I sass, crossing my arms.

"Why else would I be here with his dick in my hand?"

"Because he's drunk and doesn't know what he's doing right now," I inform her. Furrowing my brow, I wonder how he got drunk so quickly but then again, he's just topping up his system right now. The smell of liquor would probably be enough to send him to lockup if he was behind the wheel of a car.

"He's fine," she singsongs.

"Really?" I hiss. "He's so *fine* he can't even open his eyes and on top of that, you can't even get his dick hard. Either you're shit at dick handling, he's too drunk to do anything, or it's a combination of both."

"I'd only just started but you interrupted me."

"Mmmhmpf." I nod and shake my head. "You need to leave before I call the cops."

"Why would you do that?" Her tone is high-pitched at the mention of me calling the authorities.

"Well, trying to sleep with someone when they're passed out is an offense. From memory, jail time is five to ten years if you're convicted." Her mouth drops open, and I'm trying hard not to giggle right now. I have no clue if anything I just said is correct but my threat gets the chick moving. She grabs her shirt, pulls it over her head and quickly leaves.

Then I turn back to Stefan.

He's still asleep on the lounger with his dick hanging out of his pants. Even soft it's huge, and I find myself staring at it, wondering how much it will grow when he gets hard. Shaking off that thought, I walk over to him.

I can't leave him here like this so I drop down beside him, grab his dick, and put it back into his pants. It begins to harden under my touch. *Suck on that, bitch,* I think to myself, then I realize what I'm doing and I quickly drop it.

I can feel a gaze on me and when I look up, Stefan is staring down at me. His eyes are bloodshot and he looks like shit. "Don't let me stop you," he cheekily says.

"In your dreams," I spit back at him.

"Many times," he whispers.

"Huh?" I stammer like a bumbling idiot.

"Many times I've dreamed of you doing that to me."

"Huh?" I repeat again, totally confused right now.

"Have you seen you? You're hot as fuck, Wren. You're confident. You're caring. You have a killer rack, and your heart is bigger than the Specific Ocean."

"I think you mean Pacific," I place emphasis on the 'p' in Pacific.

"Potato. Vodka, but whatever the case, you're pretty awesome, Wren Brookes. You have my back unconditionally. You tried to warn me about *her* but I didn't listen and now I'm not ..." He looks up at with me sad, puppy dog eyes. Eyes that are filled with tears. "I'm not a dad, Wren, and I don't have a baby. I never did."

"Stefan," I mumble his name but I don't know what else to say. The man before me is broken. I've never seen him like this before. This whole *I'm not the daddy* debacle has really messed with his head. "What can I do?"

He shrugs at me and grabs for the bubbly and brings the bottle to his lips. Reaching out, I cover his hand and push it away from his mouth. "Uhhh uh, I think you've had enough."

"I just want the empty hole in my heart to go away."

"With time it will, Stefan, but for now, let's get you into bed."

"I knew you liked me like that."

"In your dreams, buddy. In your dreams."

A few hours later, Stefan emerges from his nap just as I'm about to go for a run.

"Morning," he sleepily says, running his hand through his hair. Even though he's hungover as hell, possibly even still drunk, he still looks good.

"Afternoon. There's coffee in the pot," I tell him and nod toward the coffee nook. "I'm going to go for a run and when I get back, you and I are going to sit down and work out a plan to save your career—" He opens his mouth but I raise my hand and stop him. "But if that's not what you want, then I'll pack my bags and head back to New York and my life. This downward spiral of yours needs to stop. Enough is enough."

After putting him to bed, again, I vowed to myself to no longer stand by and watch him implode. Stefan needs someone on his side and I'll happily be that person, but he needs to meet me halfway. I can't do it for him. Underneath his douchey exterior is a nice guy, he just needs someone to believe in him, and I do. Yes, he can be a douche at times but he can also be a sweet and kind person as well. I've come to realize I've been going around this all wrong. He wants to be seen as a person, not just as a hockey player, and that's exactly what I and everyone else have been doing. We're all just seeing him as a job when, deep down, he just wants to be loved and appreciated for him.

Not hockey.

Not his good looks.

Him. Stefan Däuchmen.

He doesn't say anything, but I'm on a roll so I continue, "You've missed games and training, and if you don't get your shit sorted out, you're going to lose your career too. Don't let her lies ruin all that you've worked for." He nods, giving me hope that when I get back, we can get things back on track, well, the ice. "I'll be back soon but, Stefan, don't throw this shot away. You've been given more chances than anyone I know. Don't let us down."

With that said, I step outside and breathe in the fresh sea air. With the possible impending doom of my career if I don't fix this kinda sorted, I put one foot in front of the other and head toward Santa Monica. I'm hoping a run will clear my mind and allow me to give this my all. I just hope Stefan is on the same page too because it will be hard to save him if his head is not in it.

Passing by Fern's, I wave, even though she can't see me and I shake my head at my goofiness as I continue along the boardwalk. There are too many people out and about today, so I head down to the sand where it's less peopley and I stroll along the beach until I reach the pier in Santa Monica.

Walking down the pier, I take a seat and stare out at the ocean. I just sit here and watch the waves. Watching them crash into the shore is cathartic.

The fresh air is just what I needed and as I sit here, I make a decision. When I get back from my run, I'll change into my swimsuit and head up to the roof for a soak. I'll see if I can convince Stefan to join me because he and I have had some deep and meaningful conversations in the tub. It's like the bubbling water is a shield and it allows him to speak freely.

With that decision cemented and my muscles starting to cool, I jump up and head home. I push myself harder on the way back, but I'm determined to fix Stefan. I needed the run to clear my mind and reset my psyche but when I return, I find the house full of people—Stefan is hosting a party.

In the short period of time I was out, it's turned into a frat house. Music is blaring from the speakers. People are bumping and grinding to the music. Empty bottles and plastic cups are discarded all around the place and my douche of a roommate is currently sucking face with a scantily clad bunny on the stairs.

Walking over to him. I clear my throat. Resting my hands on my hips, I stare at him and shake my head. "Stefan," I growl.

"Ohhh oh," he singsongs. "The unfun police is here."

The bunny giggles like he said the funniest thing ever and I roll my eyes. "Really, Stefan?"

"Ohhh, lighten up, Wren, it's just a party."

"I thought we were going to talk?" I ask him.

"We are talking," he throws back at me.

Shaking my head, I scoff. "You really are a piece of work."

"Why thank you," he says.

"Wasn't a compliment, but right now I can only handle you in small doses and even that's too much."

"That'd be right, when the tough gets tougher, everyone bails."

That comment from him is the straw that breaks the camel's back and I snap. "No one is bailing on you, you fucking douche," I yell at him. "We've all been trying but you just keep being you and we all keep expecting you to change. Hell, I moved across the country to help you and just when I think I have you all sorted, you fuck it up. But this time, Stefan, the only person to help you is you, because you're in your head and not listening." With my piece said, I turn on my heel. I need to get away from him before I say something that I'll regret, but then I spin back to face him. "Stefan, yes, it's shit what Alicia did to you but right now, you're acting like a spoiled jerk. Pull your head out or you're going to lose more than a baby that wasn't yours, and your skewed vision of people leaving will come true."

I walk out of the house with my heart racing. Sweat beads my forehead. My hands are clammy. I've never spoken to Stefan like that before, actually make that anyone, but right now I needed to bring out the big guns. Stefan has a talent on and off the ice and I'd hate to see him lose it all, but most of all, I refuse to let *her* ruin this for him.

As much as he can be a douche, when he's not, he's a great human being. One who I kinda sorta have feelings for. *Thanks Fern for pointing that out.*

My words clearly fell on deaf ears because over the next week Stefan spirals even further out of control, and I wonder if there's any chance of saving him.

28

STEFAN

IT'S BEEN over a week since my showdown with Wren and for seven days straight I've drunk and fucked away the pain, but the joke's on me because the pain is still there.

We have a game in a few hours, and I'm in the mood to cause some shit on the ice. Hockey is a great way to release that aggression, and I cannot wait to take on Vancouver. The Vikings are a strong team this season but we're stronger.

Kicking the redhead out, I climb into the shower and freshen up. There's a strong chance I'm still drunk, but I can skate even when I'm fifty sheets to the wind so tonight's game will be a piece of cake.

Walking downstairs, Wren is nowhere to be seen and I'm okay with that. After my breakdown and subsequent showdown with her the other week, I've been steering clear of her. I cannot remember everything that was said, but I do remember asking her to stay with me and she did. She snuggled with me all night long and when I woke the next morning, I was shocked to see her in my bed. Don't get me wrong, Wren's hot, but you don't shit where you eat. Besides, I think she'd rip my dick off if I ever tried that. I remember what happened after I kissed her when she first got here. That kiss was fucking hot, I can only imagine what she'd be like in bed, but I like my dick attached so that will never happen.

Ordering an Uber, I head outside to wait. I may be reckless at times but I will never drink and drive.

Climbing out of the car, I flash security my ID and make my way down the corridor. I can hear chatter from the boys and that feeling in my chest starts to ramp up the closer I get to the dressing room. Nothing is more exhilarating than taking the ice, and I realize I've missed this. I've missed hockey and the outlet it gives me.

When I step into the room, everyone stops and stares at me. "I'm heeeerrre," I sing, spreading my arms out. My smile is wide but when Coach Barber bellows, "My office, now," the grin is wiped off my face.

Dropping my bag off at my cubby, I walk into Coach's office and I find Tania and Wren in here too. Before the door even clicks closed, he's on me. "Where the fuck have you been? You've missed the last two games and every training session this week."

"I've been dealing with some personal stuff."

"Since when is fucking bunnies and passing out in an alley personal stuff?" Coach hisses at me. I have never seen him pissed like this before, but fuck him.

"The personal stuff lead to that and I can't help it if that bitch splatters my face everywhere, but who doesn't want to see this?" I circle my finger around my head.

"No one wants to see a zombie in the flesh," Tania says. "You look like shit."

"It's been a tough week," I nonchalantly tell her with a

shrug. Dropping down onto the sofa, I spread my arm along the back and stare up at the big boss lady.

"So I've heard." Her tone wavers and I offer her a sad smile, trying to buy some sympathy. "But it would have been nice to have been informed by you." I blankly stare at her. "You could have replied to any of my or Leif's messages."

"Wren knew," I throw back at her.

"It isn't Wren's job to inform us of something like this."

"Her job is to watch me—"

"No," Coach snaps, using a tone I have never heard him use before. "It's her job to overhaul your image and she was doing a great job of that, but just like that"—he snaps his fingers—"you've undone all her hard work because rather than come to us for help and support, you went on a bender and fucked up bigtime." He shakes his head. "I shouldn't be surprised though, this is typical Stefan behavior."

"She fucking lied," I hiss at him. "She fucking lied."

"And I'm not defending her but you have acted like a baby." My eyes widen at his choice of words, and I think he realizes it too from the look on his face right now. "Shit, sorry, poor choice of words there."

"Ya think?"

"Regardless of word choice, YOU fucked up here, Stefan. You should have come to myself or Tania, or even Wren. Instead, you've drunk yourself silly and right now, you should probably go and get tested for every disease under the sun. You've really gone wild this week."

"Yeah, I have." I raise my hand for a high five but he just stares at me with raised eyebrows. "Come on, Coach, don't leave me hanging." He eyes me again, and I lower my hand.

"Spoilsport," I mumble under my breath. No on speaks so I nod and stand up. "If that's all, I need to get changed.

We have a game." I go to exit Coach's office but his words stop me in my tracks.

"You aren't going anywhere near the ice tonight."

"The fuck did you just say?"

"You're not playing tonight. You've missed every practice this week. You reek of alcohol, and I doubt your head is in the game."

"But—"

"Nope, not buts. You're lucky I'm not firing your ass."

"You can't fire me! I hiss.

"He can ... as long as he has my blessing," Tania answers for Leif. She walks over to me and ushers me back to the sofa. Dropping back to the seat I just vacated, she takes a seat on the coffee table in front of me. "Stefan, you've had more chances than anyone deserves, and whenever it seems like you're finally on track, you slide right back to your douchey ways. I'm warning you, pull your head out of your ass or I will cut you from the team. No ifs, ands, buts, or what-ifs."

"Fuck this," I snort, and before anyone can say anything to me, I jump up and storm out.

All of my teammates' eyes are on me but not one of the assholes utters a word. They all remain tight-lipped and watch me exit the dressing room.

Heading back down the corridor, I walk out of the stadium and just keep walking. I don't have a destination in mind. I simply put one foot in front of the other and I walk until I come to a bar. Stepping into the establishment, I make my way to the bar and order a shot.

The barman fills my glass up and I chug it back. Tapping the sticky wooden top, he refills my glass and again, I chug it back. I tap again but the bartender looks at me. "You sure?"

Lifting my gaze to his, I see concern reflecting at me.

"Liquor isn't the answer, son. Take it from someone who nearly lost everything." His gaze travels down the bar to an elderly woman pouring a beer. "Alcohol is not the answer. Twenty times out of ten, it's the cause."

"Shouldn't you be willing to serve me?"

"There's other things to drink in a bar besides alcohol."

Nodding at him, I process his words, and me being me, I tap the bar and utter, "Another" because fuck the world.

Fuck him.

Fuck her.

Fuck them, especially them.

Fuck everyone.

I try and do the right thing and it bites me in the ass. I do the wrong thing, it bites me in the ass. No matter what I do, it bites me in the ass. I may as well have fun while my ass is being chewed out.

With a disappointed shake of his head, he pours me another drink but shocking myself, I don't drink it. I stare into the golden liquid as I twist the glass back and forth in my fingers. Resting my elbows on the edge of the sticky bar, I drop my head, run my fingers through my hair, and sigh.

"From the darkness, light will prevail," the barman says.

Lifting my head, I stare at him and mumble, "Can't rain all the time."

"Classic movie that one, but he's right. The decisions you make today will affect what happens tomorrow, and from the looks of you, that drink is not the decision you want to be making today."

Nodding at him, I throw a couple of bills on the bar and stand up ... but before I leave, I throw back the drink. "Can't let it go to waste."

The bartender chuckles and nods back at the seat I just vacated. "I'll get you a burger to soak up some of that alcohol and a Diet Coke, and *then* you can be on your way. I get the feeling you'll need to be soberish to deal with whatever's got you down."

Nodding at him, I offer a small smile as I sit back down. I watch him walk toward the kitchen. Along the way, as he passes the lady he swats her ass playfully, causing her to yelp, but the look she gives him is all-encompassing and full of love and adoration.

An hour or so later, I have a full stomach and I'm soberer than when I first walked in. Mentally, I don't feel any better, but he's right, getting drunk again won't fix this aching hole in my heart. Fucking another bunny won't heal it either. I need to focus on me and the game. With that thought in mind, I head home but when I climb out of the Uber, the last person I expect to see is sitting at my front door.

29
STEFAN

"WHAT THE FUCK are you doing here?" I sneer at Alicia, my tone giving away exactly how I feel at seeing her. As if today hasn't been enough of a clusterfuck, now I need to deal with this lying bitch too.

"I ... umm ..."

"You, umm, what?" I snap at her.

"Tyrone left me," she cries. "I have nothing now."

"Not my problem, Alicia."

"But—"

"No, no buts," I interrupt. "You lied to me. You made me think he was mine. You made me fall in love with a baby that wasn't mine. You caused me to grieve a loss that wasn't even mine to grieve. You deserve everything you get. Now, get the fuck off my property."

"Stefan, please," she pleads, reaching for me. Wrenching my arm away, I snap through clenched teeth, "Get the fuck off my property, Alicia." Then I add, "Or I'll call the police and have you arrested for trespassing and harassment."

She blankly stares at me, and after what feels like an eternity, she nods and turns. She takes her sorry ass off my front porch and walks away from me and out of my life. Shaking my head, I pull my keys out of my pocket and unlock the door.

Walking inside, the first thing I see is the ultrasound picture on the side table. It used to sit on the fridge under the hockey stick magnet I've had since I went to my first game when I was seven.

Picking up the photo, my eyes well with tears as I look at the grainy picture of the little boy who I thought was mine. I don't know what hurts more, the fact he died? Or that he wasn't mine?

Grabbing a bottle of bourbon from the wet bar and the ultrasound image, I slide down the wall and bring the bottle to my mouth and chug. I relish the burn, but it does little to ease how I'm feeling. How can I grieve someone who wasn't mine? I'm hurt. I'm pissed off. I'm broken. I'm ... every other feeling out there and then some.

My life is a mess.

Half the bottle is gone and my vision is blurry when I hear the front door open and close.

A fuzzy figure appears above me and they squat down in front of me. "Ohhh, Stefan," they coo and take the bottle from my hand and then they walk away. When they come back, a cool plastic bottle of water is placed in my hand and a soft voice commands, "Drink."

And for the second time today, I do as I'm told.

Taking a sip, I lift my gaze and the fuzzy image comes into focus. A smile graces my face when I see it's Wren. She drops to her butt next to me and stretches out her legs. A comfortable silence falls between us. We sit next to each other in the entry, each of us in our own heads. After a while, she shuffles beside me and I smile again when her thigh presses against mine, but that smile disappears when she speaks. "You really fucked up today, Stefan."

"Just today?" I retort, resting my head on her shoulder.

"Well..." Then she shrugs and my head bounces. She doesn't say anything else because what's there to say? We all know I'm not handling this very well, but how do you deal with something like this? "This doesn't happen in real life, it's only supposed to happen in TV shows," I mumble.

"I knew you liked daytimes soaps," she teases me and I can't help but chuckle.

"Shhhh, don't tell anyone. It's my secret guilty pleasure."

"It's not so secret when it appears in the recently watched section."

Another chuckle escapes me. "You'll keep my secret, won't you, Wren?"

"This secret I will keep for you, but you need to promise me something."

Lifting my head from her shoulder, I look over at her. The water has helped to sober me up but then again, I've only had half a bottle tonight. "What am I promising?"

"That you'll talk to me or someone instead of drinking and fucking your way through your grief."

"Okay," I tell her with a nod.

She shuffles to her knees and takes my hands in her. "Promise me, Stefan? I don't want to waste my time if you're a lost cause."

"I promise," I vow with a nod. "I met a man tonight and he said, 'From the darkness, light will prevail' and I think he's right because it can't rain all the time."

"Did you just quote *The Crow*?" I nod and this time, it's her who smiles. A genuine Wren smile appears on her face. When she smiles like this, it's a sight to behold. She's pretty all the time but when she's smiling-smiling, she's something else. "That was a brilliant movie and it was so sad what happened to Brandon Lee."

"Mmmhmpf," I agree, dropping my gaze back to my lap.

Lifting my face up to look at Wren again, her smile is gone and now I see nothing but concern. Then I feel guilty for all I've put her through since the shit hit the fan, well actually, since she moved in, if I'm being honest. I really am a douche and it's time for me to lose that moniker. Dropping my gaze again, I see the ultrasound photo on the floor between us. Picking it up, I stare at the image and again my eyes well with tears. "She lied," I murmur.

"She did," she confirms. "But maybe it was for the best."

"How so?" Sitting up, I shuffle around to face her and before she replies, she sits up and turns to face me too.

"Well, this way, you aren't tied to a woman who's wrong for you. You need someone who wants you for you. You want to have a baby with someone you love and want to grow old with. You need someone—" Cutting her off, I grip her cheeks and slam my lips to hers. She gasps, clearly, she was not expecting me to kiss her, but I take the opportunity to slip my tongue into her mouth. She's frozen as my tongue licks into her mouth. Just when I think she's going to shove me away, she starts to kiss me back. Her tongue pushes into my mouth and then it's on.

Sliding my hands around her waist, I slip them under her ass and lift her onto my lap. Straddling me, we continue to kiss.

As far as kisses go, this one is perfect but as quickly as it started, it stops.

Wren pulls back and stares at me. She's breathless. Her lips are puffy and her cheeks flushed. She quickly scrambles off my lap and stares down at me. Her mouth opens and closes but she doesn't say anything. Instead, she turns on her heel and races across the room and up the stairs to her bedroom. Leaving me sitting here with a hard dick and ... feelings I don't know what to do with.

30

WREN

IT'S BEEN three days since Stefan turned up for the game drunk, meaning it's been three days, seventeen hours, and twelve minutes since he kissed me senseless. Since he fucked my mouth with his tongue and left me lightheaded. Every spare second since I walked away from him has been spent replaying said kiss.

His tongue in my mouth.

His hands caressing my ass.

His hard dick pressing into me.

Sometimes it would morph into what would have happened if I didn't have my "never date a client" rule—I would have pushed him to his back, freed his cock, and wrapped my lips around his thick shaft, sucking him into my mouth with the tip hitting the back of my throat. My eyes watering as he choked me with his dick and just before he was about to come, he'd do that sexy book boyfriend move where he'd pick me up, flip me onto my back, and thrust his cock into me then fuck me into next week.

"Ugh," I groan, snapping myself back to the present

and away from Dirtyville. "I really need to get laid," I mumble, and I don't mean by Stefan because I cannot do that with a client, again. Plus, it's Stefan. No matter what Fern—or my subconscious—thinks, I do not like him like that. I do not want him to fuck the life out of me. *Liar liar, pants on fire.* Hell, even my inner whore knows I'm full of shit. Shaking away all thoughts of Stefan—kissing or fucking—I grab the remote and turn the television on. As soon as I see what's on the screen, my eyes widen and all the dirty kinky thoughts about Stefan evaporate into dreamland.

"Stefan," I call out. "Come here."

"What's up?" he singsongs, walking into the living room in nothing but gray sweatpants, every girl's kryptonite. Once again, I'm back in Dirtyville and I'm too busy checking him out to speak, so I mutely point at the TV screen.

The moment we've all been waiting for is here, Margaret from *WtB* is reporting, well gossiping, about what happened with Stefan, Alicia, and the baby. But what's shocking is she's Team Stefan.

"...the baby, unfortunately, didn't make it, but my sources confirm Stefan wasn't the father. Why women try to trap men like this is disgusting, and it explains his recent unravelling. Condolences to the parents who lost their baby and, Stefan, we're all thinking of you during this trying time."

"What the fuck?" he mumbles as we both stare at the television screen, both our eyes wide and confusion marring our faces. "Did she..."

"Yep," I agree, letting the 'p' pop. "Margaret seems to be Team Stefan."

"Pinch me," he says. No doubt it's rhetorical but just in case it's not, I lift my hand to his chest and grab hold of his nipple, squeezing and twisting. "The fuck," he hisses. "Did you just nipple cripple me?"

"You said pinch me, so I did."

"No, you nipple crippled me and that's just mean."

"Please," I refute. "There's so much muscle there"—I circle my finger toward his chest—"you didn't feel shit."

"Then why is my nipple sore?"

Shrugging, I focus back on the TV because the Margaret we all know and love, I mean hate, springs back to life. "Baby drama aside, you might wanna buckle up, buddy, 'cause word on the ice is that LA is looking for a new left defensemen when your contract is up at the end of this season."

"What the fuck? Is she right? Where does—" But his rant is cut off when a knock raps on the front door. He walks over to answer it, and I continue to listen to Margaret tear into Stefan.

Shaking my head, I stare at the screen as she talks crap about another celebrity. "You good?" a deep voice asks, and when I turn my head, I see Leif, Tania, and Maverick 'Rick' McQueen standing beside me. Every time I see Maverick McQueen, my mouth goes dry and my panties become soaked. He was a gun on the ice back in the day. Now he's killing it as the assistant coach for the Crushers and, at forty, he's still mighty fine on the eyes.

"What are you guys doing here?" I ask in lieu of a hello.

The three of them turn their attention to Stefan. "What did I do?" he hisses, and all four of us raise our eyebrows.

"Maybe it's in relation to that"—Rick points to the television—"and what happened a few days ago."

"I'm fine," he huffs, and again, all four of us raise our eyebrows at him. "Okay, well, I'm not fine fine, but I'm getting there fine."

"Why should we believe you?" Leif growls. "You turned

up drunk to a game, Stefan. You've missed every practice since this happened, and according to your bestie, Margaret, you've been out every night drinking up a storm and causing shit." He shakes his head. "You've done some reckless stuff before, Stefan, but what you did last week was unacceptable on so many levels. You're lucky that I don't bench your ass for the rest of the season."

"I—"

"No," Leif interrupts him, and I have never seen him angry like this before. "I don't want excuses because no doubt it'll just be bullshit that dribbles from your mouth. Stefan, you're an amazing player but you're pissing it away. This is your final chance to prove to us that you aren't a lost cause. In three days the team flies to Dallas, and if you're not on that plane, you can say goodbye to your career. Yes, what you've been through is shit, but you're a grown-ass man. Start acting like it."

With nothing else to say, Leif turns on his heel and walks out, leaving us with Tania and Rick.

"What he said," Tania says, breaking the silence. "Stefan, we believe in you, but you're seriously your own worst enemy. You have so many people on your side." I go to open my mouth and defend him but she Aretha's me and raises her hand to stop me. "Let us help you through this shitty time. Hell, Rick left his kids with the nanny to come here and try to talk some sense into you. And I'm aware it's shitty to refer to his kids considering what happened to you and your non-kid, but enough is enough. This is a business, my business, and you're tarnishing the brand that myself and so many others have worked hard to build and maintain. I will not let some skank and a pretty boy ruin it. Pick up your act, or you're fired and the contract renewal I've been working on with Jaxson, like you, it'll be gone too." She looks to me and she means business. "And you better make sure he's on that plane or you're fired too."

Without another word, she walks out.

"You wanna have a go at me too?" Stefan snaps at Rick and I shake my head, clearly he has learned nothing from the lectures he just got from Leif and Tania.

"Why bother because from where I'm standing, you won't listen." He pauses. "But I will say, if you let some lying woman be the downfall of your career, you aren't the person I thought you were. All respect I had for you in the past will be gone. Be the man I know you can be, Stefan, and prove to everyone that you're worth it."

Without saying anything, Stefan walks past Rick and me and heads upstairs ... on a positive note, he didn't stop at the fridge to grab a beer.

31
STEFAN

LYING on the lounger up on the rooftop deck, I stare up at the sky and play back what just happened with Tania, Leif, and Rick. The more I think on it, the more I come to the realization, they're right. I *am* a disappointment—Nanna would be so disappointed in me if she was still alive. My previous actions are clearly why Alicia and Tyrone thought they could screw me over. I guess deep down, I do deserve this because I *am* a douche. I really am.

They all clearly care because they called in the big guns, my mentor and ex-assistant coach, Rick. I cannot believe they did that but most of all, I cannot believe he flew out here ... for me, but I don't deserve his or anyone's sympathy or support. I've really fucked up and I don't deserve this second chance but now that I have it, I'm not going to throw it away.

They're all right, not that I'll admit it out loud. I'm not going to let Alicia and her deceit ruin what I've worked so hard for. Wren is right, the baby wasn't mine so I dodged a bullet by not having to spend the rest of my life with her and a kid who wasn't even mine. And the others are right in that I *am* a great player. I need to focus on the game and me, not pussy.

This is the wake-up call I need, and only I can change my future. It feels like this is my last chance to show everyone I am an amazing player. That I'm not washed up but most of all, prove that I'm a good person.

"You good, kid?" Rick questions, dropping onto the lounger next to me.

Looking over at the man who I respect and who, even after all I've done, still believes in me, I nod. "Yeah, I am. I know I haven't handled things very well—"

"No shit, but you did somehow get Margaret from *WtB* on your side."

"Until I fuck up again."

"So don't fuck up. Keep your head down. Play like a champ and be the man I know you are. Maybe it's time to lose the douche moniker and just be Stefan."

Nodding, I process his words. "I think you're right."

"Of course I am," he nonchalantly says with a Rick grin on his face.

A laugh escapes me. "It's funny. Before you came up here I made a vow to myself to change. To be a better person so I can meet Mrs. Stefan and then she and I can have a baby together. A baby that's conceived out of love and not a drunken hookup. And you know, IS mine."

"That sounds like a good plan to me, Stefan." A silence surrounds us but it's broken when Rick says, "I'm going to be a dad again."

My eyes widen at his words, I wasn't even aware he was dating anyone. Just another mark in the *you've been a self-centered ass* column. "Congratulations." I offer my fist for a bump. "Boy or girl?"

"Baby," he replies, bumping my hand. "We don't know yet."

"Are you going to find out?"

He shakes his head. "Nah, I never did with the others, and I won't this time either. There are very few surprises in life, Stefan, and nothing is more amazing than seeing the woman you love go through something phenomenal. That moment when you see the excitement in their eyes when they're told if it's a boy or girl is priceless."

"But what about you? What about what you want?"

"I want what she wants but most of all, I want her to be happy. After all, happy spouse, happy house."

"Wife, hey?"

"Not yet but after losing Rachelle, I realized life's too short not to take risks when it comes to life ... and love. We're only on this earth for a limited time and being in love is one of the most amazing feelings in the world." He pauses. "You should try it sometime and, you know, not fuck three bunnies in the house that you share with her."

A laugh escapes me and we spend the next few hours chatting. He tells me countless stories regarding his kids and life back in New York. He never lets slip who his new lady love is, but he's smiling again and he deserves to be happy. Rick was made to be a dad and husband, and I think I want that too. Not right now. Now I want to live my life carefree and unattached, but one day I can see myself with a wife, kids, and maybe even a dog. Chels used to dream of a future like that for us, but I fucked that all up. Now she's with the golden boy, but all in all, that worked out for the best ... even if he is an obnoxious goalie from Canada.

"Wanna go get some food?" Rick asks, just as the sun starts to dip. "I'm starving."

"I could eat."

"Great," he confirms, "and tomorrow before I fly home,

you and I can hit the ice and I can whip your ass back into shape."

"I'd like that," I confirm with a nod. "Thanks, Rick, I appreciate you."

"Anytime, kid, anytime."

Rick and I head downstairs, and we ask Wren to join us. While I head up to my room to change for dinner, the two of them start talking about where to eat. When Wren mentions the new Korean barbecue place that opened up around the corner, without consulting me, they call and make a reservation.

Since it's close by, we decide to walk. Plus, it's a nice night out, so why not? As Rick said, "Life's too short not to enjoy life," and walking along the boardwalk with the sun setting over the ocean is a pretty awesome way to spend the evening.

On autopilot, I follow them but I keep thinking about what I can do to change my life. There are so many people I need to make it up to. My team. Tania. Leif. Wren, especially Wren. She's gone over and above her job duties when it comes to me, and all I seem to keep doing is throwing it back in her face. If I was in her shoes, I would have walked away months ago but then again, Wren is an angel and I'm more of a devil, but that's all in the past. I'm going to stop going out. Stop drinking and start eating better. I'm going to get back into training so I can be the best player and teammate out on the ice. I'm going to leave behind my "Doucheman" moniker and just be Stefan—the best version of me.

We're seated in a booth at the back of the restaurant. Sitting across from Wren, I watch her with Rick, who's sitting next to me. She has this aura about her that makes her shine. She's an amazing woman, hell, she's put up with my douchey-ass and I'm still alive and breathing, clearly, she's a saint. I need to do something to make it up to her. When her phone rings and she sees it's her brother, she excuses herself to take the call, and I know what I can do to start making amends.

"What's that look for?" Rick asks me when Wren is gone.

"What look?" I try and play dumb but from the look he's giving me, I've failed ... miserably.

"You look like you had an 'ahhh hah' moment."

"I think I have, again," I honestly tell him, but I'm not sure I want to share the specifics, so I don't. I don't want to let those around me down if I don't live up to the expectations and goals that have been set.

"I get it, but follow that train of thought," he tells me. "I'm starting to see the Stefan from the early days bubbling beneath the surface. The kid had a future ... and if you get back to that version of you, you're going to go far in life, Stefan. You just need to believe in yourself like I do."

Nodding, I smile at my mentor and friend. "Thanks for coming out here, I ... I really appreciate it. I know I've been a douche as of late and I have a lot of people to make it up too."

"As I said, kid, I see myself in you ... just without the douche." We both chuckle at that. "We all make mistakes but it's how we deal with the repercussions that proves what type of person we are. Stefan, you *are* a good man. You just lost yourself, but now that you've seen the light, I have faith you'll get through this. Just lean on those who offer help.

We can't do it on our own and, sometimes, what we never knew we needed is right in front of us."

My gaze moves across the restaurant and it lands on Wren. My heart skips a beat within my chest, and I realize, he's right. What I need has been under my nose this whole time, but do I have a chance in hell with her?

...three weeks later

"GOOD JOB," Tania says to me as we stand in the team suite watching the guys take on San Francisco. LA is leading and with only a few minutes left in the game, the win is ours.

"I'd love to take the credit for this turnaround but it's all Stefan."

"Please," Tania scoffs. "I've seen the two of you together, if I didn't know any better, I'd think you two were getting it on."

My eyes widen at her comment, it's one thing for Fern to tease me but my boss's boss, nope, this cannot be happening.

"Yeah, I don't think so. He's my client and he's—"

"A hot motherfucker with an enormous ... ego." Shaking my head at Tania, I can't help but smile because Stefan is a hot motherfucker, as she put it. "Hotness aside, he's still on my shit list and I'd love nothing more than to fire his ass but, man, that boy glides up and down the ice like an angel, and he can handle his stick like a pro."

At the mention of Stefan and his stick, I'm once again taken to Dirtyville, and thoughts of our hot and heavy kiss play on a loop in my mind.

In the three weeks since the intervention of sorts, Stefan and I have spent a lot of time together. Since he's no longer out barhopping each night and bringing home a different bunny, we've spent many nights at home watching movies or sitting in the hot tub chatting. We haven't crossed that line again, but there have been more than a few touches that were borderline inappropriate.

"Ms. Brookes," one of the security guys interrupts us.

"Yes?" I say, turning to face him.

"There are some people here to see you."

"Me?" I screech because no one has ever come to see me before. From the corner of my eye, I see Tania grinning.

"Yes, shall I let them in?"

Standing here, I think as to who it might be, but I can't think of anyone who would visit me here. Before I can reply, Tania tells the guard to bring them in. She shuffles me toward the door of the suite and a few moments later, it opens. The guard returns and behind him is my parents. "What ... what are you doing here?"

"Stefan invited us," my mom says, pulling me in for hug.

"He what?" I ask, totally confused.

"He called and said he'd like to fly us out to visit you. He's put us up in a hotel around the corner from his place. We would have been here before the puck dropped but the flight was delayed and then LA traffic is, well, pucked, for lack of a better word."

"Hi, Mr. and Mrs. Brookes, I'm Tania," she says joining us. The game is over and LA won. By the looks of the score, another goal was scored in the last few minutes while I was with Mom and Dad.

"Please," Mom says in her mom tone. "It's Samantha and Penn."

"I thought Penn was your brother?" Tania asks in confusion, like most people do.

"Dad's Penn Senior and my brother is Penn Junior, but you can call him PJ." Then I think of him and look to my dad. "Are they here too?"

Dad shakes his head. "Fletch has school and—"

"How is that little rugrat?"

"Just as adorable as ever," my dad says, his eyes lighting up. His grandson is the apple of his eye. He'd do anything for that little boy.

"What about Penn and Tatum?"

"They're doing good. It's nice to see him smiling again." Mom gets that happy look on her face. "Told you I had a feeling." She nudges Dad in the shoulder, and I can't help but chuckle. My giggle garners her attention and she turns it to me. "You know, Wren, I have—"

"Ohhh, look, the game's over, we should go meet the team for the press conference."

"Ohhh yes." Mom nods. "We don't want to hold you back from your work."

Phew, I think to myself but then Tania speaks up. "Wren, you don't need to go. Why don't you head home with your parents?"

"Ohhh, umm, Stefan and I arrived together."

"Well, wait here." She spins her hand around the suite. "I'll send Stefan up when we're done."

Nodding, I smile and with that agreed upon, she says goodbye to Mom and Dad and heads out.

"Okay," Mom says as she links arms with mine. "Tell me everything."

Furrowing my brows, I stare at her in confusion. "We spoke like three days ago, I have nothing to tell you, but it seems this trip slipped your mind."

"We all wanted to surprise you. I was shocked when I got the call from Stefan. I thought he was calling to tell me something bad had happened."

"Mom," I whisper and pull her in for a hug.

"I'm just being silly but I still remember the day your brother called about Mads." She sniffles. "It's still so fresh is my mind."

"I don't think her loss will ever go away; she was a pretty special woman."

"She sure was. I hate thinking that now Penn is with Tate. I think she and Tate would have gotten on like a house on fire—"

"Should you really use an analogy like that when Tatum is a firefighter?"

"Ohhh, ummm, I never thought about that before."

"Tatum would get a kick out of it," Dad pipes up with a grin, saving Mom from heading into a spiral for offending someone ... even when they're not here and at the other end of the state in Lockhart Falls. "Now, what's a fella got to do to get a beer around here?"

"Well, Dad," I state. "There are these things called legs and you walk over to the bar, then you use your mouth." I circle my finger around his. "Then say, 'Duncan, can I get a Miller, please?' and then Duncan gets you your beer."

"I see you're still sassy."

"Working with Doucheman brings it out of me by the bucketload."

"Speaking of Stefan," Mom says as Dad walks over to Duncan. "Has my feeling come true yet?"

"Nope, and it won't," I defiantly inform my mother. She

gives me the eye and then I tack on, "He's my client, Mom. You know my rules about that."

"Client. Schmient." She waves her hand around dismissively. "My feelings are never wrong, and this time will be no exception. I was right about Mads, and I was right about Tatum, and I'm right about this too."

"Let's lay off the feeling talk, hey?" She just eyes me. "How long are you guys here for?" I ask, changing the topic of conversation.

"Just a few days," Dad answers, handing Mom a glass of red and a mineral water with lime for me. "Fletcher has a school play, and we want to be there to see him perform."

"What play, and what role did he get? He never mentioned anything about it."

"They're doing *Alice in Wonderland* and he's a Playing Card. It's a non-speaking role, but he's so excited and he looks adorable in his costume."

"Well, I expect pictures and a signed program from our up-and-coming thespian."

"Done."

We take a seat and watch the Zamboni buff the ice for tomorrow's game. We chat about what they've been up to recently, and of course, the stuff with Stefan and Alicia comes up. Mom was aghast when I told her what went down. "That poor boy. Luckily for him, he had you to put the pieces back together again, and I'm sure he's grateful for all you've done."

"Too right I am," the man in question says, entering the suite and walking over to us. He's in his after game suit and, fuck me dead, he looks sexy. What is it about a well-fitted suit that makes me go gaga?

"Stefan," Mom singsongs when she greets him. "You played well," she tells him and I shake my head. Mom watched like five seconds of the game and I'm sure when she did, Stefan was on the bench.

"Thank you, Samantha," he tells her, leaning in to kiss her on the cheek. I swear her cheeks darken from the kiss. Dad chuckles as he shakes Stefan's hand. "Glad you could make it, Penn. Was the flight good?"

"No dramas and the upgrade to business was greatly appreciated and not necessary at all."

"It's my pleasure. Shall we head off to dinner or would you like to check in to your hotel first?"

"Maybe the hotel to freshen up first," Mom suggests.

"Wren and I can wait in the hotel bar for you both."

"Sounds like a plan."

With the plans locked in, we all head to Stefan's car and make our way to the hotel. Traffic is light and we arrive just as the sun has set. Stefan made the decision to drop Mom and Dad off first. Then we can drop the car off at home and the two of us will walk back to the hotel to meet up with Mom and Dad.

"Thank you for this," I tell Stefan as we walk along the boardwalk back to Mom and Dad's hotel. "I didn't realize how much I've missed them. Them being here is just what I needed."

"You don't need to thank me because it's the least I can do. I know I've not been the easiest client you've ever had, and I wanted to apologize for my douchey behavior of late."

"Of late?"

"Okay, since you moved here." He pauses and stops walking. Turning to face him, he has a look on his face that I've never seen before. Stepping closer to him, I take his hand and squeeze. He smiles and continues, "I know I'm just a job, but you really are great at what you do. You have my best interests at heart and when I look back at our time together, even when I had my head up my ass, you've had my back. You've supported me, even when I didn't deserve it. And when I made a stupid decision and trusted Alicia, you were there. Even though I could tell each time she was near, all you wanted to do was rip her hair out."

"I wouldn't go that far but I did not like that woman, and I definitely did not trust her."

"You were right not to but I was blinded by, hell, I don't even know. All that aside, you had—have—my back and this, bringing your parents here is just my way of saying thanks."

"As you said, I'm doing my job."

"No." He shakes his head. "You go over and above because you care. It's more than just a job to you."

Staring at him, I'm amazed he sees me that way. This job is hard at times. Especially when your client is a douche and you don't like them as a person, but the more time I spend with Stefan, the less douchey he's becoming. I've come to realize there's hockey Stefan and home Stefan. They are two different people and if home Stefan can merge with hockey Stefan, then I will have done my job.

"You continually shock me, Stefan, and seeing you like this, it's why I do what I do. And for the record, you aren't just a job." Silence surrounds us but it's not awkward. When it becomes too much, he pulls his hand from mine and we start walking again.

Side by side, we head back to meet Mom and Dad.

They're waiting outside the hotel for us, and when I see them, I can't help but smile. "Thank you again, Stefan. No one has ever done anything this thoughtful for me before."

"You deserve all the happiness, Wren."

Before I can say anything else, we reach Mom and Dad and the four of us head off to dinner. The night is amazing and when we get back home, my relationship with Stefan once again changes.

33
STEFAN

SAMANTHA AND PENN are amazing people, I can see why Wren is, well, Wren. She's the perfect combination of both her parents with her own unique touch added for good measure. I cannot remember the last time I laughed so much.

"Thank you for a lovely dinner," Penn says as we sit in the lobby bar of their hotel. At dinner earlier, I did the sneaky "I'm just heading to the bathroom" but instead, I paid the bill. Penn demanded I let him buy a nightcap, and here we are.

"It's my pleasure, sir."

Wren and her mom laugh, garnering our attention. In the dim light of the bar, Wren has never looked more beautiful or relaxed. Earlier, when we dropped off the car, she ducked up to her room and slipped into a vibrant orange halter dress. The material caresses her curves and highlights her tits perfectly. The urge to tell her how beautiful she looks overtook me but we don't have that kind of relationship. So I bit my tongue and kept my dirty, unsavory thoughts to myself.

"We better get going," Wren says. She just caught me checking her out. Her cheeks darken but she doesn't say anything. "Stefan needs to get home, and I need my beauty sleep."

"Not that you need it," I mumble to myself. Clearly, it's louder than I intended because three people are currently staring at me. Wren in shock. Her mom has a whimsical look on her face, and her dad, well, he looks constipated with a touch of "don't hurt my baby girl."

We say our goodbyes and then Wren and I head back to the house. When we approach the bar around the corner from home, my first instinct is to keep walking. I feel proud because the old Stefan, would have wandered in for another drink ... or twelve.

Tonight, however, I keep walking.

Not even a group of bunnies purring my name or flashing their tits can sway me. Looking over—hey, I'm a man and they're boobs—I smile but shake my head and keep walking. Reaching out, I rest my hand on Wren's lower back and I increase our pace.

"You sure you don't want to stop?" Wren asks when the girls start shouting out louder.

"Nah, I'm good."

She nods and from the corner of my eye, I see a smile appear on her face. That little lip lift puts a pep in my step for the rest of the way home.

We reach the house and I unlock the front door. Stepping aside, I let Wren in first. "Nightcap?" I offer as the door clicks closed behind us.

"I'd like that," she agrees.

Nodding at her, I walk into the kitchen and get the bottle of Baileys from the refrigerator. Then I grab two tumblers and pop two cubes of ice in each. Pouring our drinks, I pick up hers and she takes the offered glass. When our fingers brush, a current zaps from her to me and her breath hitches. Silently we stare at one another as we sip on our drink.

"Shall we sit?" she asks and I nod.

With our drinks in hand, we head into the living room and I drop down onto the sofa. Wren plops down next to me. She places her glass on the coffee table and leans forward to slip her shoes off. Sighing as she does.

"I don't know why you chicks wear shoes that hurt your feet."

"'Cause they add height and these babies"—she points to her shoes on the rug—"make my legs and ass look amazing."

"Your legs and ass look amazing without them," I tell her, and hand on heart, I mean it.

Wren is the ultimate fantasy girl. Her figure is amazing. Her tits are what wet dreams are made of. Her eyes are a vivid-blue that suck you in. Her hair is as dark as a midnight sky. Normally, I like long hair but Wren's is cut in a short blunt bob, and it's the epitome of sexy. Her lips are plump, and from the memory of that time I kissed her, they're soft and delicate.

"Such a man response," she teases as she picks her drink back up and takes another sip.

"Just stating a fact."

She laughs and shakes her head. Finishing her drink, she places the empty glass down and tucks her legs up underneath her. For the next few hours, we swap stories, tell jokes, and just relax. "Tell me something honest, Stefan. Tell me something that no one else knows."

Turning to face her, I bend my knee and shuffle around. My leg rests against hers and I think about her question.

"When my nanna died. just after I was drafted to the Crushers, I thought my world was over. She had my back, no matter what. It was us against the world. That was the start of my demise. Without her guidance anymore, I was lost. Sure, Dad was there, but he had another family and would just throw money around to make my antics go away or to get me what I wanted. You could say that thanks to my dad, I became a spoiled brat. I started to lash out because life is cruel. I lost my mom and brother when I was fifteen, and then in my early twenties I lost the last of my family who ever truly loved me for me. I didn't want anyone to get close again because I would eventually lose them too. You asked me why I sabotaged my relationship with Chels, and I think it was a form of self-preservation. Things were serious between us and I got scared. Rather than acting like an adult, I self-combusted and spiraled." I pause and take a deep breath. "When Alicia told me she was pregnant, I got swept up in the idea of having a family again. I look back now and all the signs were there, but I was blinded by the possibility of having a family again. I was going to hold on with everything I had because family means everything to me."

"I had no idea." She reaches over and rests her hand on my thigh.

"And why would you? I always play my cards close to my chest. I don't easily let people in but..."

"But what?"

Looking over to her, I stare into her eyes. "I think it's time I let someone in."

She nods and stands up. "I think that's a good idea, and I'm happy you've made that choice, Stefan." Resting her hands on my shoulders, she leans down to kiss my cheek. It's nothing more than a friendly gesture but for some insane, fucked-up reason, at the very last second, I turn my head, causing her lips to land on mine.

Her eyes widen as our lips press together.

Time stands still as our lips touch.

One heartbeat turns into two.

One breath turns into two.

Our exhales mingle together and the air around us comes alive.

"Stefan," she utters my name. Her breath fans across my mouth and that one word is laced with warning and want. Before she can say anything else, I kiss her again. Gripping her ass, I pull her onto my lap so she's straddling me and I give her no opportunity to pull away. One arm bands around her lower back and the other slides around her shoulders. Slipping my fingers into her luscious locks at the back of her head, I hold on to her firmly as my tongue plunges in and out of her mouth.

Desire slams into me when she starts kissing me back. And when she moans into my mouth... Game. Fucking. Over.

We're only kissing but I could come just from the feel of her lips against mine. Her pussy rubs against my growing erection. Wren Brookes is perfect in every fucking way and then there's me. Stefan Däuchmen the mess. I have the world at my feet and somehow, I manage to self-destruct at every turn. I fucked things up with Chelsea and the Crushers. I was given a second chance with the Legends and I'm close to losing that too. I had a chance at fatherhood but it was taken away from me in the cruelest of ways. I know I shouldn't be kissing Wren, but she's the first person to show me affection—real affection. She's always on my team and the more I'm around her, the more comfortable I feel, and when I'm with her, the real me appears.

Melting into my embrace, she pulls me in closer, deepening our connection and kiss. Sliding my hands down her body, I cup her ass and squeeze. I can feel the heat of her pussy against my dick when she begins to circle her hips on my lap. She tugs my lower lip into her mouth, and I groan into the kiss.

Flipping her onto her back on the sofa, I cover her body with mine and continue to kiss her. My hands slide along her thighs and up under her dress. Cupping her pussy in my hand, I massage her slit through the soaked material of her panties. A guttural moan passes from her lips to mine. Slipping my finger under the edge of her panties, I'm about to slide in when she grips my hand, halting my movements. "Stefan," she murmurs, and I can tell from the tone she wants me to stop. I've never forced a woman, and I'm not about to start now.

Lifting myself up, I stare down at her lying beneath me. Her cheeks are flushed. Her lips puffy and swollen from our kiss, but it's her eyes that stump me. They're filled with want and confusion. It's the confusion that guts me.

"I'm so sorry, Wren," I whisper. "So fucking sorry."

"Don't be," she says. "I ... I kissed you back but, umm." She shakes her head. "I ... I can't do this. I..."

One minute I'm hovering over her and she's apologizing. The next, I'm on my ass next to the coffee table watching as she runs away from me. She takes the stairs two at a time, and then the sound of her bedroom door closing echoes around me.

What the fuck just happened?

34

WREN

LEANING AGAINST MY BEDROOM DOOR, my breaths are hurried. My eyes are filled with tears and my heart, my poor heart. It's torn and confused. I did it again, I've crossed the line with a client. Something I vowed never ever to do again, but here I am. I'm a big fat liar, liar, wet panties on fire. My panties are soaked and all we did was kiss and a little rubby rub.

It was hard to ignore the desire building between us while we were chatting. I feel like I know Stefan on a whole new level now. I discovered his middle name is Maksym, that the White Claws in the fridge are his—no shit—and that one day, he wants to go to Australia and dive on the Great Barrier Reef. In return I told him I don't have a middle name, that I knew the White Claws are his—hence why I keep replacing them—and that one day, I want to live in a house with a wraparound porch and every Sunday night I'll watch the sunset with my husband.

Just now, I saw Stefan in a whole new light. I didn't see

the douchey hockey player; I saw a sexy man who just wants to be loved. This version of him is the type of person I picture myself settling down with one day. As he spoke, a part of me wanted him to be that person but he's my client, I can't do that.

Pushing off the door, I strip off my dress, unclasp my bra, pull on a tank, and fall into bed. As soon as I close my eyes, I'm assaulted with memories of Stefan kissing me. His hands caressing my ass. Rubbing myself all over him like a cat in heat. At the memory, that spark between my legs reignites and I know if I don't sate the itch, I'll die. That's a tad melodramatic but if I don't do something, I will never get to sleep.

Reaching into my bedside drawer with one hand, I grab my vibrator and with my other hand, I slip my panties off. Circling the purple tip around my clit, I turn it on and shiver immediately in the most exquisite way. Sliding the device down my slit, it easily slips inside. I'm embarrassingly wet but I really don't care. Closing my eyes, I flick my wrist and fuck myself with the device. In and out I pump. Squeezing my breast with my other hand, I massage the plump mound as I continue to plunder myself.

That tingly feeling begins to develop low in my belly, and when I tug on my nipple, it's like I lit the fuse and I begin to violently come. My toes clench. My body stiffens, and every nerve ending in my body erupts with a massive explosion. Covering my mouth with the hand from my breast, I ride out my orgasm as fireworks dot my vision.

Collapsing back into my mattress, I remove the vibrator and toss it to the side. Staring at the ceiling, my chest heaves as I try and catch my breath. I may have just come but my body is still tense.

The clicking of Stefan's door across the hall garners my

attention, and I hope with everything I have he didn't hear me just now.

Rolling to my side, I close my eyes and try to sleep but my mind is racing. Eventually I succumb to sleep but my dreams are plagued with images of Stefan and what might have been had I not pushed him away.

My phone pings with a text and the sound startles me awake. The sun is shining, and when I look at the clock on my bedside table, I realize it's after nine. Grabbing my phone, I smile when I see my message is from mom.

MOM

What are the plans for today?

"Hide from Stefan," I mumble as I formulate a reply that doesn't paint me as the hoe that I am.

WREN

We could head to the pier and then have a picnic on the beach. I could see if Fern and Bradford want to join us

MOM

Sounds perfect.

Shall we come to you?

Not wanting Mom to see Stefan just yet 'cause she will know something happened, I quickly send my reply.

WREN

You'd have to double back so I'll come to you. Meet you in the lobby in 30 mins

MOM

thumbs-up emoji

Climbing out of bed, I quickly shower and once I'm dressed, I stand behind my closed door, psyching myself up to exit. Finally, I pull on my big girl panties and crack open the door but before I step out, I listen. I'm met with silence, beautiful silence and no roommate.

Walking briskly to the stairs, I quickly descend and sneak into the kitchen but I don't need to sneak because Stefan isn't here, according to the note he left me.

We need to talk, is never a good thing ... even if we aren't dating. No conversation that starts with "we need to talk" is ever good, and it definitely won't be after making out with your client the night before. This is one conversation I do not want to have ... ever. *Wonder if I can avoid him for the rest of my time living here?* Shaking off that silly thought, I grab a pen and write back to him.

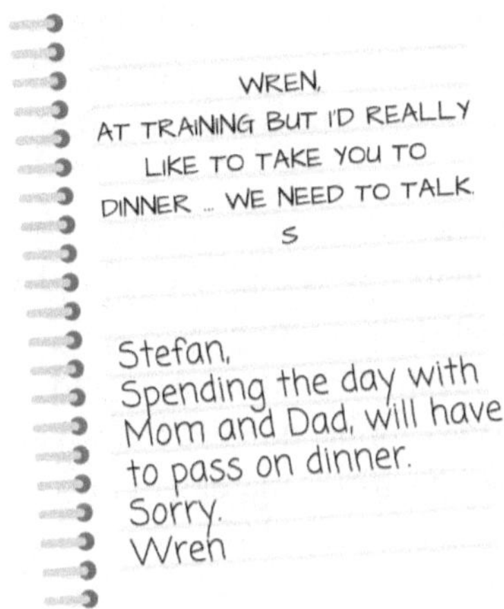

Since I'm home alone, I quickly make myself a coffee. Wrapping my hands around the mug, I savor the caffeine goodness and enjoy my hug in a mug. Then I head off to meet up with Mom and Dad, shooting off a text, letting them know I'm on my way.

Exiting the house, I step out into the morning sun and lock the door behind me. The morning rays hit my face, and I smile as the vitamin D soaks in. It's refreshing and for the first time since last night, I feel like I can breathe again ... that is until later when Mom, Fern, and I are on the beach and they ask me about Stefan.

"Where's Stefan today?" Mom asks, popping a grape into her mouth.

"Training," I reply, then I shove a cracker with some cheese and salami into my mouth so I don't have to talk anymore, but I should have known better. A mouthful of food will not sway my mom ... or Fern. Introducing these two was a mistake, and I can feel the Spanish Inquisition about to commence in three. Two. One...

"What's the go with you two?" Mom inquires.

Taking a sip of my drink, I try to bide my time but when Fern speaks up, I think it was a mistake. "Well, Mrs. B, if you ask me, what we have here is a classic case of enemies to lovers."

"Enemies to lovers?" Mom furrows her brows, not understanding where my friend is coming from. Hell, I'm not even sure what she's alluding to.

"You know, when they first meet and they hate one another but there's a connection deep down and rather than face the love, they focus on the hate. However, as tends to happen with love, it simmers to the surface but both of them are too chickenshit to act on it until one day..."

"One day, what?" Mom asks, enthralled with Fern's fairy-tale story.

"They give in. Finally kiss. Fireworks explode. Clothes get ripped off and they get jiggy with it."

"That's a very technical explanation there, Fern, and one that is a work of fiction." Even if we did kiss last night and there were fireworks. My lips are still tingling, and I'm not just referring to the ones on my face. My vibrator did *not* sate me at all.

"Please," she scoffs. "You and he are *not* a work of fiction." She places emphasis on the word not, and with her statement said and done, she pops an olive into her mouth and takes a sip of her wine.

"She's right, Wren. Maybe you and Stefan just need to kiss and get it over with," Mom unhelpfully suggests.

"Personally, I think you two should just fuck and get it over with." She looks to Mom. "Sorry for the language, Mrs. B."

"It's fine." Mom waves her off. "I think that too but voicing about you-know-whating when it's your daughter felt weird."

"I get that, but seriously." Fern turns to look at me. It's with an intensity I've never seen before. "You two just need to bump uglies."

"I'm right here, you know," I protest.

"We know," the two of them singsong together, and I just shake my head.

Mom and Fern start talking about classic enemies to lovers romances while I sit here and process what Fern said in relation to the definition of enemies to lovers. Stefan and I are one step away from being the clichéd enemies to lovers, but it cannot happen. Kissing is one thing, fucking is an entirely different story ... even if I do want to fuck him.

The next few days pass by in a blur, and I have the best time with Mom and Dad. Stefan and I have hardly seen each other the past few days, and if I'm honest, I've missed seeing him and spending time with him.

He returned just as I was about to head off and get Mom and Dad to drop them at the airport. He offered to drive, and I accepted quickly because we all know how I feel about driving in LA—and heading to LAX is the worst.

Mom was excited to see Stefan when we got to the hotel, and I prayed with everything I have that she behaves around him. *Maybe him driving wasn't a good thing after all.*

We arrive at the terminal and Stefan unloads their suitcases while I say my goodbyes. After hugging Dad, I turn to Mom. She pulls me in and holds on tight. Tighter than usual and when she pulls back, she stares at me intently. A smile graces my face, and I know Samantha Brookes is about to impart some of her motherly wisdom on me. "Sweetheart, I know he's your client but when I see the two of you together, my heart stutters. I get all warm and fuzzy. He's the milk to your cookie. You just need to jump and follow your heart." She leans in and kisses me on the cheek. "I'll call you when we get home."

With that, she walks over to Dad and the two of them walk into the terminal, leaving me standing next to Stefan's car pondering her words.

"Ready to go?" Stefan asks. Turning to look at him, I nod and we climb in. The trip back to Venice Beach is silent and just as we pull into the driveway, my brother calls.

"What up, bro?" I say in greeting.

"Just checking to see if you survived the visit with Mom and Dad?"

"I did, give me a sec." Pulling the phone away, I look over at Stefan. "I'm going to head to the beach to chat with Penn and then I'll cook dinner."

"Sounds like a plan."

He goes inside and I do as I said and make my way down to the sand to chat to Penn, filling him in about the visit with Mom and Dad.

"You sound down, what's up?"

"I'm f—"

"Do not finish that statement, Wren." I sigh and my brother chuckles. "See, not fine, what's up?"

"You ever have feelings for someone but are scared of acting on them?"

"Ummm, hello, my face would be next to the definition of that in the dictionary. Did I not do exactly that when I met Tate?"

"Yeah, you did."

"But he's my client."

"Ahhhh, so you're finally admitting to your feelings for Stefan."

"I-I, yeah, I think I am. We ... we kissed the other day and, Penn, it was the best kiss of my life but I ran away like a chicken."

"Why?"

"He's my client."

"So?" he refutes. "He's a man. You're a woman. There's no law being broken if you two get together."

"I know that but..."

"But what?"

"He's my client and I vowed never to go there again. I can't get a reputation for that."

"Look, what happened with he who shall not be named—"

"He's not *Voldemort*, Penn."

"Sucked," he ignores my statement and continues as if I didn't interrupt him. "And I will never see another movie of his again, but this time it's different."

"How can you be so sure?"

"Sis, asshat was and always will be as asshat. Stefan is not an asshat. He might be a douche but he just needs the right woman to keep him in line and, Wren, that woman is you." He pauses. "Sis, life is too short to be scared and not leap. If you want the ice cream, eat the ice cream. If you want to fuck the hockey stud into next year, fuck him ... just use protection ... I'm too young to be an uncle." I laugh. "But seriously, Sis, just take the leap."

"I wish I could be like you and leap, but I'm scared, Penn."

"Life is scary, Sis, but take it from someone who lost the love of his life and got a second chance; it was worth the leap both times for me, and this leap will be worth it for you too."

With his wise words imparted, we say our goodbyes and hang up. Bringing my legs up, I wrap my arms around them and sit here, staring out at the ocean. Wondering if it will be that easy and if I have the guts to leap.

35

STEFAN

STANDING HERE, I watch Wren walk off to chat with her brother. Things are changing between us and I'm not sure if it's a good or bad thing, but all I know is I want more with her. I haven't felt like this about a woman since Chelsea, and if I'm being honest, there's a part of me that's worried I'll fuck it all up again. I mean, my nickname is Doucheman, not much hope there.

With a sigh, I unlock the front door and let myself inside. Heading into the kitchen, I grab a beer and pop the top off. Taking a sip, I walk over to the stereo and flick it on. "Can't get You Out of My Head" by Kylie Minogue is playing and I chuckle. The universe has a warped sense of humor at times.

Opening the slider, I head out to the lower patio. I don't sit out here much but when I take a seat, I realize I can hear Wren's conversation with her brother. Not wanting to intrude, I get up to leave but when I hear her say, "We kissed the other day and, Penn, it was the best kiss of my life but I ran away like a chicken." I'm intrigued so I sit back down. I wish I could hear what her brother is saying but from what I'm hearing from Wren's side, he's telling her to go for it and it's confirmed when she replies, "I wish I could be like you and leap, but I'm scared."

"I'm scared too," I mumble to my beer bottle. Realizing it's empty, I head back inside to grab another one and get started on dinner. I'm chopping up the salad when Wren walks in. Looking up, I smile at her. "All good?"

"Yeah." She nods. "Want some help?"

Shaking my head, I continue chopping. "Nah. I got this. You just sit your pretty ass down and chat with me while I finish up the prep."

Nodding, she does exactly that. Sitting at the island, she stares at her hands and bites her lip. Walking over to the fridge, I place the salad back in and grab out the steaks to rest. "Wine? Or White Claw?" I ask her.

"I'd love one of *your* White Claws, Stefan."

Shaking my head, I hold back a smirk and grab her drink. Sliding it across to her, she catches it and offers a small thanks as I get to work on the spuds. My gaze keeps flicking to her across from me and I notice she's looking everywhere but me. Ever since our kiss the other night, she's all I can think about and since hearing her conversation with her brother just now, I want to take that final leap.

Maybe over dinner, we can share a bottle of wine, loosen up the lips, and I can see where she stands on this issue.

"What's on the menu tonight?" she asks, snapping me back to the present.

"Ummm, steak, baked spuds, and salad."

"That sounds delicious." She takes a sip of her drink and swallows. Her tongue darts out, licking the corner of her mouth. "What's for dessert?"

Without thinking, I blurt out, "You."

36
WREN

BOTH OUR EYES widen at the one word he just uttered. I sit across from him frozen, not knowing what to say or do. *Did he just say what I think he said?* I repeat to myself as we continue to mutely stare at one another.

Pulling my bottom lip into my mouth, I bite down and then lick along the indents. Stefan's gaze tracks the movement and he too licks his lips ... and then I imagine his tongue licking other lips of mine. Lips that are currently slick with arousal from his previous "you for dessert" statement. Dropping my gaze, I inhale deeply and when I look up again, he's rounded the island and is standing at my side.

He spins the chair to face him and cups my cheek in his palm. Subconsciously, I lean into it and him. His hand molds to my face as if they were carved at the same time. "Stefan," I whisper.

"Wren," he whispers back.

My name passing through his lips is filled with so much emotion. Covering his hand on my cheek, I lean forward and press my lips to his. Just like when we kissed the other night, he pulls me into his body and holds me tightly, giving me no opportunity to pull away. Unlike the other night, I don't think I want to.

Penn's words of "take the leap" flash in my mind and I decide to leap.

Draping my arms over his shoulders, I pull him into me. My breasts press into his chest and my tongue plunges in and out of his mouth. The kiss is hurried and frenzied but at the same time it's sensual and perfect.

Lifting my leg up, I hook it around his thigh, pressing myself farther into him. I can feel his erection growing between us and suddenly, I'm hungry, not for the steak and spuds, but for him.

"Stefan," I beg into the kiss, but he ignores my plea and continues to kiss me. He's fucking my mouth with his tongue; this is more than just kissing. This is everything.

He grinds his hard dick into my belly, and I moan into his mouth. He pulls back, breaking the connection. Both of us are breathlessly panting.

"Up," he demands. I furrow my brows in confusion, but he quickly rectifies my confusion when he places his hands on my hips and effortlessly lifts me up onto the edge of the counter. "Lie back, Wren." His tone is commanding, and it has my heart racing. My panties are soaked and from the heated look in his gaze, he's about to devour me; mind, body, and soul. And I can't fucking wait, but first, I need to tease him a little.

"Or what?" I defiantly throw back at him.

"Or I'm not going to have my dessert before the main meal."

Fuck me. I internally groan. The wanton hussy in me no longer wants to tease and I do as he asks. I lie back on the granite and spread my legs for him.

"Fuck, you're gorgeous," he tells me as he slides his

hands up and under the hem of my dress. He cups my mound over my soaked panties and his eyes widen. "You're dripping."

"Mmmhmpf," I agree, biting my lip to hold back the moan wanting to slip free. "What are you going to do about it?"

He stares at me lying here and smirks that sexy Stefan smirk of his. "Everything."

Before I can process his word, he pushes my dress up around my waist. He inhales deeply before kissing me through my panties. "Stefan," I whine.

"Patience, dear," he teases.

Grabbing the waistband of my panties, I lift my ass up and he rolls them down my legs. Scrunching them in his hands, he brings them to his nose and inhales. "Fuck, Wren," he growls. Slipping my discarded underwear into his pocket, he drops his gaze between my thighs. Lifting his eyes to mine, he stares at me as he traces his finger up my thigh to cup my pussy. He thrusts a finger inside me, and my back bucks off the counter at the intrusion. When he hooks his finger and wriggles it around, I clench around him and moan.

"I love the sounds you make when you come. Do you know how many nights I've stood outside your bedroom door and listened to you get yourself off?"

"What?" I hiss, lifting my head to stare at him in embarrassment.

"You heard me. It took all the restraint I have to not let myself in and help you."

I'm so embarrassed right now but also highly aroused. My arousal trumps my embarrassment and I ask, "What would you have done?"

"This," he declares. Lowering his head down, he licks me from taint to clit and continues to pump his finger in and out of me. He circles his tongue around my swollen clit and that little bundle of nerves comes alive under his touch. When he bites down and sucks, it's game over. I scream as an intense orgasm detonates. My body stiffens and I lie here as insurmountable pleasure courses through me. Dropping back to the counter, I lie here panting and smiling.

"You good?"

"Mmmhmpf. That, Stefan, was—"

"Just the starter," he interrupts.

Lifting my head, I stare down at him. His chin glistens with my release and he winks. Offering me his hand, I place mine in his and he pulls me up and off the counter. My legs are like jelly and I stumble. He wraps his arms around me, holding me up. Then he lowers his head and kisses me. I can taste myself on him and normally I'm not a fan of that but with Stefan, I don't mind it.

His hands roam over my back and down to my ass as we hungrily kiss. He palms my ass, and out of nowhere, swats my cheek. I gasp into our kiss and he chuckles. Sliding his hands down lower, he cups both cheeks and lifts me up. On instinct, I wrap my legs around his waist, digging my heels into his ass. From this angle I can feel his dick pressing into me. Even though I came only a minute or so ago, I'm ready to go again. I've never been this aroused in my life.

Without breaking the connection between our lips, he turns around and carries me up the stairs and into his room. Placing me on my feet at the end of his bed, he lifts my dress over my head and tosses it aside, leaving me only in my bra. He makes quick work of removing it, and now, I'm fully naked.

"We have a problem," I utter.

"What's that?"

"You have far too many clothes on."

"One sec," he offers, and in literally half a second, he's

as naked as the day he was born. My eyes rake over his naked form, and I can unequivocally say, the angels were having a fantastic day the day he was created.

"You right there ogling me?"

"Can you turn around please?" The cheeky man spins around and looks at me over his shoulder and the back image is just as gorgeous as the front.

"You done?"

"For now," I nonchalantly reply.

He spins back around and steps closer to me. He places his hand on my hip and stares into my eyes. I'm the only thing he's focusing on and normally I'd cower at a gaze this intense, but right now I'm lapping it up. Stefan makes me feel like I'm the most beautiful woman in the world. "You are so fucking gorgeous, Wren. How did I get so lucky to get you here?"

"Luck had nothing to do with it, Stefan."

"That's all moot because right now, I'm going to kiss you and then I'm going to fuck you into next week."

My eyes pop open at his words and breathlessly, I pant, "Yes, please."

In the blink of an eye, he's slamming his lips to mine. He kisses the life out of me and then he does just like he stated, he fucks me into next week ... and the week after.

37

STEFAN

"I'M GOING to kiss you, and then I'm going to fuck you into next week." Her eyes widen at my words but I don't give her a chance to think, I just do.

Covering her mouth with mine, I wrap her in my arms and sit on the end of my bed with her straddling me. Her amazing tits smash into my chest, her pointy nipples pressing into my pecs. The urge to taste them slams into me. Moving my lips from hers, I kiss along her jawline, down her neck and finally, finally, I reach her tits. Mashing my face between them, I inhale and smile.

"Did you just sniff my tits?" she asks. Before I can offer her an answer, I take her nipple into my mouth and suck. Her head drops back, pushing her chest into my face and I happily lose myself in the valley of her breasts. I alternate between her tits. When I'm not sucking and biting one, I'm massaging the other, tugging on her nipples.

The sounds coming from her have my dick harder than steel. My shaft slides between her ass cheeks and now all I can think about is taking her ass. "One day, Wren, I'm going to take your ass," I tell her, squeezing her ass for emphasis, "but right now, now I'm going to fuck you. Any last words?"

She shakes her head and with her eyes locked on me, she lifts up and hovers over the tip of my cock. She's smirks, thinking she's running the show when she begins to swivel her hips over my tip, not sinking down on my shaft.

Gripping her hips in my hands, I stand up and she gasps. Walking over to the window, I press her back into the glass and with a flick of my hips, I impale her on my dick. She gasps at the intrusion and I pause, letting her adjust to my girth.

"Move," she demands when I do nothing.

With a nod, I move.

Back and forth I thrust my hips, bottoming out with each stroke. Her pussy hugs my dick as if they were made for each other. She presses her lips to mine and my movements slow down as we kiss while we fuck.

I'm close to coming but I cannot come before her. "I need you to come, Wren."

"I'm close," she pants. Then she begs, "Suck my tits."

"Yes, ma'am." Lowering my head down, I suck her nipple into my mouth. Her walls contract around me, and when I bite the tip and then suck, she bucks her hips like a rodeo queen. Then she lets out a guttural growl, and it sends me over the edge too.

Together we ride out our orgasm, bucking and moaning. Drawing every last inch of pleasure out of one another.

Resting my forehead against hers, our hurried breaths mingle together. "That was..."

"Yep," she agrees, then her eyes widen and she stiffens in my arms. "Ummm, we didn't use protection."

"I'm clean," I quickly tell her. She eyes me. "I recently had a physical and asked them to test me."

She nods. "Oh, me too. I, umm, I've never not used

protection before and it's ahh, been a while since I had sex." She pauses. "And I have an IUD."

"I'm not worried," I tell her.

"You're not?" I shake my head. "I would have thought after the Alicia thing you'd be extra careful."

"Well, yeah, with a bunny I would, but I'm not worried with you."

"Why?" she screeches.

"Because you're perfect, Wren. In every way."

"I'm not perfect, Stefan." Rejecting my statement, she lowers her gaze.

"Look at me, Wren." She lifts her gaze to mine. "To me you are, and I won't hear you talk negatively. Now, let's eat, I seem to have worked up an appetite."

"Can I shower first?"

"Want help washing your back?"

Nodding her head, I place a quick kiss on her lips and walk us into my shower. We get a little dirtier before we get washed and while she dries her hair, I head down to the kitchen and finish dinner.

"Oh My God," Wren states, "That was so yummy. I didn't realize how hungry I was."

"Great sex will do that."

"Who said it was great sex?" she teases before taking a sip of her wine. We cracked open a bottle of red to go with our rooftop dinner.

"I do believe in the shower earlier your exact words were, 'Oh My God! Oh My God! Oh My God! No one has fucked me so good before' or something like that."

"I think the water in the shower made you hear things." She seductively glances at me over the top of her wine glass. "But I'm happy for you to try again. After all, practice makes perfect."

"Game on, woman."

Placing my wine glass down, I walk over to her side of the table. She stares up at me through her long lashes and smirks. Taking her wine glass from her grasp, I bring it to my mouth and drink the last sip. Her mouth pops open in shock, and she follows the movement of my hand as I return the empty glass to the table. Leaning into her, I press my lips to hers and I transfer the wine from my mouth to hers.

She wasn't expecting that, and some of the wine runs over her chin and down her neck. She licks at the corner of her mouth, while I lick the path of the wine drop. Once again, ending up in her tits. "This is fast becoming my favorite place to be," I mumble between her breasts.

"That so," she teases. Lifting my head, I nod. "So I should walk around topless from now on?"

"I'd be okay with that."

"Of course you would be." Shocking me, she rips her top off but covers her tits with her arm. "But if I'm topless, you need to come to the party too."

"I'm happy to go topless." I quickly strip my shirt off and look at her in a *what ya got now* kind of way. A smile graces her face, and I've never seen her look so carefree ... or beautiful.

"I think you can do better than that." Her gaze drops to my sweatpants, and she waggles her eyebrows. With my eyes locked on hers, I push down my pants and stand before her. Naked. My dick—which is at half-mast—is at eye height. Wren licks her lips, and once again shocks me when she grips my hips and pulls me to her. She drags her tongue over the tip of my dick, circling around the slit. Then she opens wide and sucks my shaft deep into her mouth. Lifting her hands, she holds on to my ass and begins to blow me.

My head drops back, and I stare up at the dark sky as Wren sucks my dick. Not gonna lie, I've had plenty of blow jobs over the years but never has one ever felt this good. Wren relaxes her throat and takes me all the way in. Her eyes water and she gags but she doesn't give up. She keeps sucking and when she squeezes my balls and presses on my perineum, I come. Shooting my load down her throat, she gulps down every last drop. Then she licks my shaft clean.

Pulling back, she sits before me topless, with a smug look on her face.

"Fuck me, Wren, that was ... everything." Her cheeks darken at my comment and she lowers her head. "Don't shy away from me now, not after you just sucked my dick like a pro."

"Thanks, I think."

"Definitely a compliment."

"Then, thank you, and you're welcome."

"You are something else, Wren. Who knew that underneath your ball-busting exterior was a secret wanton hussy."

"A girl's gotta have a few secrets."

A laugh escapes me. "What do you say we leave this mess for the morning and I take you to bed and show you just how appreciative I am for you and your mouth?"

"I'd like that."

Pulling her up, I slam my lips to hers. Once I've kissed the life out of her, I throw her over my shoulder and make my way down to my bedroom, where I show her just how much I appreciate her and tonight.

IN THE LIGHT of the next day, I lie here and stare at a sleeping Wren. She looks so peaceful. I'd love nothing more than to wake her up by sliding my dick into her but I know if I do, I'll be late to training and we all know I'm already on thin ice.

Leaving her a note, I grab my gear and head off to practice where Coach puts us through our paces. Considering my extracurricular activities last night, I was impressed with how I kept up with the rest of the team. When the session is over, Coach asks to see me before I leave. The rest of the guys all tease me about being in trouble and usually I'd flip them off, but I'm kinda scared because I have been good lately.

Once I'm showered and changed, I head toward his office. Knocking on the open door, he looks up and smiles when he sees me. "Stefan, close the door and take a seat," he says, and as I close the door behind me, my heart begins to race.

"How you doing?" he asks. Standing up, he comes

around to my side of the desk and rests against the edge. He crosses his arms and stares down at me, waiting for my answer.

"I'm good," I tell him, and for the first time in a long time, I mean it.

"For once, I believe you." He pauses in that stoic way he does for emphasis. "I'm proud of you, Stefan."

His words really hit home and I smile. "Thanks, Coach, I appreciate it. I know I kinda lost my way for a while there, but Wren helped me deal with that and she's..." Well, I can't tell Coach about the sex.

"She's what?"

"Threatened to kill me if I don't get my shit together."

"I never thought I'd see the day where Stefan Däuchmen is whipped by a woman."

"I'm not whipped," I refute, but I think there is some truth to that statement. I *am* whipped when it comes to Wren, but that's a secret that will stay with me and only me. "I'm seeing things from a different perspective, and I'm learning that when shit happens, there's a right way and a wrong way to deal with things. Who knew writing yourself off and sleeping with bunnies was the wrong way."

"Everyone else in the world knows that."

"And now I do too."

"Well, I'm glad because I would have hated to have had to fire you. You're one of the best players in the league, Stefan. You are going to go far and one of these days, you're going to make a fine coach."

"Thanks, Coach. I appreciate that."

"Good, now go and get out of here, I've got shit to do and you have ... I don't give a crap so long as I don't see you on *WtB*."

"I promise to behave," I tell him. And when I say behave, I mean I'm going to go home and fuck Wren. Then

I'm going to eat her pussy for dessert before we fall asleep wrapped in each other's arms.

When I get home, Wren is still asleep in my bed. Leaning against the window where I fucked her last night, I watch her sleep. I really don't want to wake her up but it's been over four hours since I've been balls deep inside of her, and I need another fix. It feels like I dumped my addiction to fucking bunnies and I've replaced it with being addicted to fucking Wren.

Walking over to the bed, I sit on the edge and run my finger down her cheek. Her lids begin to flutter and when she opens her eyes, she stares up at me. She smiles then suddenly they widen. She looks confused and shocked, not what I was hoping.

"Morning," I murmur.

"Morning," she whispers and sits up. The sheet falls away and exposes her naked breasts to me. My eyes drop to her tits, and I lick my lips. When Wren notices she's naked, she pulls the sheet up and looks mortified. "Shit, shit, fuckity fuck," she hisses. Her face blanches and then she jumps up out of bed. "This, umm, I ... I need to go." Before I can say anything, she races out of my bedroom, taking the sheet with her.

The door to my room slams closed behind her. What the fuck just happened?

39
WREN

RUNNING out of Stefan's room, I cross the landing to the safety of mine and slam the door behind me. Dropping down face-first onto my bed, I lie here, crying and shouting into my pillow. When breathing becomes difficult due to the avalanche of tears leaking out of my eyes, I roll onto my back and stare up at the ceiling, crying and berating myself for sleeping with a client again.

Letting out a sigh, I realize I'm still naked. When I ran back here, all I had was Stefan's sheet wrapped around me. Hopping up, I ball the sheet up and throw it onto the floor. I walk into my en suite bathroom to have a shower, hopefully I can wash away the shame of what I did last night. But, Oh My God, last night was the best night, and sex, of my life. The things that man can do should be taught to all men around the world. My muscles ache in the most delicious way and when I soap up my breasts, I wince a little.

Looking down, I see teeth marks around my nipple from when Stefan bit and sucked them when I demanded him too. A smile graces my face as I run my finger over the indentations ... then I gasp in shock when I realize why I'm so upset. I'm falling in love with my client ... again.

Why is love and life so confusing? Why isn't there a manual to guide you?

Sliding down the tile wall, I land on my butt and cry because we can never be. I've been here before and it never ends well for the help. They'll side with the hockey player, just like they sided with the actor last time.

Shaking my head, I think about the moment I found myself in this same predicament with Simon ...

... "I think I'm falling in love with you," Simon whispers. He and I are in his trailer in between takes. We've just finished making out like teenagers at the movies on a Saturday night, and his words just now mean everything to me. All the sneaking around while sleeping with my client has been for something. Being in love is worth the secrecy, but what if love isn't enough?

With a smile on my face, I reach up and cup his face. "I think I'm falling in love with you too but..."

"But what, Babycakes?" I shudder at the nickname he has for me.

"But you're my client. How is this going to be seen when it all comes out?"

"So we'll keep us a secret, just like we have been."

Simon and I have been sneaking around for the last three months. Six months ago, I was hired by the production company of his latest movie to keep him in line and remake his image. Simon Simon—yep, that's the stage name he went with since Simon Simdovonich is a mouthful, on both his name and his dick.

I've done my job and the production team is happy, but along the way our relationship changed. I started to fall for him and, it seems, he fell for me too. I know falling for a client is a no-no but the heart wants what the heart wants.

"I don't want to hide forever, Simon. I want to be the one to go to movie premieres with you. I want to walk the red carpet on your arm. I want to be by your side at the awards ceremony when you win. I want—"

He interrupts me, "And I want that too, Babycakes, but..."

"I'm the hired help," I dejectedly whisper.

"I knew you'd get it," he croons. Clearly misreading my words just now. "Now come here and give daddy some sugar. I'm due back on set soon but before I go, I need you."

He gives me that look that has my pussy weeping, and when he pulls his cock out and I see the tip glistening in the light of his trailer, I lick my lips. Walking over to him, I unbutton my blouse and slip it off my shoulders, leaving me in my demi-cup bra.

Coming to a stop before him, I drop down to my knees. Swiping my finger through his precum, I bring it to my lips and suck. His eyes dilate as he watches me suck my finger into my mouth.

"I can't wait to have those lips of yours wrapped around my dick."

Just as he says that, Rebecca, the head of production who hired me, walks in. "For fuck's sake, Simon, I thought you were past this. Where the fuck is Wren? She's supposed to be all over this. She's—"

"Oh, she is," Simon joyfully declares. He leans to the side, exposing a topless me and his dick to my boss.

That was the worst day of my career. Rebecca had me on the next flight out of Alamogordo, New Mexico where we were shooting, and she promised me that I'd never be an image consultant again.

With my tail between my legs, I decided to go to New York and visit my friend, Peyton, who was in town for work. She's the owner of Monty's Lingerie and was in the Big Apple for Fashion Week. She consoled me over espresso martinis and being the amazing friend she is, she knew someone who knew someone, and that's how I met with Jaxson. After promising him I wouldn't sleep with a client again, he hired me. And it was all going well until *him*.

"Fuuuuuck," I cry out and slam my palm onto the tile floor. Another round of tears explodes from my eyes. The water turns cold, so I turn it off and climb out. With a towel wrapped around me, I step into my bedroom and climb back into bed.

Rolling to my side, I curl into a ball and berate myself for succumbing to the sexy charm of Stefan and, once again, fucking up my career.

There's a knock on my door and it startles me awake. I have no idea what time it is but they knock again. "Wren, please don't shut me out." He's the last fucking person I want to see right now. He knocks again and quietly utters my name with a pleading tone.

"Go away, Stefan," I sing out. "I need to be alone."

"Please, Wren," he begs. "At least let me know you're okay."

"I ..." But I can't answer him because I'm not okay but this isn't on him. It's on me.

Thankfully he leaves me alone, but there's also a part of

me that wanted him to burst through the door and console me—I'm such a psycho bitch.

He shuffles away and I can hear him mumbling, but I can't hear what he's saying. Last night with Stefan was amazing, the best night of my life, and for me to do what I did, running away, it makes me a bitch. And ignoring him is childish, but I can't right now. I need time to process. I need time to figure out where to go from here.

A short time later, my stomach growls and I realize I'm starving. After all, it's after lunch and I haven't eaten anything since last night, and I did get in a lot of cardio last night, hence the hunger. Climbing off the bed, I pull on some clothes and turn to exit my room, but I stand here and stare at the door. "Just do it," I grumble. "You can't hide in here forever."

Reaching out, my hand is on the handle to open the door when Stefan knocks again. I jump in fright but I mutely stand here, staring at the door. *Chicken*, I hiss internally. I'm about to open the door when Stefan says, "I need to head to afternoon practice, Wren, but when I get back, we need to talk." He pauses. "No, we ARE going to talk."

Without giving me a chance to reply, he leaves. The sound of his feet stomping down the stairs echoes through my room and once again, I feel like a bitch.

Pulling on my big girl panties, I finally depart my room and by the time I get downstairs, he's gone ... it's just me and my endless thoughts.

Opening the fridge, I stare into it, looking for something to eat. I spot the bottle of wine on the shelf and think, why not? Grabbing the bottle, I pour myself a glass and I chug it back before pouring myself another. Deciding to put together a choo-choo board, I get some cheese, meats, and grapes out and go about putting together my platter.

With my food and drink in hand—including the rest of

the bottle—I head up to the rooftop deck. I've done some of my best thinking up here, and I'm hoping that today is no different. FYI, I don't think about much and instead, I drink my wine and nibble on cheese. Since I've only eaten some cheese, a few crackers, and I'm sitting in the sun, the wine hits me hard and before I know it, I'm tipsy and my bottle is empty.

On shaky legs, I make my way downstairs to grab another bottle and when I'm bent over in the fridge, Stefan returns. Standing up, I spin around and I come face-to-face with him. I see the morose look on his face and that bitch feeling resurfaces. "Hi," I utter.

"Hi," he replies.

Awkwardly we stand here staring at one another. "Wine?" I offer but he shakes his head and once again, silence envelops us.

Stefan breaks the quietness when it becomes insufferable. "We need to talk."

"So you said," I snap. I don't mean to be a bitch but with me hating myself right now, I'm projecting.

"You drive me crazy, Wren."

"Feeling's mutual," I throw back at him, but this time there's no sass or resentment. It's the honest goddamn truth. "Stefan, I know we need to talk but I can't right now. I need time to process."

"Process what?" he hisses.

"This. Us. Everything," I mumble. "Things are changing and I'm scared an—"

"Wren," he interrupts.

"No," I snap. "I need time. I can't do this."

Slamming the wine bottle down on the counter, I storm out of the kitchen pissed off. I've asked him for time and he can't even do that, *fucking douche*, but really, I should have known he wouldn't listen. Guys like him never do. They just take and take and take until you have nothing left to give. It's fine for Stefan if this all blows up because he's the famous hockey player, he'll be grand. But me? I'm just the image consultant who fucked her client … again.

Stefan doesn't let me get far, he reaches out, grabs me, and presses me into the wall at the bottom of the stairs. His body leans into mine. Our breaths mingle. The air around us sizzles, just like it did last night.

"You're really driving me crazy now," he sneers.

"Crazy attracts crazy and, clearly, you and I are both fucking crazy."

"I'm not talking about that kind of crazy," he hisses through his teeth. His eyes are filled with desire and anger. His chest is heaving. His tongue darts out and slides across his lower lip. My eyes track the movement and the douche smirks. He knows what I'm thinking right now, it's like last night synced us mentally.

Biting into my bottom lip, he stares as I drag my teeth over the skin, letting it pop back out. Our eyes meet again and there's a hunger in his gaze that has me pressing my thighs together. "I want to bite that lip more than I need my next breath, but before I do that, Wren, you need to know something. You need to know that I'm crazy about you. I can't stop thinking about you. Your taste. Your touch. Yo—"

"You just want me for sex," I snap in defense.

He shakes his head. "I want you for more than that, Wren. I want you for you. You told me to find what makes me happy, and *you* make me happy, Wren. You piss me off to no end but regardless of that, I still want you. I'm not going to push you because I'm not that kind of man. I want you to want me because I'm all you can think about. I want you to want me because I make you laugh. Because I make you happier than you've ever been before. I want you to want me how I want you."

Standing here facing off, we stare intently at one another. If I thought the air was heated before, I was wrong. Now it's a stifling inferno. Full of sexualized energy and his words hanging.

Neither of us moves.

Neither of us wants to be the one to give in but since I'm the one who ran away ... since I'm the one still running, I know I have to be the one to make the move. And I want to, but at the same time I don't, because I'm scared.

I've never felt like this about anyone before and I know, without a doubt, I want to be with him, but he's my client. And even though he's my client, he's all I can think about. He looks at me with pleading eyes and like last time, I decide to leap because fuck the consequences. Stefan makes me happy so I do as my brother suggested. I leap.

40
STEFAN

...two weeks later

THE LAST TWO weeks sneaking around with Wren have been amazing. She really is the best thing to happen to me. The more I've gotten to know her on a personal level, it's made me appreciate her in a new way. Yes, she was hired to overhaul my image, but I'm more than just a paycheck to her. She cares, really cares about me, my image, and my future.

That night two weeks ago when we slept together for the first time was the best afternoon, evening, and night of my life. Our bodies connected on a physical level and it's as if when we gave in to our desires, it unlocked our mental connection as well.

After our showdown the following day, Wren and I went back to the rooftop and we talked. She told me what happened with that asshole client of hers, and when she did, I understood her reluctance to take things further with me. I assured her I'm not like him and I promised if shit hits the fan, I'll take the blame. People will believe it was me anyway, so it's no hardship. It was me who suggested keeping us a secret, and it's not because I'm ashamed of her. I want her to feel comfortable and secure in us before we share it with the world. Apart from Chelsea, I've never had a steady girlfriend. After her it was just casual hookups and I'd never be with the same someone more than twice. I never wanted to take things further but with Wren, it's different. I want everything with her. She's a breath of fresh air and she wants me for Stefan, not Däuchmen the hockey player.

Right now, we're on a plane to New York where we're set to play against my old team. The urge to sit with her was strong but since we're sneaking around, I sat three rows behind her. I'll just have to lust over her from afar.

"You good?" Coach asks, dropping into the seat next to me.

"I am. I really am," I tell him, and like the last time he asked me that, I still mean it.

"I'm glad to see you back on track. Wren is finally earning her keep." His words about Wren have my hackles raising, but I can't say anything without it raising suspicion.

"She's been earning it from the beginning," I snip instead. The need to defend Wren is strong right now, not just because it's untrue, but I don't want her fears about her time with Simon to rear its ugly head again. I will never make her feel like he and her old bosses made her feel. We are two consenting adults and we both have made this deci-sion. If shit hits the fan, we will deal with it together. "I wasn't making things easy for her because, well, I was being a douche, but now, I see she and you and Tania only have my best interests at heart. And the team's, hence why she's arranged this charity match with my old team. Wren is amazing at her job, end of story."

Wren thought it would be good for my image to arrange a couple of games throughout the season with the New York Crushers, Colorado Dragons, and the Vancouver Vikings to raise money for charity, with myself being the spokesperson for the games and chosen charity.

Why she picked my old team or Vancouver, I will never know, but I know she picked Colorado because she's friends with the equipment manager there, Asher King, and it's a paid excuse to see her friend.

"Wow, she really has made an impression on you." He eyes me suspiciously.

"Well, when I finally pulled my head out of my ass and listened to her and Rick and Tania, I saw the error of my ways."

"What about me?"

"You ride me in a different way, and I guess you're all right, but do you think you can ease up on the bag skates?"

"Now that I know you love them so much, I'm going to drive you harder."

"Thanks," I deadpan.

"You're welcome, now rest up, I wanna kick New York's ass."

"You got it, Coach."

He nods, stands up, and heads back to his seat. Watching him walk away, my gaze drifts down to where Wren is sitting. All I can see is the top of her head, that is until she stands up. Our gaze briefly catches and she smiles, biting her lip as she steps out into the aisle and makes her way down the plane toward the restrooms. I wait until the lavatory door closes and then I get up and head in the same direction.

Hiding around the corner, I wait for her to exit. When she does, I grab her wrist and pull her into me. She lets out a squeal but I cover her mouth with mine and swallow her sounds. She's frozen for a few seconds and then she's kissing me back when she realizes it's me. But all too quickly she pulls her lips from mine. "What the hell, Stefan?" she whisper-hisses.

"I've missed you," I tell her.

"We've been in the air for like two hours."

"And I haven't kissed you since we left home."

"Stefan," she pleads. "We can't."

"Shall I push you back into the restroom and we can join the Mile High Club?"

"Oh My God, you're incorrigible."

Ignoring her, I stare into her baby blues. "I bet right now, if I slipped my hand inside your panties, I'd find you soaked."

"Maybe, maybe not," she replies. "But whatever the case, you're not getting into my panties on the team plane—"

"Game on at the hotel then."

"You're sharing with Sharpe," she reminds me.

"But *you* have a single room, and I'd hate for you to be lonely and cold. New York *is* chilly this time of year."

"Thank you for your concern but I have my flannel pj's, and I'm pretty sure the hotel has heat. I think I'll be fine."

"But what if I'm lonely and cold and chilly?"

"Sharpe can keep you company, and if not, I'm sure a bunny would be willing."

"I don't want a bunny, I want you ... and nice try trying to trap me there. I meant what I said, Wren, you're it for me. If it was up to me, I'd grab that intercom there"—I point to the device next to her head—"and I'd shout it to the whole plane that you're mine. And if I hear one more person comment on your ass or your tits, I'm going to junk punch them."

"So violent," she teases.

"Hello, hockey player, violence is my middle name."

"I thought it was Maksym?"

"Not the point," I snap while trying to hold back my smile. "Can you at least give me another kiss to tide me over?" I pause for emphasis and pout. "Please?"

"Well, when you pout like that it's too adorable not to oblige."

"I'm not adorable," I huff.

"Shut up and kiss me, Däuchmen."

"With fucking pleasure."

Grabbing her cheeks in my palms, I press my lips to hers and push my tongue into her mouth. She slips hers into mine and then it's game on. We attack each other's mouths like our lives depend on it. We pull apart when the captain asks us to return to our seats because we're about to hit some turbulence.

"Saved by the turbulence," she mumbles against my lips.

"Mmmhmpf," I mutter.

Reluctantly, I pull away. Staring at her, I take in her puffy lips and flushed cheeks and a feeling of pride takes over me. "After you," I offer in a gentlemanly gesture but really, I just want to check her ass out because like my fellow teammates continually point out, Wren has a spectacular ass ... If only they knew what her ass looks like up close and personal as my dick thrusts in and out of her from behind. Or how stunning it looks with a pink imprint of my hand, I wonder if I can convince her to let me fuck her ass? I make a mental note to see if I can get her to change her mind on the subject.

She drops into her seat just as we hit an air pocket. Taking the opportunity, I fall into the seat beside her. "Well, hello there," I croon as I fasten my seat belt. "Guess I better stay here for safety."

"Why do I feel like this was a setup?"

"Wren, I know I'm amazing but not even I can cause turbulence."

"Well, that's not entirely true, I remember it being bumpy and rocky just last night. Guess like then, I better hold on for safety." And the minx that she is, she reaches over and grabs my junk, holding on for safety. I spend the rest of the flight with a hard cock, fighting the urge to fuck Wren in front of the team.

41
STEFAN

WE LOST TO THE CRUSHERS, again, but this time it was an embarrassing loss. Like 13-0 embarrassing and to top off the embarrassment, I was sent off in the last period for my behavior. Coach and Wren are going to ream my ass when the game is over, but fuck them. Fuck this. Fuck everything.

Walking into the arena I was on cloud nine. Due to the turbulence, I spent the rest of the flight next to Wren and we may have gotten a little handsy-handsy under our blankets. I was relaxed and ready to tear up the ice but before the game, I was coming back from seeing Rick when I heard some NY fans in the tunnels. They were saying they'd love to see me get my ass handed to me on the ice, especially from Kallen. I chuckled to myself but when they brought up the Alicia shitstorm, I started to get angry. Then they went on to say I'm washed up and need to walk away from the game. All I'm good for is fucking bunnies and appearing on *WtB*. Fuck them. I'm Stefan Däuchmen and I'm a fucking amazing player.

By the time I got back to the locker room, I was fuming.

Their words irked me and when one of my old team-mates made an off-the-cuff joke about them beating us last time, that was the end of it. I saw red and lost it. Each time I'd see their smarmy faces coming toward me with the puck, I did whatever I could to take them out. I should have been focusing on the puck and scoring goals, not beating up on my old teammates.

It's no wonder I was sent off, I was playing dirty.

My body is going to hurt tomorrow after all the Kron-walling I did tonight. Storming into the locker room, I throw my helmet and growl in frustration. Ripping my gear off, I change into my street clothes and I get out of there before the game has even finished.

I'm sitting in Squires, drowning my sorrows, glaring at my phone. It's ringing, again. I have a heap of missed calls from Wren and Coach Barber. So far, neither of them has left a message but that changes when my phone pings alerting me to a new voicemail. Clicking into it, I bring my phone to my ear. "Stefan, it's Leif."

"No shit," I mumble.

"Where the fuck are you? You don't take off like that, ever. Clearly someone pissed on your Cheerios after we landed but violence aside, you played a solid game. Call me when you get rid of the bunny you're no doubt with now, but please, for the love of God, keep it in the hotel room … or her house."

I snort at his words and then sigh because I really need Wren right now, but at the same time I don't, because I know she's going to be ashamed of me.

Dropping my phone to the bar top, I order another beer and while I wait, a group of guys walk up to the bar, talking about the game and how I'm a douche. I'm about to tell them to get fucked when a chick sidles up to me.

She presses her tits into my arm and drapes hers around me.

The bartender drops off my beer. Picking it up, I hold it to my lips and chug it back, ignoring the bunny next to me but she doesn't take the hint. Finishing my beer, I order another. She leans farther into me and whispers, "Hey, stud, wanna buy me a drink?"

Turning my head to look at her, I study her face. She's pretty, but she's not Wren. I'm about to tell her to piss off when I feel someone stop and stand right behind me.

Spinning around, I come face-to-chest with a chest I know intimately. Lifting my gaze up, I stare into irate vivid-blue eyes that are currently shooting daggers at me. "Come with me," she growls.

"Ummm." The bunny, who clearly cannot read the situation, steps between Wren and me. "I was here first, bitch. Back the fuck off. You can have him after I blow him in the restroom."

Wren turns her gaze to the chick and looks her up and down. Then she locks her gaze on my hands, resting on the chicks hips. Subconsciously, I placed them there and when she lifts her head, no longer do I see anger on her face. All I see is hurt and before I can say anything, she storms away.

"Fuck," I hiss. Jumping off the chair, I shove the bunny aside and earn myself a "What the fuck?"

Ignoring the bunny, I call out to Wren but she ignores me, flipping me the bird over her shoulder while she storms away from me. All I care about is reaching Wren. Even if she hadn't turned up, I wouldn't have touched that chick. I'm with Wren now, I won't do to her what I did to Chelsea.

Finally, I catch up to Wren and I step around her. She stops before slamming into me. "It's not what you think," I tell her.

Glaring at me, she doesn't believe me. And my thoughts are confirmed when she growls, "You really are a douche."

"And you're a stuck-up bitch who's riding my ass every five seconds," I throw back at her. My anger is misguided right now and I know I'm being an ass, but New York brings out the worst in me. I hate this fucking place.

"It's my job to ride your ass," she snaps. "Stefan, you are this fucking close"—she holds her fingers millimeters apart—"to losing your career. To losing everything you've worked so hard for." There's a silent "me" in there as well, but that's neither here nor there right now. "I don't want to see every-thing go up in flames because you acted like a Neanderthal, hot-headed dickwad out on the ice."

"More like you don't want your reputation marred if I fail," I throw back at her. That was a low blow and as soon as the words pass my lips, I feel like an ass, especially when I see the hurt on her face over that comment.

"Yes, I'm so shallow that I'm all about the 'look at me' crap. I'm not conceited like you. I actually fucking care." She turns and once again, walks away from me. After a few steps, she spins back and storms over. She stops right in my face. Her blue eyes shimmer in the light with anger and hurt and pity. "You really are a self-centered, egotistical prick."

"And you're a sexy, uptight bitch."

We stare at one another, the packed bar fades into the background and it's just Wren and me. We've each said our piece and now, the hunger and desire is returning. We haven't had angry hate sex yet but I have to admit, I'm excited for it. Before anything can happen, from beside us, Kallen mumbles, "Huh, didn't see that coming." His words pull us back from whatever that just was, and both our heads swivel toward him.

Staring daggers at the asshole, I spit, "Fuck off, Jones. She's my handler. That's it."

Wren's head snaps back to me, and when I look back at her, I see hurt etched all over her face. She shakes her head and as she turns to leave, I notice tears welling in her eyes.

Standing here, I watch her race away from me. Immediately, I mourn her loss and hate myself for hurting her with my words. With words that I don't mean. She's more than my handler, so much more.

"Go after her, you fool," Kallen's voice echoes through the silence as I watch Wren race toward the restrooms.

Turning my head to him, I glare and hiss, "What?"

"For puck's sake, you two clearly have the hots for each other. Go. After. Her," he enunciates the last three words, spelling it out for me, but I have more than the hots for her. I've fallen for her but after my actions just now, I think I've lost her.

Remembering that we're supposed to be keeping this on the down-low, I huff, "Do not." But we both know I'm full of shit. Wren Brookes is an amazing woman and she's the one person on my team who has had my back, no matter what, but when it comes to her, I keep fucking things up.

Looking back to Kallen, I'm at a loss of what to say. "I—"

"Go," he says again and this time it sparks me into action. Turning on my heel, I head off in the direction Wren went and hope I haven't fucked things up completely because I don't want to lose her.

42
WREN

STEFAN and I are arguing in the middle of a bar. Normally, we argue behind closed doors and not in such a public place, but seeing his hands on that bunny bitch fired me up. The barbs started flying and neither of us were backing down.

When the goalie from The Crushers says something, indicating he knows we're hooking up, we both look over to him. I'm too shocked to reply but Stefan snaps at him. Then he utters eight words that hurt, "Fuck off, Jones, she's my handler. That's it."

I know to everyone else, that's all I am. So I don't know why I'm so upset over his words but I'm more than that, and hearing him verbalize it crushed me. This is why I should never have gotten involved with a client, even in secret. Tears well in my eyes and before anyone can say anything else, I race away from him and head toward the restrooms for a breather.

Swinging the restroom door open, I meet a stunned Chelsea when the door flies into the wall with a thud. Then

I see her friend and the Crushers PT, I think that's her role. Pushing past them, I head into a stall and lock the door behind me.

Leaning against it, I close my eyes and swallow back a sob.

"Fuck off, Jones, she's my handler. That's it."

Those words hurt more than anything he's ever done to me.

Covering my mouth, I shake my head as the first tear falls. I need to get out of here, I can't be here when he just thinks of me as his handler because I feel more.

I

Love

Stefan Däuchmen.

I'm so in love with Stefan Däuchmen but, right now, I pucking hate to love him. He really is a douche. I should have known better.

Dropping my head back, I stare up at the fluorescent light above me and shake my it side-to-side. "I fucking hate him," I mumble. Taking a deep cleansing breath, I unlock the door and when I open it, I come face-to-face with Chelsea. I totally forgot she and her friend were in here. She has concern etched on her face but I can't deal with her, or anyone, right now so I mumble, "Excuse me."

Looking at my feet, I race past them and pull the door open. Stepping out into the hallway, I walk toward the exit. I've only taken a few steps when an arm reaches out and grabs me. A tiny yelp slips out, and I'm spun around and slammed into the wall of the corridor. A muscular body cocoons me, and I close my eyes in fear but when I'm assaulted with a scent I'd recognize anywhere, I open them and stare up into his chocolate-brown eyes.

I don't want to talk to him right now so through clenched teeth, I growl, "Back the fuck up, Stefan." I press my hands into his chest but he doesn't move, even though the tone of my voice means business.

Stefan utters two words that I never thought I'd hear him ever say, much less to a woman. The words "I'm sorry" pass through his lips.

What the actual fuck?

Stefan Däuchmen just apologized.

"Stefan, I ..." But I don't know what to say. "I need to go. I ... I can't do this right now."

With a strength I didn't know I possessed, I push him away from me and make my escape. Racing through the bar, I head back to the hotel where the team is staying. I know my job is to look out for Stefan but, right now, I need to look out for me.

Arriving back at the hotel, I cross the lobby and enter the elevator. It stops on the pool level and Leif enters. "Wren," he says by way of greeting.

"Coach," I offer with a smile.

"Everything okay?"

"Just peachy," I lie, and from the look he gives me, he knows I'm full of shit. "I'm handling Stefan's antics from tonight," I tell him.

"At least he answered you. He ignored my calls."

I wish I could ignore him. "Guess I'm doing my job then." I smile at him as the elevator arrives at my floor. "Night," I whisper and before he can say anything, I exit and head to my room.

Opening the door, I kick off my sneakers and climb onto the bed. Resting my back against the headboard, I pull a pillow to my chest, hug it, and cry.

A few minutes later, my bladder lets me know it's full, so I climb off the bed and head to the bathroom. With my bladder empty, I open the mini bar and grab the bottle of wine. It's a chardonnay, not my favorite variety, but it's alcohol. And to add to my night, it's one with a cork. With the bottle finally open, I forgo a glass and chug straight from the bottle.

My face scrunches up at the taste, and I place the bottle on the counter. As much as I need alcohol, I cannot do the chardonnay. My phone pings with a text; it's Evie.

EVIE

> You want me to come to your hotel and we can drink wine and throw darts at Doucheman's face?

WREN

> As much as that sounds like fun, I just want to be alone. Tonight was…

But I don't know how to explain it to her without spilling my secret, but before I can make something up, she texts me back.

EVIE

> I'm here whenever you're ready

> … and if you need an alibi, I'm your girl.

WREN

> Thanks, babe … Nite

EVIE

> Nite nite Xo

Walking back to the bed, I strip off my clothes, leaving me in the sexy lingerie set I bought for tonight. At least I can appreciate how good I look. Falling onto the mattress, I stare up at the ceiling and the last thought I have before sleep overtakes me is that I need to start looking for a new job.

The sound of my phone ringing startles me, and I'm confused for a few seconds. Reaching over to the bedside table, I grab it. "Hello," I sleepily mumble. The digits on the alarm clock let me know it's super early in the morning.

"Hey, Wren, it's me," Stefan morosely says.

"Why are you calling me at stupid o'clock, did you do something stupid?"

"Yeah, I, umm, can you bail me out?"

Sitting up, my eyes widen and now I'm wide awake. "For fuck's sake, Stefan, what did you do now?"

"I kinda got into a bar fight with Kallen, and we both got arrested."

"Fucking hell," I groan. "Which station?" He tells me which precinct he's at. "I'll be there soon."

Pulling on last night's clothes, I put my Chucks on and grab my things to head to bail out my client.

STRETCHING OUT MY LEGS, I stare at the back of the chair in front of me while I wait for Stefan to be released and let out a sigh. It's nearing lunchtime and I'm still waiting. In hindsight, I should have gone back to sleep and made *him* wait.

This is NOT how I pictured this trip going.

After what happened on the plane, I was looking forward to a sexy night between the sheets with Stefan. After a game he's always ready and roaring. After the defeating loss to the Crushers, I was hoping to make him feel better ... instead he shredded me like the Crushers shredded them on the ice.

The door opens but it's not Stefan walking out, it's Kallen Jones. He walks over to David Maxwell, the coach of the Crushers and his girlfriend's father. Kallen looks sheepish and ashamed as David ushers him out. Before he exits the precinct, he looks to me and nods.

This morning while waiting, he and I put our heads together and have come up with a plan to deal with the rivalry between Kallen and Stefan once and for all. I'm sure they're both going to whine like little bitches, but enough is enough.

A few moments later, Stefan emerges. He's sporting a black eye and a split lip. "Hey," he hesitantly utters when he walks over to me.

"Hey," I reply, the urge to hug him is strong but I need to keep my hands to myself. I do, however, tell him what I'm feeling. "As much as I want to give you another black eye to match your current one, I also really want to hug you."

"You do?"

"Yes, you may have acted like a douche yesterday but deep down, I still kinda like you. Now, let's get back to the hotel so I can hug you."

"Okay." He nods and we exit the building while I order us a car. "Ummm, how are we getting back since the team jet left thirty minutes ago?"

"You bought us first class tickets on a United flight leaving first thing tomorrow morning." He nods but doesn't say anything. "I wasn't sure when you'd be out but I guess I can call the airline and change to a flight tonight.

"Or we can have a night together here, and I can make it up to you."

"Or we can do that," I agree with a smile.

He reaches out and grabs my hand. A spark jolts between us and I look at our hands then I lift my gaze to his face. "I'm really sorry, Wren, I fucked up in so many ways last night, and I took my issues out on you. You didn't deserve that. I wish I could go back in time and do it all over again."

"What would you do differently?"

"Rather than telling Kal that you're just my handler, I'd tell him I'm puck over stick in love with the most amazing woman in the world."

"Stefan," I whisper his name.

"I mean it, Wren. You're the most amazing part of my life. I just wish I saw what was right in front of me sooner. I want to shout from the rooftop how amazing the woman I love is—"

"But—"

He presses his finger to my lips. "But I know you want to keep us a secret and as much as that pains me, I'd do anything for you, Wren."

"Guess now's the time to let you know that you and Jones have been benched for three games. His coach, myself, and Leif feel that's punishment enough. You will each also be fined ten grand and at the upcoming Christmas charity day for underprivileged kids, you and Jones will be required to give a talk on team bonding and how to deal with big personalities."

"For fuck's sake," he hisses, but I ignore his outburst and continue.

"And so the two of you don't go all WWF again, I've arranged for a few teammates each to accompany you both. I will also be there as a buffer to keep the two of you in line. The three of us feel it's time you two learned to play nice together."

"I just want you there," he says. "With you by my side, I can conquer anything." I find myself nodding and feeling all gooey inside that he wants, no needs, me.

"I'd be there regardless but it's nice to be wanted."

"I want you more than you know and I will do anything to make you happy ... even do a presentation with my mortal enemy."

"That's going a bit far, isn't it?"

"No," he hisses. "I fucking hate him."

"Why do you hate him so much? Are..." I hesitate to ask my next question.

"Are what?

"Are you still in love with Chelsea?"

"No," he quickly refutes. "I fell out of love with Chelsea long before we ended. I should have manned up and dumped her but instead, I—"

"Was a douche?"

"Yeah." He nods and chuckles. "And for what it's worth, what I felt for her is nothing compared to how I feel for you. It's funny, sitting in my cell, all I could think about was how I disappointed you. Coach's wrath means nothing to me; I'll accept the bag skates and move on. But the thought of you walking away, that was something I couldn't bear."

Our car arrives and takes us back to the hotel. Silently we head up to our room, I let us in and enter first. When the door closes behind Stefan, the click of the lock engaging echoes around the room. Turning around, I gasp when I realize Stefan is right there.

"Hi," I whisper.

"Hi, yourself," he replies and before I can say anything else, he covers my mouth with his and kisses me. His tongue licks into mine and I moan into his kiss. Draping my arms over his shoulders, I pull him into me, deepening our connection.

He walks me backward and my back collides with the wall causing the frame next to my head to rattle. Reaching behind his neck, he grabs my wrists, lifts my arms, and presses them into the wall. Covering both my wrists with one of his hands, he slides his palm down my arm. His fingertips gently graze over my neck causing goosebumps to appear. His hand travels lower, over my chest and he cups my boob. Squeezing, he caresses my mound. Pulling my shirt and bra down, his fingertips trace over my nipple and I moan into the kiss. Tugging on my nipple, I grind myself into his growing erection, but the moment is interrupted when my phone rings from within my pocket. Ignoring it, I lift my leg and hook it around his hip. It stops, only to immediately start ringing again.

"You gonna get that?" Stefan asks against my lips.

"Nope," I reply, letting the 'p' pop.

"Good," he agrees. "Keep your hands up," he demands, and then, with a force I didn't know he could possess, he tears my shirt down the center, leans down, takes my nipple into his mouth, and sucks.

"Ohhh God," I pant.

"It's Stefan," he cheekily says, "but you can call me anything you want when you let me do this to your tits." He pulls down the other cup, licks across the valley of my breasts, and kisses my breast.

My phone rings again. He slips his hand into my pocket and pulls it out.

Jaxson's name flashes on the screen. "Answer it," he commands but I shake my head. I need to compose myself before I talk to my boss but I should have known better, Stefan answers for me and puts it on speaker. "Jaxson, my man—"

"Why are you answering Wren's phone?"

"She's a little tied up right now." He chuckles and my eyes widen. "How you doing?"

"How am I doing?" he growls. "I'll tell you how I'm doing. I'm kind of pissed off right now," he snaps. "My client who I thought was behaving himself got into a bar fight last night and was subsequently—"

"It was just a little scuffle," Stefan nonchalantly interrupts, sliding slides his hand down my abdomen.

"Yeah, a little scuffle that resulted in an arrest," Jaxson snaps at Stefan. He's still pissed it seems. When I called him this morning to give him an update, he used some colorful language to express his anger.

With extraordinary dexterity, Stefan manages to pop open the button on my jeans with one hand, lower the zipper, and slip his hand beneath my panties. "Stefan," I mouth, but he just grins and slides his finger down my folds and presses inside me. Biting my lip, I try to stifle my moan as I keep my arms up like Stefan demanded.

"No charges were filed, Jax, because Wren and someone from the Crushers got the charges dropped."

"How you keep getting away with shit, I will never know."

"It's because Wren is amazing at her job," Stefan defends me and when I stare at him, I realize he really means it. He winks and then presses a second finger into me. I have to bite my lip to stop myself from crying out.

"How she hasn't stabbed you in your sleep yet is beyond me."

"I'm stabbing her with my fingers right now," he whispers into my ear before biting my earlobe.

"She there?" Jaxson asks.

"Yeah, I'll just get her for you." Pause. "Wren, phone, it's Jaxson."

"I'm coming," I call out and I mean it in both senses right now.

Somehow, I manage to stifle my moans as I come hard all over Stefan's fingers. Stefan is grinning like a fucking carnival clown ... and me? I'm mortified I just orgasmed while my boss is on the phone, on speaker no less.

"Jaxson," I breathlessly say his name.

"You sound wheezy, are you coming down with something?"

"No, I'm fine," I tell him. "What's up?"

"Just checking in to see how it all went this morning?"

"Fine. Stefan is now under my watchful eye, and we

will not be leaving this room until it's time to leave for the airport tomorrow."

While I'm speaking with Jaxson, Stefan begins to strip his clothes off. It's like my very own *Magic Mike* show but instead of "Pony" by Ginuwine playing, it's my boss going off to the fact that my client is a degenerate, and then he's praising me for being a saint for sticking by him.

Stefan is now gloriously naked, and he's fisting his giant dick. *Why is it so hot watching a guy pleasure himself?*

Finally, I hang up from Jaxson, not really sure what I agreed to, but I do as we told him. Stefan and I do not leave the hotel room until it's time to head to the airport the next morning. And for these twelve hours, we christen every surface in the room ... some of them twice.

44

STEFAN

WREN and I are back in New York for the underprivileged kid thing. Kallen is still pissed at me because if looks could kill, I'd be six feet under right now, but if anyone should be pissed, it's me. For the last week, my phone and email have blown up with his people and mine trying to come up with a game plan for today. Luckily for me, Wren has everything sorted.

"It's go time," Wren says, walking up to me. I want nothing more than to pull her into my arms and kiss her, but we're still hiding our relationship. It's funny, you'd think it would be me wanting to hide us, but all I want to do is hold her hand in public and attend an event with her on my arm as my girlfriend and not in the background as my handler/image consultant. "Do you know where Kallen is?"

Looking around, I find him and Chelsea together. They really do make a cute couple and I'm glad to see her happy ... but I don't give two fucks about him. He can fuck a hockey stick sideways for all I care. Pointing him out, the two of us walk over to the happy couple.

"Sorry to interrupt," Wren says with a smile, "but, Kallen, it's time for you guys to give your speech."

"Sure," he replies. He looks to Chels and sternly adds, "We'll finish this later."

Kallen and I follow Wren to the front of the room. We stand to the side of the makeshift stage and Wren begins explaining what's about to happen and the timeline of events. Kallen is not paying attention and his lack of respect for Wren and what we're doing pisses me off.

"Focus, Jones," I snap under my breath so only he can hear.

With the plan of events locked in, we have a few moments before this thing officially starts. So I take the opportunity to head to the restroom but before I make it to the men's room, I bump into Chelsea when she exits the ladies'. She looks like shit but when she sees me, her face pales further.

"Shit, Stefan, I'm sorry. I didn't see you there."

"Are you okay, Chels?" I reach out and rest my hand on her arm in concern. She drops her gaze to where I'm touching her and quickly pulls her arm free.

"I'm fine, Stefan."

"You look a little green, Chels. You sure you're okay?" She nods again to reassure me. "I thought for a minute there you had a bun in the oven." Her eyes widen and I realize that she is. "Fuck me, you're pregnant?"

"Yes," she hisses, "but Kallen doesn't know and you can't tell him. Don't be a douche and ruin my Christmas surprise."

"You're the worst secret keeper ever. How does he not know?" I question because Chelsea Maxwell, well, Jones, is the worst secret keeper ever.

"Please," she begs, ignoring my secret jab. "I ... I, please don't tell Kal."

"Don't tell Kal what?" the man in question asks when he joins us.

"That she's still in love with me," I cockily taunt him.

"Yeah, I call bullshit on that." He looks to Chels. "What are you not telling me, babe?"

The two of them chat about her recent bouts of sickness and I wait for the moment to click in his brain, but he must be dumber than I thought because he still has no idea. Me being me, well, I can't help but be a douche. "Maybe she's pregnant."

Chelsea glares at me and Kallen stands next to his wife in shock, but it soon morphs to excitement and now I kind of feel bad for ruining her surprise. I think back to when I found out that I was going to be a dad, even if it was a lie, I was so excited. No one should have a moment like this taken from them so I tune back into their conversation, and I decide to help Chels. Fake gagging, I push between them and race into the bathroom behind us, pretending to vomit.

"Maybe you both have food poisoning?" Kal suggests and to keep up the ruse, I fake spew again. There's a knock then Kallen asks, "You okay, Däuchmen?"

"Fine," I yell out.

Wren comes barreling in. "Stefan, Oh My God, are you okay?"

"I'm fine," I reassure her. Then I whisper, "I'll tell you later. Now let's get this thing over with, we have a hotel room to christen." Her cheeks darken and we exit the bathroom. Kallen leaves Chelsea with her friend and we give our speech.

I'm not really paying attention to what Kallen's saying but my ears prick when he says, "Sometimes you'll come across people you clash with, and that's okay. It's how you deal with those people that shows the kind of person you really are. Like a puzzle piece, the right pieces fit together perfectly and with the help of those around you, you get the complete picture."

Shit, I hiss to myself that's going to be hard to top. Taking the spot in front of the microphone, I take a deep breath and begin. "I think Kallen summed up everything perfectly, and he's right, we may be different but together we're part of one big picture. Sometimes that final piece may be hard to place but when you do, it's perfect in every way. And with that being said, I'll wrap things up but before I do, I need to offer an apology." This is my way of finishing the puzzle that is New York and my troubled past. "I need to apologize to my former teammates and my old coach. I really was a douche when I was playing here in New York. I thought my shit didn't stink and the world owed me. I hurt a lot of people along the way. Sorry for not being the teammate and man I should have been, but I guess it worked out well because you married a pretty great chick." Turning to face my nemesis, I add, "Kallen, you're pretty great too. I know we've had our differences, on and off the ice, but that's all in the past and I hope one day we can become friends." He looks shocked at my words but nonetheless, he smiles and nods. I'll take that as a win. "I also need to thank Wren for keeping my ass, I mean butt, in line and putting up with me." I catch her eye and wordlessly, we say what we mean to each other. Then I look back to the crowd. "Most of all, Kallen and I need to thank you guys, our fans. Without fans like you, we wouldn't have the desire to win. You guys cheering us on is always the push we need to play at our best. Sure, some of you root for the wrong team." The Crushers in attendance boo and I chuckle. "And yes, I know I used to be a Crusher, but I'm now with the far superior team." Now it's my teammates turn to cheer. "But rivalry is good, when it's handled professionally and left on the ice. I think Kallen will agree with me, life is much simpler when we don't have management, or Wren, riding our butts."

Kallen steps up to the microphone. "I don't know about Wren riding my butt 'cause, well, I'm not a douche, but I do have a wife and father-in-law who keep me in line."

Leaning into the mic, I shove him away. "Boys and girls, don't hook up with the coach's daughter because the coach will push you harder, on and off the ice."

"It's worth it if you ask me." Kallen must spy Chels because he gets this look on his face, and it's one I recognize; it's one of unequivocal love. Pushing that aside, I get back to my speech. "Life is hard and we aren't always going to get along with everyone, and that's okay. But we need to treat each other with respect. Life is difficult enough without making it harder for ourselves by focusing on the negatives." Finding Wren again, I stare at her as I say, "A wise woman once told me to show respect to everyone, even those who don't deserve it because it reflects on you and your character in how you treat them." Looking to Kallen at my side, I focus on him. "Jones, I'm sorry for being a jackass to you." Then I find Chelsea. "And, Chels, I let my insecurities fester and it wasn't until I was about to lose it all that I realized, only I can change what happens in my life and dragging you down with me, what a shi—crappy thing to do."

"I...ummm, wow, I don't know what to say," Kallen stammers from next to me.

"You don't have to say anything, just know I'm sorry and I'm sure you'll make a great dad." My eyes widen at my slip of the tongue and then I quickly tack on, "One of these days."

"Thanks, man, and truth be told, I'm sorry too."

"What are you sorry for?" I furrow my brows because Kallen hasn't done anything wrong. All the animosity between us was because of me and my insecurities.

"I'm not sure exactly but after you're heartfelt speech, I felt like I needed to say it too. I'm sure I did just as many douchey things as you did."

"Let's leave the past in the past and focus on the future?" I offer him my hand and he shakes it.

The crowd claps and when I look up, Chelsea is walking toward us and I notice she's wiping at her eyes. "You guys, that was amazing," she says when she reaches us.

"I meant it, Chels, I'm sorry. I was horrible to you when we dated and the things I did to you, I'm ashamed of myself."

"As you said, it's in the past. I've moved on ... and I think you might have too." She head nods toward Wren who is talking with one of the organizers, but her eyes are locked on me. She quickly averts her gaze when she realizes we are watching.

"I'm trying, but she's stubborn." I need to get her to admit we are a thing publicly because this hiding, it's not sitting well with me. Secrets never stay secrets, trust me, I know. I want us to tell the world on our terms but if secret is all I can get for now, I'll do it because she's worth it.

"Is she worth the fight?" Chelsea asks and smiles because it's like she was just in my head.

"Yeah, she is."

"Then don't give up," Chels tells me. "Be the man I first fell in love with, and she'll have no choice in the matter."

"Why are you being so nice to me?"

"Because I'm happy and, Stefan, that's all I ever wanted for you. Sure, you and I didn't work out and you did the worst thing possible to a girl, but I never wanted you to be alone and unhappy. Everyone deserves happiness, Stefan, even douches who cheat."

"Thank you," I tell her.

She shocks me when she wraps her arms around me and

whispers, "And thanks for earlier." She pulls back. "It was eye-opening all around."

"It really was," Kallen agrees. "Thanks for making this fun, I was really dreading it."

"You and me both." I nod in agreement. "As it turns out, you're not so bad after all, but just know, the next time we play you guys, I'm going to wipe the ice with your ass."

"And the douche is back," he teases.

"Once a douche, always a douche." Saying goodbye, I step around them and walk over to Wren.

"Wanna get out of here?"

"Yeah, but one question, what's going on between you and Chelsea?"

Filling her in on what transpired in relation to her being pregnant, she smiles up at me. "That was a really nice thing you did."

"I can be nice."

"I know you can ... I just wish you showed this side more often."

Me too, I think to myself as we walk out of the event that was eye-opening in more ways than one, because I realized today that I love this woman more than I love myself.

45

WREN

...five months later

THE SEASON IS ALMOST over and there's a chance LA could win the Cup. Of course, they're facing off against the Crushers and Stefan is out to win. Even if it wasn't against New York, he'd still be fired up but considering who they *are* playing, he's even more gung-ho now.

This morning I met with Tania and Leif, and let's just say, the meeting did NOT go in my favor, well it did, but it also didn't.

... "Wren, you really are a miracle worker," Tania praises. "It's been nearly five months and Stefan hasn't been caught with his pants down or appeared on WtB once." I chuckle to myself at that reference because I've had his pants down on many occasions in that time. "I think at the end of the season, you can return to your life in New York and put Stefan behind you."

Sitting here, I continue to listen to Jaxson, Leif, and Tania sing my praises, but I'm trying to figure out a way to be able to stay because the thought of leaving Stefan hurts. Maybe I can ask Jaxson to transfer me to the LA office?

I knew this day was coming. Now that it's here, I'm not ready to leave but at the same time, I'm not ready to have our relationship splashed on *WtB* and in the tabloids either. I keep thinking about the fallout of my time with Simon Simon. I know unequivocally, Stefan is nothing like that slimeball asshat, but no matter how you look at him, he's my client ... and not sleeping with Stefan was why Jaxson hired me. His words were something along the lines of "you won't let it happen again because I know you've learned your lesson" but, clearly, I haven't because here I am, hopelessly in love with my client because I slept with him.

But like exposing our relationship, I'm a big chicken and don't ask him. At the end of this season, I'll be returning to New York to work with Colton Bolton—yes, I still chuckle at his name every time I say it. The guy's had a tough time since joining the Crushers and, let's just say, he's giving Stefan a run for his money when it comes to who's the biggest douche.

Thankfully, the season will be over, which means Stefan can come visit me. However, if I just put my big girl panties on, I could just stay here and live happily ever after with my hockey stud.

The whir of the garage door motor kicks in, and I know it's time to face Stefan and tell him I'm leaving, but how do you tell the man you love you're moving twenty-eight hundred miles away 'cause you're a chicken?

46

STEFAN

AS SOON AS I walk inside and look at Wren, I immediately know somethings wrong. "Wren, babe, what's wrong?" I ask, pulling her into my embrace.

Instead of answering me, she wraps her arms around my waist and holds on to me. I love having her in my arms, yes, I'm officially pussy-whipped but whatever. She sighs heavily into my chest. "You're scaring me, Wren."

She lifts her head and instead of seeing her usual vivid-blue eyes, I see dull, almost gray ones. Her mouth opens and closes, "I ... I have to go back to New York," she morosely whispers. "Come the end of the season, Tania and Leif are ending my contract with the Legends."

Processing her words, I nod. "Oh," is all I can muster in reply. "So, you're leaving?"

"Mmmhmpf," she says, also nodding.

"You're going back to New York?"

Again, all I get is a nod and a "Mmmhmpf."

"Should I go out and do something stupid so they rehire you?"

"No," she hisses and laughs. "You are not going to ruin everything you've done just so I stay."

"Then what do I do to get you to stay?" He pauses. "I don't want you to go, Wren. You're the best thing to happen to me. I love you more than I love myself. I don't want to lose that. I don't want to lose you."

"I don't want to lose you either, but my job is in New York and yours is here."

"You could work in the LA office?" I suggest.

"I could, but won't it be suspicious if I ask that?"

"I don't care. I just want you. Maybe it's time we come clean?"

"No," she shouts, and who knew that a two letter word could cut so deeply.

Scoffing, I step back from her and shake my head. "I ... I need some air." Without waiting for a reply from her, I walk out, slamming the door behind me.

Walking down the boardwalk, I head for the nearest bar. Taking a seat at the bar, I wait for the bartender and when she arrives, I realize it's a chick I've fucked on several occasions. "The fuck you want?" she hisses at me.

"A beer, please." I smile at her, earning myself a scowl.

She pours my usual and slams it down in front of me, beer spills down the side. Without another word, she walks away, not before muttering under her breath, "Asshole."

"What up, douchehole?" a chick says, taking the stool next to me. Turning my head, I smile when I see it's Wren's friend, Fern.

"Wren's leaving," I tell her.

"What did you do?" she snaps at me before ordering herself a margarita.

"Behaved." She looks at me with confusion all over her face. "Since I've been behaving—"

"She's no longer needed," she interrupts and guesses in

one. "And you're upset 'cause you and her have been fucking like rabbits and you'll miss her."

My eyes widen. I thought this was a secret between us. "What? How?"

"Dude, you have a glass front door that you can see the kitchen from. Let me just say, I will always wipe down your island bench before putting food on it."

"Oh ... how long have you known?"

"For a while," she tells me. "You two have a connection that is smoking fucking hot." She fans herself. "How others haven't figured it out, I do not know, but you two fucking aside, what's this about her leaving?"

"Tania and Leif fired her, well, come the end of the season, she'll no longer be employed by them since I'm well-adjusted now."

"Just do something stupid to get you in the headlines and then BOOM, they'll hire her back."

"I thought of that, but me doing something stupid will look bad on her."

She nods. "Yeah, okay, I get that. Why not come clean with your relationship and then she can just move here. Doesn't LTS have an office here?"

"I suggested that but she shot me down."

"Why?"

"History."

"Huh?"

Seems Wren hasn't opened up to Fern about that dick-wad. "It's not my story to tell but she doesn't want her reputation marred."

"And hooking up with a client would do that?"

"Something like that."

"Do you love her?"

"With all my heart," I honestly tell her, and I mean it. Wren is a breath of fresh air. She makes me a better person.

She made me realize the world doesn't revolve around me and it certainly doesn't owe me a thing. She's opened my eyes to so many new things.

"Then you need to let her go. You need to let her spread her wings but when her heart aches from being away from you, you need to be there for her and she *will* come running back."

"How can you be so sure?"

"Because Bradford once pushed me away, but our hearts were already intwined and we found our way back to each other. That will happen for you guys too."

"I hope so because ..."

"You love her."

Grinning, I nod. "I do, I really fucking do."

"Then remind her that you love her. That you support her and once she knows, the rest will right itself."

I really hope Fern is right because I don't know what I'm going to do without Wren in my life. She's become the beacon of light in what was a dark life. I'm a better person when she's around, and I kinda like the person I'm becoming with her guidance. Deciding to take Fern's advice, I head home to discuss my feelings with Wren ... like a mature adult.

47
WREN

STARING at the door Stefan just walked out of, my eyes well with tears. I wish I could be brave about this but I'm scared, shit fucking scared. My career won't weather another scandal like this, but my heart won't handle losing Stefan either. I love the douche, with all my heart. It feels like I'm screwed no matter what I choose.

My phone rings and when I see Mom's name on the screen, I silence it but at the last minute, I answer, "Hey, Mom."

"What's wrong?" she says instead of saying hello back.

"I ... ummm, Mom."

"Talk to me sweetheart, you're scaring me."

"I'm going back to New York," I tell her.

"And you're upset to be leaving LA and Stefan because you're in love with him, but you don't want what happened with that double named twat to happen, hence, why you've been sneaking around."

A laugh escapes me and really, I'm not surprised Mom figured this all out. "So you knew, huh?"

"Anyone with eyes could see that you two are gaga for each other."

"But he's my client, Mom."

"Well, technically, when you go back to New York he won't be anymore."

"But—"

"No, sweetheart, no buts. You two are meant to be; I just know it."

"It's not that easy, Mom."

"Love never is, Wren. You just need to decide what's more important, Stefan or your job."

That statement stops me in my tracks and really gives me something to think about. Mom and I spend the rest of the call catching up, and by the time I hang up, I feel better but I still don't know what I'm going to do.

After tidying up the already clean kitchen, I grab a White Claw and head up to the rooftop deck to think. Lying back on the lounger, I sip on my sickly sweet drink and I think. I know I want and love Stefan, but I can't get past the fear of what exposing our relationship will do to my career. It sounds selfish but I've worked too hard to get where I am, and I don't want to see it wasted.

"Hey," a gruff voice says, scaring the shit out of me and I jump in fright.

"Shit, Stefan, you scared me."

"Sorry," he sheepishly says. Putting his hands in his pockets, he stands there, staring at me.

We both say each other's name at the same time and we

laugh. Sitting up, I cross my legs and pat the lounger next to me.

He takes a seat beside me, and I hate the awkwardness that's between us.

"Wren," he says, speaking first. "As much as it pains me, I know you need to go back to New York for you. It's only a five hour and twenty-five minute flight from here to there and there's FaceTime." Mutely I stare at him and process his words. Then he adds, "Plus, it'd be super sexy to watch you play with yourself like that."

"Perve," I tease.

"Only for you because, Wren, I love you." He reaches over and cups my cheek. Turning my head, I place a kiss on his palm. "I want the best for you, but know I'll always be here, no matter what."

One minute he's holding my face and the next, his lips are on mine and he's kissing me. This is a kiss from the movies. It's soft and sensual but at the same time, it's heated and full of emotion.

Stefan sure knows how to kiss, and with each lash of his tongue against mine, everything in the world feels right again. I know without a doubt that I want him. I just need to figure out a way to make this work that's fair for both of us.

48
STEFAN

ANOTHER SEASON HAS COME to an end and unfortunately, we lost to the Crushers, 4-1. Kallen Jones was on fire tonight, and he blocked all but one puck. And I'm man enough to admit that he's an excellent goalie. Our goalies could learn a thing or two from him.

Unlike last offseason, I'm not being shipped off to Tania's ranch and then a private island due to my douchey ways, instead my heart is being shredded. Wren is heading back to New York and already I miss her. Tania and Leif are extremely happy with my behavior and after a meeting with them before the playoffs, they feel I no longer need her. If only they knew how much I really do need her.

Wren is due to start back in the NYC office a week from Monday. I've tried to convince her to stay until the Sunday before, but Wren being Wren wants to get back and be settled before starting work there again.

I still wish she would let us be honest with the world but as Fern said, I have to bide my time until she sees what's right in front of her—me. Even if the seeing me is through a phone screen.

Fern convinced her to go to Vegas for a last hurrah, but Bradford and I hustled our way into the trip as well, so the four of us flew to Vegas early this morning for a weekend of gambling, drinking, and fun.

Bradford knows a guy, and we're staying at the Bellagio in a penthouse suite with a view of the fountain.

Walking into the penthouse, the girls squeal over the view. Bradford and I just sit back and watch them run around excitedly. He and I grab a beer each and he pops open a bottle of bubbly for the girls.

"A toast," Fern states when they finally join us. "Cheers, to a Veg-tabolous weekend."

We all tap our glasses together. The girls crank up the music and we spend the afternoon in the room drinking.

To be honest, I just want to spend time alone with Wren since she's leaving soon, but seeing her so happy and excited with Fern, I push my wants aside and go with the flow.

Fern wants to try out some famous steak house and I'm not one to turn down a good steak, so I pull a few strings and manage to get us a table this evening. Sometimes it comes in handy to be a famous hockey player.

Fern and Bradford head to their room to get ready and Wren and I do the same. I let her shower first since, well, she's a chick and will take longer than me to get ready. When I step out of the en suite, my mouth drops open when I see Wren. She's wearing a figure-hugging, strapless white dress that looks like a second skin. She's fucking stunning. Looking down at my black slacks a with white button-down, I feel underdressed.

"Hey, handsome," she singsongs when she spots me.

"Wren, babe, you're fucking gorgeous. It's going to be so hard to keep my hands off you tonight."

"Back at ya, stud." She walks over to me and adjusts my collar. Sliding my hand around her waist, I bring her in for a kiss. It's only supposed to be a quick peck but as with anytime I kiss Wren, I can't help myself and it becomes ravenous.

My hand slides down and I cup her ass in my palm, giving it a little squeeze. She moans into my mouth and hooks her leg around my thigh. Slipping my hand along her skin, I slide under her dress and my eyes widen when my finger slips into her slit. "Umm, Wren, where are your panties?"

"I haven't put them on yet," she purrs and looks at me seductively.

"Fuck, babe, thinking about your naked cun-pussy has my dick hard."

She pushes on my chest and grabs her panties from the bed. She steps into a skimpy thong. I watch as she pulls the flimsy material up her stunning legs, and it somehow is more erotic *with* her wearing panties.

"Think of the fun we'll have once we get back here and you tear these off of me. But since you've been a good boy and haven't appeared on *WtB* recently, as a reward, I can blow you now to tide you over."

"Don't tempt me, Wren."

With her eyes locked on mine, she drops to her knees and makes quick work of pulling my dick out. She sticks her tongue out and slides it over the bulbous head of my cock. Opening wide, she sucks my shaft into her mouth and begins to bob her head up and down. I watch her intently as my dick slides in and out between her lips. She moans around my shaft, and I realize she's fingering herself through her thong. That thought lights the fuse. My balls tighten and I come down her throat. She licks and sucks every drop from me.

My dick pops out of her mouth, and she falls back to her ass. She spreads her legs, pulls her thong to the side, and gives me an unobstructed view of her fingers in her slit as she brings herself to climax.

Watching her pleasure herself has my cock once again twitching and before I say fuck it and fuck her, Fern sings out that the car will be here in five minutes to take us to dinner.

"We're going to pick this up when we get back from dinner."

"Mmmhmpf." She nods and removes her fingers, they glisten with her arousal and my mouth waters. Reaching out, I grab her wrist and bring her fingers to my lips. I lick the juices off her fingers and moan. Wren has the most unique taste, and I cannot wait to have her for dessert.

"Oh My God," I groan after finishing the last mouthful. "That was the best steak I've ever had."

Everyone nods in agreement. We pass on dessert but the girls would like a nightcap so we decide to head to a cocktail bar on the Strip near our hotel.

"I'm just going to use the ladies'," Wren says. Sitting here, I watch her walk away and I smile as I watch her ass sway side to side.

Our waiter brings the bill, and Bradford and I argue over who's paying. We end up agreeing to split the bill but while I am getting my card out, the asshole pays the whole thing. "You can get the drinks," he says, just as movement at the back of the restaurant garners my attention.

Pushing my chair back, I storm through the restaurant toward Wren and a man. He just back handed her and without thinking, I grab him. It's Simon Simon. Rearing my hand back, I slam my fist into his face and push him aside. Turning around, I focus on Wren. She's pressed herself into the wall. Tears are cascading down her cheeks. Without thinking, I pull her into my arms and I hold on to her tightly as she breaks down.

Fern and Bradford join us. "Look after Wren for me," I tell Fern. Fern pulls Wren into her arms, and I turn my attention to the piece of shit sitting on the floor holding his bloody nose. Dropping down to his level, I grab the collar of his shirt and jerk him toward me. "You ever touch my woman like that again and I'll kill you."

Throwing him back to the ground, I stand up, turn, and walk back over to Wren. Placing my hand on her back, she looks at me over her shoulder and when she realizes it's me, she throws her arms around my neck and holds me.

A camera flash nearby grabs my attention but Wren's body begins to shake like she's in shock, and all I can focus on is her. Whispering, "Shhhh," I tighten my embrace on her.

"I want to leave," she mumbles into my chest.

"Let's go," I tell her. She pulls away from me and stumbles in her heels. Reaching out, I sweep her off her feet and up into my arms. Bridal style, I carry her out of the restaurant and as luck would have it, there's a taxi waiting and the four of us climb in.

Once we're buckled in, with Wren still on my lap, the driver pulls away from the curb.

"Thank you for saving me, Stefan," she tearfully whispers into my shoulder.

"You don't need to thank me." Placing a kiss on her temple, I hold her tighter.

"You're always saving me." Her statement is mumbled into my chest.

"No, Wren," I adamantly state while shaking my head. She lifts hers up and stares at me. "You're the one who's always saving me. From the moment you moved in, you've had my back. Even when I didn't deserve it." A small laugh slips free and she smiles. Reaching up, I cup her cheek and gently run the pad of my thumb over her cheekbone where Simon hit her. "Even when I was at my douchiest you believed in me. I've never had anyone in my corner like you. I've had no one since Nanna."

"Well, when you aren't a total douche, you're kinda awesome, Stefan Däuchmen."

"Well, Wren Brookes, you are always awesome and I'm glad to have you on Team Stefan."

The taxi pulls up outside of the hotel. Shuffling out, I try to keep Wren in my arms but she insists she's okay to walk. Reluctantly, I place her down on her feet but I take her hand in mine. I'm never letting her out of my sight again.

Entering the hotel, I head for the elevators but she tugs on my hand. "Can we get a drink before we go to our room?"

"Anything for you, babe. Anything." Turning to Fern and Bradford, I ask, "You guys coming?"

"Ummm, we might head on up," Bradford replies. Nodding at him, I waggle my eyebrows at him but he just shrugs. Going by the smirk on his face, he's going to take the opportunity to fuck Fern while we aren't there.

Fern hugs Wren and then we split up.

They head up to the room, and Wren and I head to the lobby bar where the evening takes another unexpected turn.

49

WREN

WAKING UP, I crack my eyes open but I quickly shut them again; the brightness is blinding. My mouth tastes like the bottom of a dirty ashtray, well, I presume this is what a dirty ashtray tastes like. There's also a throbbing in both my head and between my legs, clearly I had a good time last night—if only I could remember the fun.

Lying here, I focus on my breathing but it's hard because my stomach is doing somersaults. The jitters are not from my hangover, these are nervous and excited butterflies. *Why am I excited and nervous while I'm hungover?*

The events of last night are fuzzy. I remember dinner and then Simon and sitting in the lobby bar having a drink and then nothing. Clearly, I drank waaaaaaay too much and had a little fun between the sheets because as I stretch my arms above my head, my body hurts in that *you had lots of energetic sex* kind of way.

Opening my eyes again, I squint and look around. I'm in a hotel room but I have no clue how I got here. It's also a different hotel room from the one we shared with Bradford and Fern but it's just as stunning, waaaaay above my pay grade. Glancing around, I take in the decadence of the room and that confusion from before ramps up once again.

Where's Stefan?

Shaking my head, I close my eyes and will myself to remember, but I've got nothing.

In frustration, I close my eyes and sigh. Lifting my hand, I rub my forehead and temple to try and ease the jackhammering in my brain, then I freeze.

My eyes fly open and when I pull my hand away from my face, my gaze focuses on my ring finger. I stare with laser focus at the metal band sitting on my left hand's fourth finger. "That wasn't there yesterday," I mumble. I try and remember but I got nothing. I don't remember anything from last night. "What the fuck did you do, Wren?"

Blinking rapidly, I stare at the glittering gold band and accompanying diamond ring. And holy diamond, Batman. This thing must be at least two carats and even though it's on the larger side, it's stunning, fucking stunning.

Lifting myself up, the sheet falls and the cool air of the air-conditioning pebbles my nipples and I shiver. Quickly I pull the sheet back up and climb out of the most comfiest bed I have ever slept in. Padding over to the windows, I pull the curtain open. My eyes widen, again, when I see the Vegas Strip before me. "I'm still in Vegas," I mumble, stating the freakin' obvious. The view this morning is different, the Bellagio fountains are now across the road and I'm staring at the Bellagio Hotel behind the fountain. "Why am I in a different hotel?"

Shuffling over to the sofa, I drop down on it and just like the bed, it's soft and comfy. The sound of the electronic lock on the hotel room door beeps. Turning my head toward the sound, I wait to see who enters and when I see who it is, I smile. "Phew," I hiss, it's not some crazy stranger. I wasn't abducted.

The sound causes him to lift his head my way. He smiles at me in a way that takes my breath away, and then he utters three words that shock the ever-loving shit out of me. "Good morning, wife."

50
STEFAN

"GOOD MORNING, WIFE," I call out as I enter the penthouse suite. It's not as grand as the one we shared with Fern and Bradford, but I didn't want roommates on my wedding night, and I'm glad because last night was off-the-charts erotic. *Who knew my wife was such a sex fiend?*

Dropping the shopping bag by the door, I walk farther into the room with breakfast. I want to start married life with my balls intact, so I ducked out to get coffee and OJ. We all know Wren doesn't function until she's had her morning glass of OJ and her coffee.

"W-w-w-wife?" she stammers.

Nodding, I walk over to her and place a kiss on her lips. Grabbing the juice from the tray, I hold it up. "Drink this and once you've had your bitch juice and debitch, we can talk."

"Can't you just call it juice, like a normal fucking person? And I'm not a bitch, no sane person likes mornings. Whoever invented them should be shot and then boiled in a vat of pig shit."

"Case in point, wife, you're bitchy first thing in the morning."

"I'm not bitchy; I'm just hungover. And stop calling me wife."

"Would you prefer ball and chain? Missus? Other half? Old lady? Nah, that won't work. I'm not a biker dude and you're not old. How about—"

"Just shut up and give me my juice."

"Yes, ma'am." Twisting off the lid, I pop in a straw and finally hand it to her.

"Thanks," she whispers and when she wraps her lips around the straw. I'm accosted with a memory of her in the shower last night ... or was it early this morning?

...Wren is on her knees staring up at me. Water cascades over her shoulders, and I watch the rivulets track between her breasts. She has her hand on my cock and is pumping my dick like her life depends on it. Then she leans forward, kisses the tip, and covers the head with her mouth. She pumps the base and wraps her gorgeous lips around my shaft.

Shaking away that thought, I readjust my hardening dick but when I notice the ring on her finger, I'm transported back to the shower.

...The ring on her finger sparkles in the light and I smile.

My wife is giving me a blow job and life is great. She takes my dick to the back of her throat, and the sound of her gagging is music to my ears. "Wife, you suck my dick like a champ. I can't wait to spend the rest of my life gagging you and getting blow jobs from you."

She murmurs her agreement around my shaft, and then she relaxes her throat and takes it all. Her nose presses into my stomach, and the feeling is indescribable. She squeezes my balls and it's game over. Grunting, I spill my seed down her throat. She sucks every last drop. My cock pops out of her mouth and she wipes at the corner, my gaze catches on her ring and I can't help but smile. She's mine.

Once again, I find myself grinning and Wren stares at me. She drops her gaze to where I'm staring and her eyes widen. She flicks her gaze from her ring finger to me to my ring finger and back again. Placing the empty juice bottle on the coffee table, she asks, "What happened last night?"

"We got married," I tell her.

"I figured that but, umm, how? How the fuck did we get to that point? The last thing I remember is heading to the lobby bar with you after Simon hit me at dinner." *Simon fucking Simon.* I want to pummel that asshole's face again. Apparently, he hit her because she refused to blow him. Not that I blame him; Wren is fantastic at that, but no means no and she's mine. Literally. Now I have the piece of paper to prove it.

"While you drink your coffee, I'll fill you in."

She picks up her coffee, and I open the paper bag. Reaching in, I grab a pain au chocolat—we are at the Paris Hotel now, so a French breakfast is called for—and hand it to her. Grabbing mine, I drop onto the sofa next to her.

Nibbling on her breakfast, she tucks her legs underneath her. The sheet slips open, giving me an unobstructed view of her tits. Tits that I remember losing myself in just a few hours ago.

. . .

...Pulling down the top of her dress, I quickly unclasp her bra and flick it to the side. Cupping her tits, I lean down and suck on her nipple before I bury my face in the valley of her breasts, and I breathe in deeply. "I love your tits," I mumble before I take the other nipple in my mouth and gently bite down. I could lose myself in her tits and that's exactly what I do for the next few minutes.

"Stop looking at my boobs," she snaps, readjusting the sheet to cover up her chest.

"That's not what you were saying a few hours ago while I was sucking and nipping at them. I distinctly remember you asking me to fuck them and for me to coat your face in cum."

"I did no such thing," she hisses, but from the pink tinge glowing on her cheeks, she remembers me doing just that. And from the way she's subtly pressing her thighs together; she wants it to happen again. I will happily fuck my wife's tits anytime she wants. After all, happy wife, happy life, and what's better than titty fucking?

Licking the crumbs off her fingers, she reaches over and grabs her coffee again. Taking a sip, she closes her eyes and savors the flavor.

"Is your coffee black like your soul enough for you?"

"Yes, it is." She pauses and smile. "And thank you. I appreciate it."

"You're welcome."

A comfortable silence befalls us and we quietly sit here and drink our coffees. I can see her brain running a million miles a minute and when her face scrunches, I know it's time to fill her in, and that thought is confirmed when she says, "Okay, tits and coffee aside, how did this"—she lifts her left hand and wiggles her ring finger—"happen?"

"When we got back to the Bellagio, you suggested a nightcap. Fern and Bradford ditched us to no doubt fuck, so you and I went into the bar off the lobby. You and I started drinking martinis, and at one point we had a drink that came covered in smoke—"

"I remember," she excitedly says. "It's called a Poof! And it's whiskey based."

"That's the one. Anyway, we had more than one nightcap. You went to the restroom at some point and when you came back, you were crying. You sat back down next to me and declared, 'I need to get shitfaced drunk to forget' and that's what we did."

"Did I ever tell you why I was crying?"

Nodding, I mumble, "You did."

"And what did I tell you?"

"You told me you received a text. It was a video ..."

At my words, she jumps up and searches for her phone. With trembling hands she taps the screen to wake it up and her eyes widen when it does. She turns her phone around and her lock screen image is a picture of the two of us inside the chapel. I've dipped her back and I'm about to kiss her. We both look drunk but we also look happy and in love. She pulls her phone back and unlocks it. Her hands fly over the screen, and I know the moment she sees the cover image of the video. Her eyes well with tears as she presses play, but I quickly jump up and snatch her phone from her. "Are you sure you want to watch it again?"

Looking at me, she tearfully nods.

Handing her back her phone, she hits play again. Standing across from her, I watch her as she stares at the screen. Simon Simon is sinking his dick into some skinny chick while a tattooed, muscular steroid junkie steps behind Simon and eats his ass before he slides his monster cock into Simon's ass. But the most shocking part of the video? Wren is lying on the other side of them. Her eyes are closed, it looks like she's passed out.

"I have no recollection of that night," she sobs, then she laughs. "Simon always told me anal was disgusting."

"Babe, I'll fuck your ass anytime."

She laughs. "Thanks, but that's the last thing I'm thinking about right now."

"What are you thinking about?"

"Why did he send this to me? And how did I go from watching my ex-boyfriend be part of a gangbang while I'm passed out to marrying you in Vegas?"

"That's a very good question but before I answer, you need to put some clothes on and th—"

"Bet you've never said that to a woman before?" she teases.

"It is a first, but I can't concentrate on this story knowing you're naked under that sheet, when all I want to do is tear said sheet off of you and fuck you into next week ... again."

51

WREN

MY EYES WIDEN at his words. I've heard Stefan use lines like that before but for some reason, right now, it doesn't feel like a line. He means it. He really WANTS to fuck me and not in the wham-bam-thank-you-ma'am kind of way. He wants to sleep with me because I'm his whole world but it doesn't change the fact that in a few short days, I'm moving back to New York.

"You can't say stuff like that to me," I tell him.

"I can say whatever I want to my wife."

"I'm not your wife, Stefan."

He reaches out, grabs my hand, and points to my new bling. "These rings and the piece of paper on the table over there say otherwise."

"Where the fuck did you get a wedding set from anyway?"

"When you have money and you're me, you can get what you want when you want."

"Brag much?"

"It's the truth, baby. Now, go get dressed."

"Where are my clothes?"

Both of us look around the hotel room and there are clothes spread from one end of the place to the other. I spy my thong but when I bend down and pick it up, I see it's shredded. "What did you do to my undies?" He nonchalantly shrugs at me. "Stefan, I can't leave this room with no panties on."

"You threatened to last night," he throws back at me.

"Yes, threatened but in fact, I wore a thong." I wave my shredded panties in front of his face. "I didn't go to dinner last night with no panties on and in the light of the day, the same rules apply."

Stefan walks over to the door and picks up the bag he dropped when he walked back in. "Here," he says, shoving the bag at me. Peeking inside I see underwear and a royal blue maxi dress. "You bought me clothes?"

"Well, I knew you wouldn't want to wear your wedding dress out of here so I stopped at a store and grabbed you another dress."

"Thank you," I honestly tell him.

He steps over to me and cups my cheek. "I'd do anything for you, Wren."

We silently stare at one another, the air around us thickens but before I do anything stupid like fuck him, I turn on my heel and walk into the bathroom.

Closing the door behind me, I lean against it and sigh. Sex is not what I need right now. I need my head clear so I can fix this. I have no clue how I got here or why I married him but, deep down, I know Stefan cares. This is the side of him that kept me going. The caring and considerate Stefan. This is the Stefan I fell in love with but marriage? What the hell?

"What's this I hear about Doucheman getting married last night?" Jaxson bellows into the phone as I finish another coffee after my shower. Stefan's in the shower now, and I was just about to log into my emails to see if this has gotten out but Jaxson beat me to it, confirming that, yes, the news of our marriage is out.

My eyes glance to the en suite door but it's closed, sequestering Stefan away from this conversation and my firing. "It's true, he got married last night," I mumble, more to myself than him.

"It's all over the fucking news, Wren," he huffs. "Margaret is having a field day with this."

"Shit," I hiss. "Stefan and I will take care of it."

"Do you know who this bimbo he married is?"

"I, umm, ahh..." Shit, this next part is going to be hard to tell him. There's no use in hiding it, so I bite the bullet and just spit it out. At least it's over the phone and not face-to-face. "Yes, I know her and, as I said, I'm dealing with it." I'm not but he doesn't need to know that and, thankfully, he's several states away in New York.

"How are you dealing with this, Wren? 'Cause from where I'm sitting, it's every fucking where."

"I'm dealing with it," I repeat. "I've got a plan." There's got to be a courthouse around here to get this annulled. I mean, shit like this happens all the time in Vegas. We can get in annulled and all will be fine again.

There, game plan sorted.

Stefan and I will go to the courthouse and get an annulment. With it being the weekend, we'll have to wait till

Monday but we can be there as soon as they open and by lunchtime, it'll be like the marriage never happened.

Crisis averted.

We can chalk it up to a drunken prank.

While I was in my head planning this, Jaxson was talking but I have no clue what he said. Now, a silence has fallen between us. The only sound is his heavy breathing and me chewing on my bottom lip.

"Wren, why do I get the feeling you know more than you're letting on right now?" Fucking Jaxson and his perceptiveness. I'm unsure as to what to say next but when he draws my name out with six extra e's, I know I have no other option but to tell him the truth.

Deciding to just spit it out, I blurt out seven words I never thought I would utter. Ever. "Last night, Stefan and I got married."

"I'm sorry, did you just say *you* and Stefan got married?"

Nodding my head, I purse my lips. "Mmmhmpf, yep, that's what I said." Silently I add, *I'm Mrs. Stefan Däuchmen.*

"For fuck's sake, Wren. I'm coming over and—"

"That might be a problem," I interrupt.

"Why?" he bellows, and I have to pull the phone away from my ear and the shrillness of his tone.

"Because he and I are still at our hotel in Vegas."

Even through the phone I can see the disappointment on his face. He trusted me with this gig. He put his faith in me that I could rework Stefan's image and not fall for his charms. And I didn't, I fell for Stefan, the man, not his bunny-taming charms. I fell for the person he's kept hidden from the media and everyone else, and this reaction is why I didn't want to go public with us. "I thought I could trust you with this, Wren."

"You can," I defend. "Stefan is—"

This time it's him who cuts me off. "Do not leave that hotel room, Wren. You and him are to stay in that room. I'll be there later tonight and then we can come up with a game plan."

"I already have a plan."

"Clearly you can't be trusted when it comes to Doucheman. Just stay fucking put, Wren."

"Okay," I dejectedly reply then I quietly add, "I'm sorry, Jaxson."

"Yeah, me too." That comment stings but at the same time, I deserve it. I vowed I would not do this but here I am. Only this time, I'm ten times deeper in the shit. "Don't leave that hotel room," he reiterates, and without another word, he hangs up.

Swallowing deeply, I hold the phone to my ear, shaking my head. My eyes well with tears and in frustration, I throw the device across the room. I just fucked my career, again, but this time, there'll be no coming back from it.

Plopping down to the sofa, I drop my head back and stare at the ceiling. The sound of the en suite door opening garners my attention and when I look up, Stefan is standing in the doorway. My eyes roam over his body, he's only in a towel and it showcases his muscular torso and that V muscle that causes woman to go gaga ... and the reason why Jaxson got him the underwear endorsement with Monty's. Come to think of it, I'm pretty sure Peyton signed every hockey player represented by LTS to her latest campaign. And what a campaign it will be. All those hockey players in nothing but their underwear, yes pucking please.

Snapping my attention away from him before I do something stupid, like fuck him, again, I pick up the remote and flick the television on. Of course, it's Margaret from *WtB* focusing on Stefan and what happened last night. She's trying to figure out who his mystery bride is. *At least I'm hidden*, I think to myself. For the first time since my call with Jaxson, I smile because it's a win. A little win but still a win.

She always seems to be there when shit goes down. She's like a magnet for gossip. Anytime someone does something headline worthy, she's there, and it's out there for everyone to know ... Thankfully, she missed *my* headline news the first time round and once again, I want to keep my private life just that—private.

"You okay?" Stefan asks, coming to stand before me. Lifting my head, my eyes slowly roam up his body to his face. A face that has a knowing smirk on it.

"No, I'm not okay, Stefan. My career and reputation are about to be ruined because we got married."

"It'll be fine," he nonchalantly says with a shrug.

"For you it will be. You're the star hockey player. But me? I'm the consultant who fucked up for the second time..."

"Second time?"

"Simon Simon," I huff in frustration. Rearing my hand back, I throw the remote in my hand to the floor. "What matters right now is that you'll be fine and I'm fucked and I—"

"You're not fucked," he interrupts.

He drops down to his knees and in doing so, the towel separates and I'm given an up close and unobstructed view of the most beautiful dick in the world. If we stay married, I could have access to the most beautiful dick in the world whenever I want, but him having a beautiful dick is no reason to stay married. What we did was reckless and stupid. Clearly, I was dick drunk last night as well as drunk-drunk. That can be the only reason as to why I married him, but when I think back to last night, I vaguely remember his words after the video debacle.

...“If you were my wife, I would never allow something like that”—he points to my phone—“to happen.”

“Well, I’m not your wife, so it’s moot.” I chuckle. “Moot is such a fun word to say. Moot. Mooooot. Discombobulated is also a fun word to say.”

“You’re fun, Wren, and one day, I’m gonna marry you.”

“You say that to all the girls,” I tease.

He shakes his head. “Nope, I’ve never wanted the whole marriage thing before, but you make me a betterer person, and I’d happily marry you. Anytime. Anywhere.”

“We should do it,” I suggest with a smile.

“Do what?”

“Get married.”

“We should,” he agrees, smiling brightly. “And then you can stay and I can be betterer all the time. So what do you say, wanna get hitched?”

Clearly, I said yes because, well, we’re currently married.

The memory of our wedding and when we got back here has my pussy quivering for another taste of my husband’s dick, but I need to think right now. And I need to think with my head and not my vagina. But when I look up and see Stefan staring intently at me, I don’t know if I’ll be able to control myself. “I’m so fucked,” I mutter.

52
STEFAN

"YOU'RE NOT FUCKED ... YET ... ANYWAY."

Before she can say anything, I reach over, pick up the remote, and pop it onto the coffee table. Shuffling between Wren's legs, I look down at her and it reminds me of last night when we got back from the chapel. Whereas now she's complaining about her career, last night, she was complaining about her feet.

... Leaning against the wall with my ankles crossed, I watch my wife walk into our room. She brings the bottle of Bollinger to her lips and takes a sip. She moans as the crisp flavor of the bubbly dances over her tongue. My focus intensifies when some of the liquid spills out the side of her mouth. It slides down her throat and between the valley of her breasts. Whatever bra she's wearing tonight, I need to send a thank you note to the designer because it makes her always amazing tits look phenomenal. "Fuck my feet hurt," Wren whines as she drops down onto the sofa.

Without thinking, I squat down in front of her and lift one of her stiletto-clad feet to my knee. Undoing the buckle, I remove her shoe and drop it to the floor before repeating the action to her other foot. Taking her foot in my hand, I rub my thumbs into the arch, earning myself a moan that heads straight to my dick. Repeating the action with her other foot, she ends up sitting back in the sofa with both her feet resting on my knees.

Sliding her foot up my thigh, she presses the ball of her foot into my growing erection. Swallowing deeply, I run the palm of my hand up her calf and between her thighs. Slipping my hand under the hem of her dress, I continue up to her thong. The material is soaked as I rub my finger up and down her slit. She moans as I press my finger between her lips. Finding her clit, I press my thumb into her bundle of nerves. "Stefan," she huskily whispers.

"Mmmhmpf?"

"What ... what are you doing?" she asks as I push her thong to the side and finally get skin-on-skin contact. Her lips are puffy, hot and wet. I want nothing more than to bury my face in her mound and breathe in her scent before devouring her delectable pussy.

With my eyes locked on hers, I tell her exactly what I plan on doing ... which surprisingly, does not involve my face between her legs. "I'm going to finger my wife, and then I'm going to fuck her until she can't remember her name." Before she can reply, I grip the side of her thong and tear it from her body. Dropping the shredded material to the carpet, I slide my hand back between her thighs and push a finger into her.

"Fuck," she pants.

Thrusting my digit in and out of her, her walls clench my finger. Her breathing becomes erratic but I'm not ready to let her come yet. So I pull my hand out and bring it to my lips but at the last second, I reach out and press my finger into her mouth. She licks her juices from my finger.

"Stefan," she pleads.

"Tell me what you want, wife?"

"I ... I want your fingers and your dick. I ... I just want you."

"As you wish," I tell her.

Shoving two fingers back into her, she grips my shoulders for support and squeezes tightly as she rides my hand. Once again, I begin to thrust my fingers in and out of her. Her head drops back in ecstasy. Inserting a third finger, I bring her to the edge. "I'm close," she hisses through clenched teeth. Just when she's about to come, I pull my hand from between her thighs. Her head snaps up and she growls, "What the fuck?"

With my eyes locked on hers, I bring my fingers to my lips and suck. Her juices are tangy and sweet but right now, I want to fuck her. I want her to ride me and scream my name when she comes. I want the whole hotel to know my name, but right now my wife is pissed off at being left hanging.

Shocking the shit out of me, she slaps my hand from my mouth and pushes on my shoulders. She knocks me onto my ass and throws her leg over me. Leaning down, she covers my mouth with hers. Her tongue licks into mine and she twines her fingers into my hair and pulls in punishment for edging her.

Tensing my core, I push myself upright and hold Wren to me. She wraps her legs around me as our tongues battle it out.

My cock is painfully hard within my pants, pressing into her slit. The only barrier between us is my clothes. She swivels her hips and I feel her smile into our kiss when I groan at the sensation.

Pulling back, she's breathlessly panting. She stares into

my eyes and huskily demands, "Dear husband of mine, I want you to fuck me now."

Her words snap me back to the present, and I smile when I realize she said the same thing last night. "What did you say?"

"I said, I want you to fuck me now. Make me forget the clusterfuck that is my life. Give me a moment of pleasure before I have to face reality."

"What my wife wants, my wife gets."

Before she has a chance to second-guess her decision, I throw her over my shoulder and march into the bedroom. Tossing her down onto the mattress she squeals and giggles. Shuffling up to the pillows, she lies back and stares at me. The air around us is thick with desire.

"You seem to be overdressed, wife."

"I'm not your wife," she throws back at me as she reaches down and shimmies about to pull her dress off, leaving her in her bra and a G-string.

"Better?"

Ignoring her, I rest my knee on the mattress, grip her ankle, and drag her toward the end of the bed. Gripping the edge of her panties, I rip them from her. The flimsy material disintegrates from the force.

"That's the second pair of panties you've shredded."

"Maybe you should stop wearing them."

"Not gonna happen."

"Then deal with the shredding. Now, remove your bra and let me make you forget about all your worries for a few hours."

"Hours?"

"Yep, hours."

...a few hours later

"FUCK ME," I pant, flopping to my back.

"We just did ... several times," he gloats with a pinch to my nipple.

"I thought you were joking about the hours thing."

"When it comes to sex, I never joke." He winks and the wink has my pussy throbbing again. *Down girl. Momma needs a rest,* but there's something about this man that turns me into a wanton hussy. I know fucking him is not going to fix this dilemma I find myself in but Stefan Däuchman aka my husband is like crack, one romp and I'm an addict. "You should know that by now. Now, you're going to give me one more orgasm. Then we're going to shower and go for a walk. After our cardio, I'm going to feed my wife. And then we will have some more bedtime cardio."

"Jaxson said to stay inside."

"Do you always do what you're told?" He begins tracing

his finger around my nipple, it pebbles under his touch and that ache between my leg intensifies.

"When it's from my boss and my career is on the line, yes. Yes, I do."

He stares at me for a beat. "Fine, new plan. You're going to give me two more orgasms. One here in bed and another in the shower. Then we're going to order room service and we're going to watch a movie, and then some bedtime cardio."

"My vagina is going to die if we keep fucking like this."

"I've never broken a vagina in my life."

"I don't want to hear about all the other vaginas you've been inside while mine is still buzzing from my last orgasm."

"Then let me put my mouth to better use."

In the blink of an eye, Stefan is down between my thighs. My legs are thrown over his shoulders and he's definitely putting his mouth to better use. He licks me from taint to clit, and when he pushes a finger into me, I start moaning like a cat in heat.

The things this man can do with his tongue should be illegal and even though I orgasmed only a few moments ago, my pussy zings back to life and my orgasm quickly builds. He devours me with his mouth and fingers.

My hands move to his head and I wring my fingers through the strands of his hair as he coaxes another orgasm from me that has me crying out his name. Adding about five extra e's to his name.

I'm still coming back to Earth when he shoves his cock back into me. I'm lost in the bliss of my never-ending orgasm, and I miss seeing him reach his peak. I think this is the first time we haven't come in unison.

Collapsing to the mattress next to me, we are both breathlessly panting. I lie here with my eyes closed, but I can feel his presence next to me. I'm too exhausted to open my eyes or even move. I'm content to just lie here and bask in the remnants of my orgasm.

Stefan begins to trace his finger up and down my sternum, causing goosebumps to break out and I shiver. Cracking my eyes open, I turn my head and I see him staring at me. He's on his side and is resting his head on his hand.

"You're staring," I tell him, stating the obvious.

"Just admiring my wife."

"Stefan," I protest just as my phone pings with a text. Knowing that Jaxson will be here soon, I climb out of bed and grab it.

JAXSON

Just parking my car. I'll check into my room and be at yours within the hour. Need anything?

A time machine, I think to myself, but then I catch a glimpse of Stefan lying next to me and I don't know that I necessarily want one after all.

WREN

All good here. See you soon

"That was Jaxson. He's arrived and will be here within the hour."

"So what you're saying is I have fifty-five minutes to pleasure you."

"No." I shake my head. "It means we need to shower and be ready to tackle this mess."

"There's nothing to tackle."

"Stefan, we're married. We need to face that. We can't just brush it under the rug."

"So we shout it to the world."

How is he so blasé about all of this? Not wanting to get into an argument before Jaxson gets here, I ignore him. Hopping up, I walk into the bathroom and close the door behind me. My eyes glance at the massive tub and as much as a bath sounds wonderful right now, I don't have time. All I have time for is a quick shower, plus I need to get my game head on.

After scrubbing myself raw and washing my hair twice, I climb out of the shower and wrap a towel around me. Stepping back into the room, I find my bra and put it back on. Searching for my panties, I find them but Stefan shredded them, again. "Looks like I'm going commando," I mumble to myself.

"Nothing wrong with that," Stefan states from the bed.

Ignoring him, I pick up my dress and pull the maxi Stefan got for me back on. It's soft and long and I'm thankful for that. The last thing I need is for a hoo-ha flash to be added to my list of shit things happening to me at the moment.

Looking at Stefan lying there naked, I take a moment to appreciate him. We both speak at the same time. He says, "That color suits you," and I say, "You need to get dressed. Jaxson will be here soon."

A silence overtakes us and then without acknowledging what each of us said, he climbs out of bed, walks into the bathroom, and closes the door behind him. Meanwhile, I shake my head and exit the bedroom. Walking over to the mini fridge, I pull out a water and place the cool bottle on my neck.

Leaning against the wall, I take a sip and close my eyes. I inhale deeply because I need to regroup. I'm on edge and without a clear head, there's a possibility I'll make a stupid decision, again.

Pushing off the wall, I head over to the sofa and drop

down onto it. I'm fidgety, my leg bouncing since my nerves are rattled.

When there's a knock at the door, my head snaps in that direction but I don't move. I'm frozen on the spot, I just sit here and stare at the door. My body is rooted to the sofa, the complete opposite of how I was a few seconds ago.

"Wren, it's Jaxson," he calls out. No doubt he thinks I'm ignoring him and, to an extent, I am, because when he enters this room, it all becomes real. Realer than it is now.

"I'll get it," Stefan states from behind me.

He crosses the room and I notice he's in a pair of cargo shorts and a black Henley. I watch his ass as he walks to the door but then I internally slap myself, this isn't the time to be perving. Swinging it open, Jaxson waltzes in and when he sees me sitting here looking like I'm going to throw up, he stops in his tracks and worry mars his stoic face.

"Wren, you okay?"

"Am I okay?" I repeat. "I'm..."

"She's grand," Stefan answers for me as he walks around Jaxson. He drops down onto the sofa next to me and takes my hand in his, lacing our fingers together. My eyes drop to the new bling on my finger and that feeling of utter failure slams into me with the force of a player being Kronwalled.

Not wanting to show affection in front of Jaxson, I pull my hand free and jump up. Space is what I need right now but when Jaxson speaks, I want nothing more than for Stefan to pull me into his arms and make me feel safe.

"So," Jaxson says, walking farther into the room. "You two got hitched and are now Mr. and Mrs. Däuchmen; wanna tell me how that happened?"

54

STEFAN

WREN SEEMS to have lost the ability to speak, so I answer and fill Jaxson in on everything relating to Wren and me. From sneaking around. To Simon Simon and the text. The drinks and then our wedding. I leave out the sexy parts but the lingering sex smell in the room kinda gives that away.

"What? How? What?" he stammers. This is the first time I've ever seen Jaxson Scott speechless and rocked to his core ... and I've done some crazy shit over the years. "You've been sneaking around for months?"

"Yep," I reply letting the 'p' pop.

"So this marriage, it's real?"

Wren and I both answer but it's with different responses. Mine is a resounding, "Yes," and hers is a stern "No," accompanied by a headshake.

"What the fuck do you mean no?" I snap at Wren.

"Exactly that, we can't stay married Stefan."

"Why the fuck not?"

"We got married 'cause we were drunk, Stefan."

"So?" I hiss back at her.

"It needs to end, Stefan."

I'm pissed the fuck off that she's talking about ending this ... and I don't know if she's referring to our nuptials or us in general. The thought of losing her completely doesn't sit well with me.

"What are you suggesting, Wren?" Jaxson asks her. Finally his tone is less angry and the urge to punch my agent in the face is no longer there, but now I want to throttle my wife for suggesting we end this.

"Well, I think Stefan and I need to get an annulment. We can head down to the courthouse and with a few signatures, boom, we're no longer married."

"That won't be happening, sweetheart. We are NOT getting an annulment."

"Uhhh, yeah, we are," she sasses back at me.

"Think again, wife," I throw back at her. My anger levels have risen to a level I have never felt before, and I'm a hockey player. Aggression is in our blood but this, this is next level.

"Stop calling me wife," she snaps, and from the expression on her face, she's as angry as I am now ... just at the opposite end of the scale. I love when Wren gets fired up like this. Seeing her all hot and bothered gets me all hot and bothered. If Jaxson wasn't here right now, I'd bend her over the back of the sofa and fuck her so hard that she'll forget about this annulment shit.

It's funny. Of the two of us, you'd think I'd be camping out at the courthouse eagerly waiting to get this annulled, but I don't want that. I *want* to stay married. I want to be Wren's husband. I want to grow old with her. In layman's terms, I just want her. Wren brings out the best in me, and

I'm a better person with her by my side. She's tenacious and focused. She's fun to be around and between the sheets, she's a spitfire. She's perfect in every way, and I want her as much as I want hockey.

"Well, *wife*," I emphasize the word. "You and I fucked, several times, therefore we consummated the marriage. The only way you're getting rid of me is to divorce me."

"Fine," she hisses. Staring defiantly at me, she stands up, cocks her hip to the side, and rests her hand there. With her eyes glued to mine, she growls, "I. Want. A. Divorce." She emphasizes each word with a pause.

"No," I adamantly state.

"No," she repeats and I've never heard her use that tone before.

"That's right, Wren, no. N-fucking-O! No! This happened for a reason. You love me and I love you—"

"Love isn't a reason to get married while drunk in Vegas."

"Are you listening to yourself right now, Wren? Love IS the reason you get married," I place emphasis on is. "Wren," I lower my tone, "it's the ultimate reason to *get* and *stay* married. Those who love one another want to get married and buy a house with a wraparound porch so that every Sunday night they can watch the sunset together. They want to get married because they cannot imagine a life without the other. They want to get married because the other person makes them happier than they've ever been before. Love is the whole reason for marriage and, Wren, you and I love one another. Marriage was inevitable for us."

Her eyes widen and her breath hitches. "You ... you remembered."

Crossing the room, I stop in front of her. Cupping her cheeks in my palms, I stare into her baby blues. "I remember everything about you, Wren 'no middle name' Däuchmen."

She rolls her eyes at that but there's also a hint of a smile. "I've never been more sure of anything in my life, Wren. I love you with everything I have and then some. I really want to stay married to you but the question remains, do you want to stay married to me?"

DO *you want to stay married to me?* That's the fifty-four-million-dollar question.

"Yes. No. I don't fucking know. This was supposed to be a fun getaway before I go back to New York. I wasn't supposed to marry you ... or anyone."

"Well, you did," he snaps. He drops his hands from my cheeks and takes my hands in his. He brings my left hand to his lips and kisses the rings on my ring finger. "I can't get you out of my head, Wren, but I know without a shadow of a doubt, you and I could be something amazing if you'd just give marriage and me a go."

"Stefan—" He presses his finger to my lips, shushing me.

"Don't talk, just listen. I love you, Wren. I really, really love you. As I said, I can't get you out of my head. We've been sneaking around for months now, but when you drunkenly said we should do it, I jumped because I want it. I want you. I want us. You make me a better person, and the last six months with you have been amazing. Can't believe I'm saying this but getting arrested with Kallen was the best thing to happen to me because he made me realize you're worth it, Wren. You. Are. Worth. It." Leaning into me, he places his lips on mine and when our lips touch, a spark ignites. It sets every nerve ending in my body ablaze. My soul comes alive in a way that I cannot put into words. It's true, Stefan and I have this chemistry. It's indescribable. I've never felt it with anyone before and in the last twenty-four hours, it's intensified greatly, but are we just caught up in the hurrah of Vegas?

"Stefan, I..." I don't finish because I don't know how to articulate what I'm feeling. But he's right, the last six months sneaking around with him have been amazing, but what's the world going to say when it comes out that I've hooked up with a client? Going by the text from *him* last night, he won't sit back and keep his mouth shut regarding us from years ago. He's a vindictive pin-pricked weasel, and after what happened last night, he's going to be pissed. Especially since I didn't react to the text he sent, well, I did react, I got fucking married.

I need air and I need to think. I have to get out of here. "I ... I n-n-need to go," I stammer and before he or Jaxson can say anything, I'm out the door.

Thankfully, the elevator doors open and a couple steps out. Smiling at them, I jump into the waiting car and punch the button for the lobby. When I look up again, Stefan is standing in the hallway. He has a melancholy look on his face, and that look alone has me second-guessing my actions.

I reach the ground floor and when I step out into the lobby, my phone rings. I smile when I see Fern's name on the screen. "Hey," I say in greeting.

"Don't hey me, you bitch. You didn't sleep here last

night, why did you not answer any of the million texts I sent? But most of all, where the fuck are you?"

Shit, I internally hiss, I really am a shitty friend but I think when you wake up married to your client after a bender in Vegas you're entitle to a free pass, right? "Across the road at the Paris—"

"Why the hell are you there?"

"Long story, but umm, can you and I meet. I ... I." But words elude me. My eyes well with tears and in the middle of the Paris Hotel lobby, I cry into the phone while my friend listens on the other end.

"I'm on my way," she says, in the background I can hear her shuffling about. She calls out to Bradford that she'll "be back soon" and then I hear a door close. "I'm going to stay on the line while you cry. When I get to you, I'm gonna hug you and then I'm going to kick whoever's ass made you cry."

"I think you might need to kick mine," I tell her.

"Well, you let me decide on whose ass I kick."

A laugh escapes me and I listen as Fern tells me about the amazing breakfast she had. Ten minutes later, she walks across the lobby, pulls me into her arms, and hugs me. As soon as her limbs wrap around me, I fall apart.

She ushers me into a bar off the lobby and we grab a table on the outdoor patio that overlooks the Bellagio fountain. Fern orders us some cocktails and then she stares at me. "Okay, spill."

"I need a drink first." Thankfully fate is on my team because the waiter returns with two glasses of what looks like sangria. "Keep 'em coming," I tell him. He nods and leaves.

"Okay, you have your drink, start talking."

Nodding, I take a sip ... and another ... and then I fill her in on everything that's happened since we parted ways last night.

"Holy shit," she hisses. "What are you going to do?"

Before I can answer, she flags the waiter down and orders a round of shots to go with our sangria. Then she looks at me expectantly and awaits my answer.

"Get a divorce, I guess."

"Divorce. Schmivorce."

"Really, schmivorce?"

"What word I used isn't important. What's important is that you love him and he loves you." I open my mouth to dispute that fact, but she raises her hand and gives me a look that has me sitting back in my chair while I mime zipping my lips. "That man loves you, Wren. Unconditionally. I told you before you two even started sneaking around that it would happen and I was right. Just like I'm right when I tell you, divorcing him will be a mistake. He remembered your dream house for fuck's sake, who does that? If that isn't a sign of unconditional, unwavering love, I don't know what is."

"But we were drunk," I say all defensively.

"So?" She nonchalantly shrugs. "Liquor loosens lips and causes you to be honest and, clearly, you two wanted to get married. Why not give it a go? If it's shit in six months get divorced then. Don't give up before you even try, but from where I'm sitting, this is just the beginning of your epic fairy tale."

"Ugh, you're such a romantic."

"No, I'm calling it as I see it. Now, show me that bling again and then go back upstairs and tell your husband that you've reconsidered the divorce. Then fuck him silly to apologize for being a butthead. Then you can both head back to LA and live happily ever after."

"I head to New York next week."

"Put in for a transfer."

"You sound like Stefan."

"Then he must be a very wise man." I laugh. "But seriously, you should listen to the two of us."

The waiter returns with our shots and another drink. Smiling, I thank him, and as I shoot back the tequila, I decide that yes, I need to speak to Stefan.

Chugging back my drink for liquid courage, I excuse myself and head back up to the suite to face my husband.

56
STEFAN

STANDING in the hallway and watching the elevator doors close, taking Wren away from me, is the hardest thing I've ever had to endure, but I know Wren needs time.

"You good?" Jaxson asks from the doorway to our room.

Looking at him, I shake my head. "Not even fucking close."

"Come back inside and we'll come up with a game plan for you to win over the girl."

"I thought you wanted to kick my ass?"

"Ohhh, I still want to do that but, Stefan, if two people are meant to be together, it's you two. I don't know how I didn't see it."

Smiling at him, I walk back into the room, kicking the door closed behind me. "So, you went and fell in love?"

"Mmmhmpf," I mumble with a nod. "Puck over stick in love."

"I'm happy for you ... and me."

"Why you?"

"Because now you're whipped you'll stay out of the

media spotlight, which means more endorsement deals and more moola for my pocket."

"I need a new agent."

"Pffft, no one is as good as me, and you know it."

Shaking my head, I grab two beers from the mini fridge and, together, Jaxson and I come up with a plan to win over my wife.

He heads out, leaving me here waiting. I'm nervous, game day nervous. It's not every day you have to try and convince the woman you love to stay married. My phone pings with a text, and I quickly grab it, hoping it's from Wren, but it's not.

FERN

> Your wife is on her way back to you but if you fuck her over, I will kill you

STEFAN

> I won't ... I love her

FERN

> You make me sick ... but yay ... and if all else fails, tie her to the bed and fuck her into submission

Shaking my head, I smirk. I've never met anyone like Fern, and thank fuck there is only one of her out there. The sound of the door unlocking garners my attention, and I throw my phone to the side, stand up, and wait.

She steps into the room and stops when she sees me standing here. Silence fills the space around us. My hearts starts to rapidly race, it feels like it's going to beat right out of my chest.

"Hey," she finally speaks.

"Hey, yourself," I reply.

More than anything else in the world, I want to storm over to her, pull her into my arms, and hold her tightly and beg for her to reconsider this divorce. But I know Wren and that won't work. I need to let her process and assess everything before she decides.

"We need to talk," she says, breaking the silence that fell between us.

"That statement is never followed by good news," I grumble.

She smiles and I study her while I wait for her to speak. Like the poker-faced player she is, I can't read her. She's playing her cards close to her chest, but I notice her eyes are red-rimmed, indicating she's been crying. I hate the thought of her being in pain over this. Over us. A part of me feels bad for pushing her. Maybe it will be for the best if we divorce and go our separate ways, but the thought of not having her in my life hurts.

She walks into the room and takes a seat on the sofa. In the same spot where I went down on her last night and my dick twitches. It's at half-mast at the memory, but I quickly think of fat naked men in saunas and my dick quickly softens.

Taking a seat in the armchair, I focus on her. I'm sitting in the farthest one from her because if she's in reach, I'm gonna wanna touch her and I think that's the last thing she wants. "I'm sorry I walked out earlier. It was suffocating being in here. Jaxson was mad. You were voicing what you wanted, and me, I was confused and scared."

"Why are you scared?"

"Stefan, I have so much to lose if this all falls apart. You're the hockey God, you'll be fine—"

"We've discussed this, Wren, I won't let that happen. I will protect you. Ring or no ring."

"I know you will but ... but I don't want you to just protect me." My heart breaks at that statement and I drop my gaze to the floor. "I want us to protect each other, it's what married couples do, right?"

My head snaps back up. "Say that again?"

"I want us to protect each other."

"Not that, the other part."

"It's what married couples do because, well, we are married. I have the rings"—she lifts her left hand and waggles her ring finger—"and the piece of paper to prove it."

"So you don't want to get divorced?" She shakes her head. "You want to be my wife?" She nods. "I can tell the whole world you're mine? That we got married in Vegas and that we've been sneaking around for months?" Again she nods.

"We can tell them everything, Stefan. I don't want to hide us anymore. You came into my life like a wrecking ball, causing havoc at every turn, but I got to know you and underneath your douchey exterior is an amazing man. I want everyone to know my husband is the sweetest most caring man I have ever met. I want the world to know he loves sweet coffee. That he's an excellent cook. That he's the most thoughtful person out there but most of all, I want them to know I love him with all my heart."

"And I want them to know I love you will all my ego." She furrows her brow at that analogy. "My ego's bigger than my heart ... I was going to go with dick but I have to PG it up, otherwise, my handler will get mad."

She chuckles and it's music to my ears. I have my wife back. I know it's only been a day since we said "I do" but it's been the best day of my life—minus the last two hours when she was freaking out.

"You done? Or do you still have some ego to fill?"

"I'm good," I throw back at her.

"Good. Now come here and kiss me."

I've never jumped up so quickly. Pulling her upright, I

slide one hand around her waist, and with the other, I cup her cheek in my palm. I stare into the most gorgeous eyes I've ever seen, and I see nothing but love radiating back at me. "I love you, Wren."

"I love you too, Stefan. Now kiss me."

"For you, wife, anything."

Covering her mouth with mine, I kiss her. I kiss my wife like she's never been kissed before, and I know together we can overcome anything.

...a few weeks later

"EVIE," I cry when she walks over to me. "This is amazing, thank you so much." Evie has thrown Stefan and I a belated wedding reception, and it's more than I could have hoped for.

"It's the least I could do. I mean, you saved my ass years ago, and I know this isn't the same thing but it makes me feel better."

Recently, things haven't been easy for her but she's paved out a fantastic life for herself. Yes, it's been marred with tragedy but she's finally found happiness with Miller and their son, Tyler.

"Please. I did not save your bacon."

"Umm, hello, you supplied the Skittles and coffee. Without those two key ingredients, I would not have survived USC."

"Whatever," I singsong like Cher from *Clueless*. "But

seriously, Eve, this is more than Stefan and I could have hoped for, so thank you."

"Anytime, babe, now go, enjoy yourself. We can catch up properly later."

Pulling her in for a hug, I hold on extra tight. It's been rough for her in recent weeks, but it's nice to see her smiling again ... and it's all to do with Miller Wentworth and a little matchmaker named Tyler.

Standing here, I watch her head back to Miller and Tyler. My already big smile increases when Miller lights up when he sees her walking toward them. He tugs her into his embrace and it's magical watching the two of them together. I'm so, so happy for them.

"Drink?" my brother asks, pointing at the empty glass in my hand. Nodding, he links arms with me and guides me over to the bar.

"I still can't believe my baby sister is married," my brother states while we wait for our drinks. He pulls me in for a side hug and kisses me on the head. Then, Penn being Penn, adds, "Clearly, you had to get the groom drunk to marry your sorry ass." His tone is teasing and it's accompanied by a belly laugh, and even though he's laughing at my expense, I'm happy to see him laughing.

"Hardy har har," I reply, slapping him upside the head. "Cleary, you had to drug two women to marry your sorry ass," I throw back at him with a wink.

"Hey, whatever works to get your happily ever after," he teases. "For what it's worth, I've never seen you happier."

The smile on my face widens at my brother's words and he's right. I have never been happier than I am right now. The fallout of my and Stefan's surprise wedding and relationship wasn't anything like I expected. Most people were happy for us. Sure, the bunnies hate me, but that's the same for all the other wives and girlfriends, or WAGs as we're affectionally referred to as. It's so weird to refer to myself as a WAG, but those women know what it's like and I now have a bigger friend group. And Stefan's ex, Chelsea, has become one of my best friends. She already knew I was Stefan's mystery bride because right after us, Lexi and JJ were waiting to get hitched. They eloped due to some bet JJ lost with Kallen. Chels and Kallen were attending via FaceTime since she was ready to pop, and with a screen flip, they saw us stumble out of the chapel.

In the aftermath of our Vegas wedding, Chelsea reached out to me. I'd totally forgotten they saw us on account of being drunk. During our conversation, she told me I was good for Stefan and she was happy for us both. From that moment, a friendship was forged. I can't ever see Kallen and Stefan being as close as us but, thankfully, their grudge has been squashed and they can tolerate one another now.

"For what it's worth, I haven't seen you this happy in a long time either. Seems the time is right for both Brookes siblings."

"Hello, it's 'cause we're awesome," he emphatically states, then his eyes widen. "Do not look at the dance floor."

So what do I do, I look at the dance floor because when someone tells you not to do something, you always do it. My face scrunches up when I see our parents out there; they're basically dry humping one another. "Ugh, I could have gone my whole life without seeing that, but is it wrong that at the same time I'm happy to see them enjoying life?"

"You're fucked in the head, Wren Brookes—"

"It's Däuchmen now," Stefan interrupts, joining us. He slides his hands around my waist and I relax back into him. I love being able to do things like this now. If only my pride hadn't gotten in the way, we could have been doing this for longer but that aside, we can now do it forever.

"Okay, I'll rephrase, you're fucked in the head, Wren Däuchmen."

"And why is my wife fucked in the head?" Stefan questions.

"For enjoying that." Penn points to the dance floor. Thankfully, Mom and Dad have moved on from dry humping and are now, I have no idea what they're doing, but from the look on each of their faces, they are having the time of their lives. They're happy and in love, just like me.

"They're happy, so what? And just so you know, that'll be your sister and me in twenty years' time."

Penn begins to fake gag, and I shake my head at my brother's antics. On reflex, when it comes to my brother, my hand flies out and I slap him in the stomach, causing him to hiss from the force of my actions.

He says he's going to find Tate and get her to kiss him better. Shaking my head, he wanders off, leaving me with my husband. Spinning around, I drape my arms over his shoulders and gaze lovingly at him.

"You're a dangerous woman, Wren Däuchmen, but I'm so glad you're mine. Now, take me to our room. I'm done with peopling."

With a smile on my face, I nod up at my husband and smack a quick kiss on his lips. Removing my arms from around his neck, I take his hand and lace my fingers with his. Then I lead him toward the exit.

As much as I've enjoyed our belated wedding reception, I'm looking forward to some private time with my husband. I'm so glad he convinced me to stay married. Yes, it was reckless drunkenly getting married in Vegas, but it was the push I needed to admit to the world he's mine. Do I miss sneaking around? Sometimes, but walking into a room with Stefan by my side is indescribable.

"Where are you two sneaking off to?" Mom asks us, just before we make our escape.

"Bed," Stefan tells her with a waggle of his eyebrows. Like I did to my brother earlier, I smack him in the stomach. Whereas Penn's abs are pudgy, Stefan's are rock-hard and my slap does nothing to him.

"Without saying goodbye to everyone?" She looks hurt.

"We didn't want to make a spectacle," I tell her, but just as I say this, Dad cups his mouth and calls out. "The happy couple is sneaking away, come say your goodbyes and let them go make me a grandaddy."

"Daaaaad," I scoff. "You did not just say that?"

"Yeah, I did." He beams at me. "Fletcher needs a cousin."

"Dad, we've been married for all of five minutes. At least let us enjoy being married for a bit."

"Fine," he relents. "I give you till Christmas."

"A few months. That's so generous of you."

Stefan leans into me. "We can still practice, right?"

"Get me out of here and we can start practicing in the next five minutes."

His smile widens. His eyes dilate and fill with desire. He turns to our guests and shouts, "Laters everyone." Before I have a chance to breathe, he throws me over his shoulder, and slaps my ass. Our guests cheer and holler as Stefan marches out of the room and down the corridor toward the elevators.

That night, we practice making babies several times, and in the early hours of the morning, I fall blissfully asleep in my husband's arms. I'm woken a few hours later with his head between my legs, which I have to say is my new favorite alarm clock.

I'm coming back to Earth when my husband stares up at

me from between my thighs. "Puck me, baby, one more time."

"Did you just Britney me?"

"I guess I did but the offer still stands. Wren, puck me now, baby."

"I will ffffuck you," I place emphasis on the "F," "if you promise never to say puck me, baby, again?"

He chuckles and nods in agreement. "Deal, now jump on and p-fuck me."

Stefan rolls to his back and fists his dick as I move into place. I throw my leg over and I p-fuck him. I p-fuck the hell out of my husband, and I'm gonna be waddling like a cowgirl when we leave this hotel room, but I'm okay with that. Stefan knows how to p-fuck, and I'm always up for a good p-fucking ... especially when it goes into overtime. I'm so pucking screwed—literally—when it comes to Stefan, and I'm not upset by that at all.

"WHERE ARE YOU TAKING ME?" I ask from the passenger seat. It's late in the afternoon, and all I want to do is sit in the hot tub, drink wine with my husband, and watch the sky.

"It's a surprise," he tells me.

I'm currently sitting in the front seat of his G-Wagon with my eyes covered. He's been sneaky, sneaky for the past week and, to be honest, I thought maybe he was cheating on me. Stupid, I know, but the mind does crazy things when you're in love. It was after a chat with Fern my worries eased, but there's still a small part that thinks she's wrong.

Forty minutes later, the car comes to a stop. "Wait there," he commands as he turns the engine off.

"Like I'm going anywhere by myself blindfolded. I have no clue where I am but if you've led me to the woods to murder me, just know, I'm coming back to haunt you."

He laughs but doesn't say anything. He slips out of the car, leaving me sitting here by myself. My door opens and he unbuckles my seat belt and spins me to face him. Stefan removes the blindfold but tells me to keep my eyes closed. Then he takes my hands in his and guides me out of the car. We take a few steps and then we stop.

My heart is racing but no longer am I scared, I'm excited for whatever my surprise is.

"Open them," he whispers from behind me.

Opening my eyes, I stare ahead and my eyes widen as I take in the house before me. When Stefan and I found this house a couple of weeks ago, I immediately fell in love with it. It's a Victorian-style, two-story house with a wraparound front porch. He told me we were outbid, and I was crestfallen.

"We weren't outbid, were we?" I mumble with tear-filled eyes.

"Nope, we weren't. I wanted to surprise you with your dream home." He wraps his arms around my waist, and I lean back into him. Standing in the driveway of *our* home, I stare at it gobsmacked.

He leads me over to the front steps and sits down, motioning for me to sit between his legs. Walking over, I take a seat and lean back into his embrace. He places his hands on my belly. "One day we will sit here with our kids and watch the sunset with them."

"I fucking love you, Stefan Däuchmen," I tell him. Looking over my shoulder at my husband, I'm filled with every emotion out there.

"I love you too, Mrs. Däuchmen." I snuggle back into my husband and wrapped in his arms; we watch the sunset together ... on the porch of *our* home.

It's funny, I pucking hated him when I first met him but over time he grew on me and now, I can't imagine my life without him. I'm finally at peace. No longer does it feel wrong to have fallen in love with my client. I'm exactly where I should be, and I'm so pucking happy I love him. So. Pucking. Happy.

EPILOGUE - STEFAN

...one year later

"DO YOU REMEMBER US?" two young guys stop and ask as Wren and I walk away from the stadium after practice.

"Sorry, I don't," I honestly tell them and they look heartbroken.

"I'm Brandon, that's Dylan. We used to have a podcast and we interviewed you in your second season with LA."

"Ohhh, I remember you two now. You're a little bigger than when we first met."

"Yeah, we are. We're seniors now and we graduate later this year."

"Still doing the podcast?"

"Yeah, we are. Dylan and I are going to go to NYU to study journalism and make a go of this."

"That's awesome, congrats."

"Thanks, do you, umm, think we could get a photo?"

"Of course," I tell them.

"I'll take it," Wren offers.

"Thanks," Brandon says. He hands Wren his phone and looks quizzically at her. "Hey, I remember you. You're his handler."

"Wife," I correct him. Draping my arm over her shoulder, I pull her into me and kiss her temple and then I remember something. "Actually, you have her to thank for the interview back then."

"Really?" Dylan asks her.

"Yep, I managed every aspect of his life back then."

"And you still do," I tell her, earning myself a whack to the stomach.

"Pussy-whipped," one of them coughs.

I laugh. "Best pussy to be whipped by."

"Stefan," Wren scolds me and slaps me in the stomach again. "You can't say that to kids."

"We're not kids anymore, we're almost college students an—"

"Still kids," Wren interrupts, "and Stefan knows better." She gives me her *handler* look, but I also see nothing but love in her eyes radiating back at me.

"Sorry, dear," I deadpan. "Now take this pic because we have somewhere to be."

After snapping a pic with the guys, I tell them I'll have tickets waiting for them for our next home game behind the bench ... and a check for their tuition at college.

When we get home, I listen to their podcast and they have come a long way since the dumpster of an interview I did with them. Those two are going to go far in life and if I can help them achieve their dreams, I'll do what I can.

With the right people on your team, you will go far in life. Trust me, I know.

I was lucky to have Wren rooting for me because if it wasn't for her, I wouldn't be where I am today. In fact, without her on my team, I'd be a washed-up player with no career and no prospects. Wren Däuchmen being assigned as my image consultant/handler is the best thing to ever have happened to me. I'm the man I am today because of her, and I cannot wait to grow old with her and watch the sunset on our wraparound porch ... just like she'd always dreamed.

EPILOGUE - WREN

... three months later

"SHIT! SHIT! SHIT!," I hiss, my fingers moving quickly as I flick back through my calendar. "I'm late. I'm late, ohh, fuckballs, I'm really late," I mumble. It's been nearly three months since my last period. How the hell did I not notice it's been three months? And how the hell did I not realize I'm pregnant? Well, I presume I am, but surely, you'd know if you were, right? I mean, my boobs are the same size. Looking down at my chest, I pull the top of my strapless dress out and I inspect the girls. They're still the same size as always and I still don't need a bra with this dress. Yes, my belly is a little plump but I put that down to a change in my diet ... a diet that now has me craving PB and J sandwiches and chocolate milk at all hours of the day. "Ohhh fuckballs, I'm pregnant."

"Honey, I'm home," Stefan sings out while I sit here in our home office at my desk freaking the fuck out.

"In here," I shout and a few moments later my husband

appears in the doorway. Leaning against the doorframe, he crosses his arms and ankles. *He really is good-looking,* I think to myself as my eyes roam over him. He's in dark sweatpants—hello, my kryptonite—and a Legends tight fitting tee. The material clings to his muscular arms and chest. Biting my bottom lip, I hold in the moan that wants to slip out.

"You keep looking at me like that, and I'm gonna be forced to bend you over your desk and fuck you six ways till Sunday."

Shaking my head, I grin at the picture he just played out ... a picture that happens quite often in this room. Then I begin to wonder if it was one of those times that led to me being in this predicament. I look into his eyes and the teasing look that was on his face evaporates when he takes in my expression. "Wren, babe, what's wrong?" He pushes off the frame and walks over to me. Spinning my chair around, he drops down to his knees in front of me and rests his hands on my thighs.

My mouth opens and closes but no words come out.

"Wren, you're scaring me."

"IthinkI'mpregnant." Those four words whoosh out of my mouth in a jumbled flowing one-worded mess.

"Huh?"

Taking a deep breath, I calmly utter those four words, well, five words, because I add his name this time. "Stefan, I think I'm pregnant."

I'm met with silence.

Stefan sits between my legs, blinking rapidly and not saying anything. All I can hear is the beating of my heart. It echoes in my ears as I stare down at my mute husband. Then I start thinking of that time with *her* and wonder if he'll be happy like he was back then.

Stefan and I have come so far since then. Sure, we've

discussed kids in passing, but we never really discussed-discussed the topic. Going by his reaction, well non-reaction, I'm guessing this is not what he wants right now. *Shit, he's going to leave me 'cause I'm pregnant, and I'll be a homeless single mom.*

"Wren," he shouts my name and then I realize, while I was internally freaking out, he's been speaking to me.

"Sorry, I missed that, what did you say?"

"I said, how far along are you?"

"I ... ummm, I'm not sure." He looks quizzically at me. "I haven't taken a test."

"Then how do you know you're pregnant?"

"I ... ummm, I was looking back in my diary and noticed when I marked my last period and, I ... umm, then thought about it, and I, ummm, it's been three months."

"So you don't know for sure?"

"I ... ummm, no, not for sure."

He nods and then, without saying a word, stands up and exits the office. Then I hear the front door open and close. A few moments later his car starts and he backs out of the driveway, gunning it down the street.

Sitting here, my body becomes numb and my eyes well with tears. I can't believe he just drove off. I thought he'd be excited or at least yell. I didn't expect him to just leave. Standing up, I walk out of my office and head to the front porch, my happy place.

Dropping down to the top step, I bring my knees up to my chest and hug them. The first tear falls, and I silently sit here and sob. Dropping my head to my knees, I cry and cry. I'm so lost in my grief that I startle when a hand touches my shoulder.

Lifting my head up, I squint into the afternoon light and when my eyes focus, I gasp.

"Wren, babe—"

"You left," I whisper.

"Huh?" he questions, and I get a sense of déjà vu from earlier in my office.

"You left," I repeat.

"I left to get these." He lifts a bag with the logo from the pharmacy around the corner.

"But you left without saying anything. You left and I thought…"

"Babe, no." He shakes his head and drops down next to me. He puts his arm around my shoulders and pulls me into his side. "I'm sorry I did that, but it was not what I expected to hear when I got home earlier and I got all excited. I just want to know if we are."

"But what if I am?"

"Then we'll have a baby."

"But—"

"Nope, no buts, Wren."

"You remembered," I joke.

"Trust me. I'm not going there … ever. You bucking back and slamming your head into my nose is enough of a reminder that the butt is a no-go zone with you." Stefan and I were doing it doggy style one night, and he tried to slip his finger into my ass. My butt is a one-way zone, and that way is out, not in. In shock, I reared back and my head connected with his nose. There was blood everywhere, and Stefan was sporting a black eye for a week after the incident. "Anal aside, Wren, we'll deal with this together but trust me when I tell you, I cannot wait to have a baby with you. Seeing your belly grow with our child is going to be amazing, and you're going to be an awesome mother."

"Stefan," I cry. Reaching up, I cup his cheek. "You continually amaze me."

"What can I say, I'm pretty awesome."

"And there's the douche I first fell in love with."

He shrugs. "How about we head inside and you can pee on a stick and we'll find out for sure if I managed to get one past the goalie?"

"And they say romance is dead," I say with a laugh.

He just smirks.

Standing up, he offers me his hand and he pulls me up. Wrapping his arm around my waist, he pulls me in for a hug. "I love you, Wren."

"I love you too."

We share a quick kiss and then he lifts me into his arms and bridal style, he walks us inside and into our bedroom. He crosses the room into the en suite before placing me on my feet. Reaching into the bag, he pulls out three different boxes. "I didn't know what to get so I grabbed the first three I saw."

Looking at the boxes, I laugh. "Well, this one is an ovulation test, so that's out."

"Okay, so, do we go. Box A or Box B?"

"B," I tell him.

"B for baby," he says, and I smile that he was thinking what I was thinking. Opening the box, he pulls the stick out and hands it to me. He leans against the vanity and stares at me expectantly.

"Ummm, what are you doing?"

"Waiting to see if I'm a dad."

"I'm not doing this in front of you."

"Babe, you pee in here while I'm in the shower. This is no different." He raises his hand to stop me. "Pee. I'm not leaving."

Shaking my head, I try and hold back my smile, but I do as he's demanded and I pee on the stick while he watches me. Placing the test on the floor, I wipe, and pull my pants up. After flushing, I wash my hands and when I look in the mirror, I notice Stefan is staring at me. There is nothing but love and admiration reflecting at me. He pulls me into his arms and I rest my head on his shoulder.

"I'm sorry for freaking out," I mumble.

"I'm sorry for not telling you where I was going."

Lifting my head, I look up at my husband and realize that no matter what, we'll be fine. Gripping his cheeks in my palms, I press my lips to his. He licks into my mouth and what started as a soft kiss quickly turns heated.

Stefan slides his hands down my back and cups my ass. Lifting me up, I wrap my legs around his waist. He spins us around and rests my ass on the edge of the vanity. He massages my breasts and I moan into the kiss. Ripping the top of my dress down, he exposes my chest and quickly covers my tits with his mouth and hands.

"Yes," I mewl, grinding myself on his growing erection.

Slipping my hands between us, I try to pull his sweats down but there's not much room to move so he steps back, allowing me to push his pants down and expose his dick. His beautiful dick. From the corner of my eye, I spot the test on the mat by the toilet. "Shit, the test," I state.

"Shit," Stefan hisses.

Turning his head, he looks at the test and I lean forward. Even from my spot on the vanity, I can clearly see the pink positive sign, waving its sparkly jazz hands at us.

"We're pregnant," I utter. "We're having a baby."

Moving my eyes from the test to Stefan, I see him smiling and I've never seen his smile so bright. He turns his attention to me and somehow, his smile widens. "We're gonna have a baby."

Words elude me so I just nod in agreement. He slams his lips to mine, kissing the life out of me. Slipping his hands under my ass, he lifts me off the vanity and walks out of the bathroom with me in his arms. He lowers me to the bed and pushes me down. Lifting my dress up, he situates himself between my thighs and cups my stomach. "Hey, baby, it's your daddy. I love you and your mom more than I love hockey. I cannot wait to teach you all the things, but most of all, I cannot wait to hold you in my arms and love you forever."

He presses a kiss to my stomach and I realize, I had no reason to worry. Then we finish what we started in the en suite earlier.

Life is a game and I've just scored the ultimate goal, the unconditional love of my husband and a baby.

The Pucking End!!!!!!!!!!!!!

Coming next in the Pucking Love series, It's Pucking Fake. It's available for preorder now.

Surrounded by sleazy men and desperate puck bunnies, Jett Jensen, New York Crusher's left wing, and I become each other's saviour. Fake dating at events is the game, and saving each other from awkward situations is the goal.

However, the rules change when Jett takes me as his date to his sister's wedding. It's hard not to be swept away in the moment and the romance of a Valentine's Day ceremony.

Our fake relationship suddenly becomes more real than either of us expected. Between whispered confessions and slow dances, our fate is sealed.

Until the next wedding...

ACKNOWLEDGMENTS

These things never get any easier and I'm sure I miss someone each and every time so this is a blanket thank you to everyone who I have met along the way and who has offered advice, thanks and praise. You all pucking rock <— totally bad pun I know.

Karen Hrdlicka from **Barren Acres Editing**; thank you for everything you do for me. You are not only my editor but you are also my friend ... let's not leave it seven years between hugs now.

Victoria from **Cruel Ink Editing;** thank you for checking all my I's are dotted, my T's are crossed and my commas are correct.

Renae from **R.L. Cover Designs**; thank you for bringing Kallen to life. This image is perfect for him and you nailed it. And **Kristie** from **Vanilla Lily** for the alternate cover. As soon as I saw the set, I had to have them and we've managed to allocate them to each character perfectly ... without even realising it.

Lainey from **DS Promotions, Ena** and **Amanda** from **Enticing Journey** and all of the bloggers, thank you for helping me share IPHTLY with the world.

My beta babes **Bec, Lana, Margaret, Sarah, Stef and Vi;** I would be lost without you ladies. You give me advice when I second guess everything and you helped to bring this story to life. Thank you from the bottom of my heart.

Troy, my husband, my everything. You really are

awesome at what you do and you are an even better husband and father. Love you long-time dude.

To my munchkins, **Piper** and **Kade**. You two are my greatest achievement and I'm so lucky to have you both in my life. Love you long-time guys and I look forward to the day when you are forty and can finally read my books.

And finally, **you, my reader**. I hope you love Stefan as much as I do. Even douches deserves love and we all know, he's the douchesiest douche of all.

Cheers,

Dana XoXoX

PLAYLIST

Silhouettes - Of Monsters and Men
Breath of Life - Florence + The Machine
Can't Get You out of my Head - Kylie Minogue
You'll Be Mine - The Pierces
Hate That I Love You - Rhinna, Ne-Yo
Decode - Paramore
I See Red - Everybody Loves an Outlaw
I Don't Wanna Love Forever - ZAYN, Taylor Swift
I Wanna Be Yours - Arctic Monkeys
Small Doses - Bebe Rexha
All I Need - Within Temptation
Poker Face - Lady Gaga
Mirrors - Justin Timberlake
Just Give Me a Reason - P!nk, Nate Ruess
Dark Horse - Katy Perry, Juicy J
Wrecking Ball - Miley Cyrus
I Knew You Were Trouble - Taylor Swift
Come & Get It - Selena Gomez
I Need Your Love - Calvin Harris feat. Ellie Goulding
Burn - Ellie Goulding

Lost - Linkin Park
You're So Vain - Carly Simon
Feel Invincible - Skillet
Paparazzi - Lady Gaga
Apologise - Timbaland, One Republic
Only Girl (In The World) - Rhinna
Can't Remember to Forget - Shakira feat. Rhianna
Bad Romance - Lady Gaga
Dangerous Woman - Ariana Grande
Blank Space - Taylor Swift

This playlist can be found on Spotify.

ALSO BY DL GALLIE

STAND ALONES

Antecedent

Doc Steel

Oops

Off the Books

Deck...the Balls

Secrets and Sunrises

Always in the Cards

Fractured

The Christmas Ornament

Before the Ashes

After the Ashes

Love Me Like You Do

Never Let Me Go

Seven Nights

Seven Kisses

PUCKING LOVE SERIES

I Pucking Hate That I Love You

A Pucking Good Christmas

I Pucking Hate That You Love Me

I Pucking Hate To Love You

It's Pucking Fake

...and a few pucking more

FALLING NOVELS

These men make it hard not to fall for them

Falling for Dr. Kelly

Falling for Dr. Knight

Falling for Agent Cox

Falling for Agent Cruz

Falling: The Complete Collection

LORDS OF CRESTWOOD PREP

Co-write with Tara Lee

Thatcher

Reign

Hendrix

Saint

THE UNEXPECTED SERIES

When it comes to love, expect the unexpected

The Unexpected Gift

The Unexpected Letter

The Unexpected Package

The Unexpected Connection

The Unexpected series: The Complete Collection

THE LIQUOR CABINET SERIES

Liquor has never been so disturbingly saucy

Malt Me (Book 1)

Tequila Healing (Book 2)

Wine Not (Book 3)

The Final Shot (Book 4)

The Liquor Cabinet: Series boxset

All of these books are available on Amazon.

ABOUT THE AUTHOR

DL Gallie is from Queensland, Australia, but she's lived in many different places all over the world, including the UK and Canada. She currently resides in Central Queensland with her husband and two munchkins. She and her husband have been together  since she was sixteen, and although they drive each other crazy at times, she couldn't imagine her life without him.

Shortly after her son was born, DL began reading again. With encouragement from her husband, she picked up the pen and started writing, and now the voices in her head won't shut up.

DL enjoys listening to music, drinking white wine in the summer, red wine in the winter, and beer all year round. She's also never been known to turn down a cocktail, especially a margarita.

FACEBOOK ~ INSTAGRAM ~ BOOKBUB

GOODREADS ~ WEBSITE

dana@dlgallieauthor.com

Sign up to my newsletter

www.ingramcontent.com/pod-product-compliance
Lightning Source LLC
Chambersburg PA
CBHW020329120726
47904CB00002B/343